THANH DINH

Chronicle of a Love Foretold

A Novel

First edition

ISBN: 978-1-0694998-4-4

Editing by Nicole Fegan

This book was professionally typeset on Reedsy. Find out more at reedsy.com

For every queer immigrant kid who always feels like they don't belong. Your voice matters, and you are what makes this life more beautiful. With love, from an immigrant adult.

Contents

Acknowledgments

This book could not have come into being without the invaluable guidance of Nicole Fegan, an editor whose kindness, precision, and commitment I deeply admire. Nicole, your care and attention shaped this work in ways I will always be grateful for.

The striking cover artwork was created by Tiago Araujo, an exceptionally talented freelance designer on Behance. His work stands out for its beauty and originality, and I am fortunate to have his artistry represent this book.

I extend my heartfelt thanks to my parents and sister, whose unwavering support has carried me through the most challenging parts of this journey. To my dear friend Hoang-Anh Nguyen—whose bridal dress shop in Moncton, New Brunswick, is as lovely as her generosity—thank you for offering your help so freely. To my longtime friend Tam Nguyen, who has patiently waited since our grade-nine days to hold a copy of my novel, your faith has been a quiet but steady source of strength.

To all of you who have believed in me: thank you for reminding me that the path forward is always possible.

With gratitude,
Thanh Dinh

Chapter 1: Enchanted

Dong perks up his ears; his hand stops writing. The pencil hangs mid-air as the name rings in his mind, echoing in the chamber of his soul. His Simon. His lost Alexandra. With bated breath, he listens to Ames and Lizzie's conversation, waiting for a perfect opportunity to jump in, to tear right through the thistle, to catch the prey, to once more seize what is rightfully his.

Dong is glad to suffer the pain, bearing it in his heart and calling it living. His heart throbs inside his chest every time the name gets brought up in the short span of fifteen minutes. Unable to tolerate the suspense anymore, he carefully turns his head, pretending he doesn't care, feigning his heart is not bleeding, acting as if the name is not gouging out his lungs, making him gasp, and says, "Did you mention that a certain Simon will be there?"

"Oh, yeah, the Charming Prince will be there. I thought he told you about the party already, didn't he?" says the girl with the freckle spots spread across her beautiful oval face, sucking on her apple lollipop.

Dong tries to suppress his oncoming hyperventilation. He can feel the air escaping him in quick succession as if he is going to die again and again. How can he help it? With Simon, he tasted the bitter poison from the cup of Aphrodite on a winter's night. He doesn't think he'll ever recover from the sip of that hot cocoa, the soft lips, the tender gaze, and the phrase "No matter what happens, remember I love you."

Heaving a sigh, Dong says, "Nah, we parted ways before high school. He's in a Catholic private high school. I'm only a lowly public-school prisoner. Ames, give me your math homework. You are doing question 2 wrong."

Despite feigning a nonchalant facade as best as he can, deep inside, Dong's guts are churning. *Simon will be there, Simon will be there, Simon will be there, oh my God, Simon will be there.* Dong keeps repeating the sentence until it crystalizes in his mind and turns into a fact that no one and nothing can steal from him. He swallows. The name tastes like fresh blood dropping on the rotten autumn leaves.

"Huh? But you guys are childhood friends, no? Don't you guys, like, keep in contact and whatnot? I mean, you must have his phone number at least, don't you, D-dog?" Ames says, pushing her math homework toward Dong while reaching for another lollipop. "And I'm not doing anything wrong. You are just bad at teaching. Anyways, about that Prince Charming—"

"Simon."

"Yeah, whatever. Simon." Ames rolls her eyes, tearing the apple lollipop and sucking on the sweet treat with relish. "He has quite a fan club for a boy our age.I mean, why should a teenage boy have a fan club? Imagine getting letters and being surrounded by girls all the time, eh? You guys ever talked about that?"

"Ames, it's not that simple." In his mind, Dong wishes it *were* that simple.

"Aw, D-dog, to you, nothing is that simple, isn't it? It's always,

'Ames, you did that question wrong,' 'Ames, you should not use ketchup with eggs,' 'Ames, spring rolls are not supposed to be eaten that way,' 'Ames, blah blah blah.' It's always my fault. Is anything ever your fault?" Ames says, teasing the boy until his ears turn red.

But she isn't successful this time. Dong's facial expression turns soft with sorrow. He looks down at the carpeted floor of his room, plucking the thread. His eyelashes quiver slightly at the memory of the day when he finally learned that there was something worth living for and dying for. The day the world finally emerged before him in every shade of vivid color, but he ruined it. It was his fault. It will always be his fault.

His eyes are hazy, calculating the future, mourning for the past. Everything is happening so quickly in front of his eyes, and Dong feels like he is watching a movie in reverse. Should he go to the party? Should he not? After all, Simon hasn't written him back since the day of the incident.

Dong bites his thumb. His whole body is burning for all the possibilities that could or could not beat the party, an event he doesn't even know if he will be allowed to attend. His parents won't let the word "party" be whispered in their presence, let alone allow him, their precious son (is he even that precious? He doesn't know), to go to the place "where all the degenerates are present." Unconsciously, he pushes his notebook away and crawls into himself.

"D-dog, you okay?" asks the girl sitting opposite him with a tinge of concern, finally joining the conversation. She munches on the beef jerky while scribbling furiously on her math homework, knowing that she won't get a good grade when she hands it in tomorrow.

"Oh, I'm fine. It's just…" Dong says. His voice breaks a little

3

at the end. He coughs to hide it.

"Fuck your 'I'm fine.' I mean, pardon the French, but you seriously need to stop that habit. Just say whatever you are feeling. Don't make it that complicated. Our life is hard enough as is. Anyway, you guys have known each other since elementary school, right? Why don't you just call him?" Lizzie asks and stares at Dong for exactly thirty seconds, then goes back to chewing her jerky while scribbling even crazier answers in her homework.

Dong breathes in and feels the air fill up his entire being. *Don't think about it,* he thinks to himself. *If you don't think about it, it will be like it'd never happened.* But it had happened, and he had tried his best to forget, but even his best is not enough to erase the day from existence.

"He probably won't answer if he knows it's me calling. He probably will block me. We parted on bad terms." Dong inhales again. It takes him every molecule not to spill all his guts on the bedroom's floor. "Very bad terms."

"Then just go to the party. You'll meet him there, and you can solve all your misunderstandings. I heard from my girlfriends at Appleby that Simon is a pretty decent guy. And you are just a sweet, little goofball. I can't fathom how you two could have parted on bad terms," Ames says, slurring on her words as she sucks on the apple lollipop and copies the notes from Lizzie's English notebook. She knows her essay about *Hamlet* will surely get at least a D.

"As I said, we parted on *very* bad terms. He'll probably leave the moment he sees me and—"

"Then don't go," Lizzie retorts, expressing her annoyance in clear, short words.

"But if I don't go, this could be the last chance for us to—"

"Then fucking go!" Ames snaps. "Do you have anything left to lose? I mean, come on, D-dog, it's not like he will eat you. Keep your worries to yourself. Besides, apparently Simon is nice. He'd forgive you even if you set fire to his house. That's how nice he is. Well, that is, if my girlfriends from Appleby aren't lying to me. Which might be the case. Which will render everything I said null. Agh, I'm losing my mind over our homeboy Shakespeare here. Lizzie, why does Hamlet say this?"

"Alright, alright, give me that. You guys are always exaggerating." Dong chuckles.

Of all people, he knows best how nice and gentle Simon is. From the warm palm that used to ruffle his hair to the bright smile that shines on him every time Dong needs an escape or a place to call home, Simon has always been the nicest and gentlest person. *And yet, I just had to go and do that.* Dong immerses himself in his memory as if it were just yesterday. *I just had to lose him.*

Sometimes, people mistake kindness for love. And for people like Dong, whose name is a constant joke, whose sexual identity is a forbidden topic at his home, whose grades can *never* be below an A, a simple touch of kindness is a fountain of spring water amidst the vast, empty desert. He had walked for so long only for the holy taste of a few drops, and just when he thought it was okay to be greedy, the fountain disappeared.

"Simon looks dope, though. Hey, you never told me how hot he is." Ames pulls Lizzie close to her and they look at the photo on the phone screen. "Lizzie, look, isn't he just super handsome? Are all guys from private school this hot?" The girls giggle. Dong scoots over to their side and takes a sneak peek.

5

On Ames's phone, the photo shows Simon playing basketball, shooting a ball. His dark skin glistens with sweat. His hair combed back, his forehead covered with an elastic band, his dark eyes focused on the goal. Dong feels his heart jump up to his throat. He can sense Simon's intense breathing in the air—Simon always has that habit of open-mouth breathing when he focuses on something he likes—and he can smell the scent of burned cedar on Simon's collar bones.

Simon, sweet Simon, who never joked about Dong's name or his ethnicity, who never told him that he smells like dead fish, who always ruffled his hair when he got a grade below A, who always smiled and told him that things would be okay because Simon was by his side. Simon, sweet Simon—the nectar of his spring and the snowstorm of his winter—and look at what he did to that little spark in his darkness.

Dong leans back against the bedframe. He's made up his mind. This is his only chance. All those years, all the distance, all the longing that he put into the lengthy letters that he sent Simon every day has led to this one chance. He knows he must go to the party, no matter the cost. This time, he will fix everything. And if worse comes to worst, it won't mean anything to him now. After all, isn't life about losing everything?

"Hey, this party, when is it, and where is it?"

The two girls stop their giggling and stare at him, awestruck.

"Seriously, you plan on going?" Ames asks with a tinge of disbelief.

"You said a few seconds ago that I should go."

"Yeah, but I didn't actually think you'd go. I mean, considering the kind of guy you are…and that helicopter mom of yours."

"Hey, what kind of guy?" Dong laughs. "The kind that is always stuck up in his room doing homework and teaching other people math? The kind that always gets straight A's and is a teacher's pet and all that? And my mom, I suppose I can do something about her." He scratches his head, but no plan appears.

"Yeah, hon. You are all of that in a combined mess. And your mom is just a sweet cherry on top, isn't she?"

"This time, I want to get out of that mess."

"Simon means that much to you, huh?" Lizzie asks, still chewing on her beef jerky.

"It's not Simon," Dong says, twirling his pencil in his hand. "It's me. I just…I need to get out of that mess." He looks up and smiles at the puzzled look on both of his friends' faces. "I have a burden on my shoulders, and this is my one chance to let it go."

Lizzie and Ames glance at each other. The girls seem to sense something in the light voice and the hazy eyes of the boy who's been helping them since grade ten, their first year of high school. Now they are entering the final year of their carefree life, yet the boy who is always too timid to speak his mind and too shy to make any decision on his own remains the same. The boy who is the son of poor Vietnamese refugees, always the subject of rude jokes and passive-aggressive racism disguised as laughter and kindness. He bears it all without a single word of complaint and just smiles at the stones thrown his way until the girls find him crying in the corner of the school staircase. That boy now says that he needs this one chance. Liz and Ames nod in agreement.

Ames turns to Dong and says firmly, "Okay, then count us in. We will get you there and back safely. I will confirm Simon's

7

appearance with my friend and get you an invitation, and Lizzie will act as a double agent to blindfold your mom. We will plan together and see to it that you get your so-called burden off your shoulders. And remember, no matter what the results are after you let it go, we will always be by your side."

"Ames is right, D-dog. Without you, my math tests would score no higher than an F," Lizzie says, laughing.

"Yeah, and I wouldn't even know if Shakespeare was a writer or the name of a rising actor. I mean, his portrait looks handsome to me. That's all I know about Shakespeare."

The three of them let the silence sink in. When that truth eventually comes out like an avalanche of burning, hidden emotions, Dong knows that Lizzie and Ames will always be there for him. A sudden flower blooms in his frozen heart, then a smile and the touch of a freezing hand and the phrase "No matter what happens, remember I love you."

Chapter 2: Alexandra Leaving

Lizzie and Ames say their goodbyes and the laughter leaves Dong's life like a soft breeze.

He walks with light feet on the cold tiled floor to the dining room. Greeting him are his only dates: a cold dinner wrapped in foil paper on a table that hasn't known a human's touch for God knows how long, and the weight of the solitude that is scratching on the window frames. Outside, the night is falling. A storm is threatening to come. The dark cloud is pregnant with malice.

Dong draws the curtains of the living room windows. He tries to distinguish in his foggy existence between the possibles and the probables. Nothingness seems to be the only thing left in his hands, trickling through the cracks of his broken facade to form the monster of his shadow under the sun.

Looking at the cold dishes with no appetite, Dong puts his dinner away. He can already hear the shouting, the arguments, and the blame coming from his parents when they come home, but he will deal with the consequences when they attack him later. On a better day, his parents would just go straight to bed, and he could fib his way out of not having eaten dinner. It's not like they would check the fridge. Dong smiles ruefully at his own hypocrisy. He isn't a good person, and yet, everyone

9

refuses to believe that. He is tired of wearing the costume, but it isn't time for him to drop the role.

His father works for a car manufacturing factory. His mother works for a nail salon near home, and sometimes, she takes on night shifts at a Vietnamese restaurant in the nearby Chinatown. Since the day of his birth, Dong has known how hard his parents' lives are. He knows it, and yet—

And yet, what about me?

Dong shuts the door to his room. He leaves the light off. The darkness embraces him with the warm bosom of a true mother. He lies on the floor, pulls out his phone with the photo of Simon still on the screen, and traces the lines on the boy's figure. A fire kindles in the pit of his stomach and spreads everywhere, leaving him a burning pile of passion and ashes of a boy still too young to know how to survive after love. He slowly pulls down his pants and kisses the phone screen, his eyes closed, his mind back to the eve of the winter years ago when two bodies entangled in a slow dance of innocence. He whispers in a hoarse voice, the forest fire on the tip of his tongue, "Simon, dearest Simon..."

"Dong, do you ever wonder what love is?" Simon asked amidst the tune of Leonard Cohen's "Alexandra Leaving."

"I don't know." Dong blushed. "I've never thought much of it." But he did. He thought too much of it that he even saw it in his dreams in the shape of the boy sitting by his side, whispering sweet nothings in his ears. Both were still young, only getting on to grade nine. But Dong knew what love was. Or, rather, Dong knew who love was.

"Well, I do," Simon said, his eyes staring with a vacant look at the dark ceiling as if it were a universe filled with the golden mythos of Aphrodite and Athena, of the bitter taste when one mingled love

and war; of hope, of living, of death.

"Have you figured it out?"

"That's what I mean, D-dog," he said with a laugh. "No one knows what it is. I doubt anyone ever will. Listen, I've been trying to figure out the hook for this song on guitar. Let me get it."

Simon stretched his hand over Dong's chest to reach the old guitar that was leaning on the edge of the bed. A sudden surge of heat quickly seeped through the thick layer of Dong's wool vest and shirt. He closed his eyes and took a deep breath. Simon smelled like a forest of pine in the fresh morning, wet and heavy with fog and dewdrops. The heat on Dong's cheeks rose with each of Simon's heartbeats. The music in his ear was muted. All he could hear was the whisper of something darker, something that had always been there but had only recently gotten the chance to slowly lurch toward his heart.

He wanted to say that Simon should stay there, that he would get the guitar. He wanted to say that he would get everything Simon wanted, if only Simon would request it—if Simon would always be here, lying on the floor, looking at the ceiling, and feeling the void of existence. But before he could open his mouth and commit the most atrocious of sins in his life, Simon had resumed the old position and strummed along the strings. In the hoarse voice of a boy almost turning into a man, he sang,

"It's not a trick, your senses all deceiving
A fitful dream, the morning will exhaust
Say goodbye to Alexandra leaving
Then say goodbye to Alexandra lost"

"Do you think I got it?" Simon asked, strumming the strings a few more times, trying to find a place among the melody where he could fit in. A place where he belonged.

"I don't know." Dong turned away, his tears rolling down the

bridge of his nose and forming a tiny dark circle on the carpet. "I'd rather we just sleep." Feeling stupid, he scolded himself as the words escaped his mouth. Who would want to sleep now?

"But it's early." Simon laughed, ruffling Dong's hair with a loving tenderness he would never find anywhere else, or in anyone else.

"It's eleven p.m. I don't think it's early."

"Well, that's just your opinion." Simon put the guitar back in its place, and he lay down with his face to Dong's back. As the warm breath tickled his spinal cord, he shuddered with an unknown feeling—a sensation that was too strong to put a name to.

"Why don't you sleep on the bed?" Dong muttered, beads of sweat forming on his forehead.

"I'd rather sleep on the floor." Simon wrapped his arms around Dong's waist, yawning into his pale nape.

"There's no point trying to reason with you. Just like a child."

"But I am a child." Simon beamed mischievously. "At least, for now."

He moved closer and pulled Dong in his tight embrace. Under the duvet and the makeshift blanket tower, they were the only two living people in the dark world. Dong turned around, and in the palpable heat of the moment, Simon kissed him, slow and tender, with all the innocence of a person who had not known yet which sins were forgivable and which were not. Dong returned the kiss with hesitation at first, then he dove deep into the burning passion that was always buried within his heart, and for the first time, he understood what was meant by letting go.

In that burning moment of fervent passion, they tasted the forbidden flavor of each other's bodies with trembling hands and nervous laughter. The feeling of skin sticking together then separating only to find out that there were no other places for them to be but here made them fully aware of the sensation of living, and *in that fleeting moment, before either of them could fully grasp the meaning of their actions, Simon moved the kisses further down in a chaos of tumbling emotions.*

Dong was breathless because he thought he must have died a thousand times over only to live for this moment. Simon was smoldering because he knew full well before it all began that he was and forever would be this timid boy's moment. And though the world was cruel to these young boys, the Earth underneath their naked bodies moved until they became one again with the history of mankind.

Just when Dong thought that this was all, and Simon's feverish eyes told him that it was not, they heard the loud noise of plates and glasses breaking on the floor, shattering their first dream of love. Simon's mother was standing in the dimly lit hallway, staring at them, eyes wild with fear more than bewilderment. She whispered, "What on Earth are you doing to my son?"

Dong wakes up from his reverie and stares at the sticky fluid on his hand in a daze. He must not let his parents know the sinful dreams in his head. He fears that they will drag him back to the innocence of Earth again. Dong reaches for the tissue box; beside him, the photo of Simon is there, lit up in the darkened room like a fleeting hope of escape at the end of the tunnel.

Dong looks at the phone screen. He thinks he can see a fleeting glimpse of happiness, but all he can feel is a nauseating sensation churning up inside his stomach. The insults, the stares, the laughter. The words. They all come back to him in this moment of solitude, and he can't fight against them; after so many years of tolerating them, he can't help but believe they are the truth.

They say, "Man up," and he replies, "When was I not a man?"

while thinking to himself, *Aren't we all human? What is wrong with a human loving another human?* And that is when the laughter begins.

The odd one out. The weirdo. The Asian guy who refuses to be close with anyone because he knows everyone will leave in the end. Then Lizzie and Ames came into his life. The girls picked him up, broken and shattered as he was—a bird flailing his wings in the dark, a moth with its wings torn—and they sheltered him in their hearts. They taught him to outgrow his madness. When everyone else in his life rejected his existence, Ames and Lizzie taught him to go against the world. Perhaps that is why he is still alive at this moment. The three of them are the outliers in a school full of perfect statistics and circles, and he revels in it.

Dong imagines for one moment that he is not expected to be a straight-A student, a scrawny, yellow-skin boy with the scent of fish sauce, or even a clown who can only laugh at the cruelty his classmates pour on him. But he knows nothing is that simple. He can't change who he is, and Dong doubts that he could ever learn to love that being with his whole heart.

While he is lost in muddled thoughts, his phone screen lights up. It is Ames. She texts: "Are you okay, D-dog? Lizzie's mom agreed to get us to the party and back."

He sits up, leaning against the bed, and after a long pondering moment, he presses the call button.

"What do you mean 'Are you okay?' It's not like I suddenly broke after you left," Dong says immediately when Ames picks up, laughing.

"Oh, I don't know. I just get this feeling after leaving your house, you know. A woman's intuition. It tells me that you don't want to be alone right now."

"Well, whatever that intuition is, you should use it more. It's scary good. Thanks. I'm fine. It's just…my parents won't be home until midnight. So, I *am* alone, at least for now,," Dong says, and after a moment, he adds, "Say, will you stay on the line with me for a while? Just talk about whatever you want. I will listen."

"I'd love to do that, but my family is having dinner soon." Ames hesitates. Dong can picture her biting her nails. She has a bad habit of biting her nails and chewing her lips whenever she is flustered and frustrated. She continues softly, her voice urgent with worry, "Are you sure that everything's okay? Your voice is shaking."

"That's alright. Sorry for asking. I'm being silly. And yes, I am okay, it's just—no, never mind, thanks Ames."

"D-dog, I—"

But Dong hangs up before Ames can finish her sentence. He can tolerate a lot of things. However, the one thing he can't bear is pity from other people. He was raised to be strong, his father used to say. And being strong in his father's eyes means not breaking into pieces. There's no place for pity, for mercy, for love. He is a man, his father says, and a man doesn't need such feminine feelings.

Dong sometimes wonders why men and women are built so differently in his father's mind. He once asked, "But *ba oi*[1], aren't we all human?" to which his father replied with a beating because he wasn't permitted to doubt his elder's words. So, Dong is used to it—living the life other people expect of him, faking the smile people want to see, and pretending to be a person he is not.

---

[1] T/N: father dear

Until today, when Simon has suddenly come back into his life with this party and the chance in a lifetime to get out of these enclosed walls. He thinks about Simon's words. "No matter what happens, remember I love you."

Dong finds that he has long forgotten how to be loved. He has buried those words so deep under the Earth. Now that it has been resurrected, he has no armor to fight against its weapon. He simply surrenders to the tender love that burns like embers in his heart. Dong let himself immerse in the reminiscence of Simon's laugh the last time he saw him in his room. Hearts beating in their ears. Burning skin under the touch of hot fingers, and Simon was so near to him, his happiness was so near to him. Dong says out loud, "Hey Siri, call Alexandra."

The phone replies, "I'm sorry, I can't find a person with the name 'Alexandra' in your directory."

It is better that way, Dong thinks to himself, alone in the dark, his face between his knees. *It is better that way. Because my Alexandra is leaving.* He smiles, overwhelmed by the darkness of his solitude. *My Alexandra is lost.*

Chapter 3: Letter #1

Simon, my Alexandra, my light, my freedom, my will to live,

If only I could call you that and still have you beside me. I'm breathing through dreams mingled with harsh reality. What can I do? We are living in hard times. Remember when you told me about that Charles Dickens novel? It is the best of times, and it is the worst of times. This is my way of asking, "How are you doing?"

You might say—and I can hear your voice ringing in my ear with laughter—that I'm being melodramatic. Oakville and Mississauga are not that far away. A thirty-minute trip could cover everything I want to say in an embrace. I can smell summer on your clothes. But never mind.

It is very bold of me to write you a letter considering how we parted ways. However, I'm holding on to your word that I can send you these good-for-nothing letters. It's worth noting that I'm also secretly holding on to "Alexandra Leaving." So here goes nothing, again.

I had an interesting encounter with Leonard Cohen's "Dance Me to the End of Love" today, sung by the man himself. The raspy voice and the poignant lyrics make me think about so many things. Most of them are sad, so I will not be bothering you with that. But I also think of good things. Like how a human heart can feel so much from something so simple. Like how Leonard Cohen is a genius at tugging at the audience's heartstring through words. Like how my parents are screaming downstairs while I'm putting on my headphones and cranking up the volume—doing everything I can to stop the hurt. If only I could express with words how badly I wish you were in the room with me and holding me in your arms, telling me that the thunderstorm will pass.

Or like how we don't appreciate peace enough as it is.

So, it's getting sad. Other news: I made friends. They are nice. You don't have to be here physically to protect me anymore. Should I imagine you being happy with that? Or would you be sad that the boy who was writhing, crying in your arms a few years back has now grown up—not into a strong person who can beat his bullies, but into a person who can tolerate the abuse?

Hey, have you ever read Pablo Neruda? I bought his book and hid it under my pillow. My parents would probably take me to weird places if they know I'm still "up to the same shenanigans and that weird sexual stuff." It might not be the best decision for now, but I am high on the guilt. At least I have no regrets. You can say that I bite off more than I could chew. But in the end, I always eat it up and spit it out. "My Way" reference.

Among the burning of the Amazon Rainforest and the African jungles, the looming war in the Pacific Ocean, and the rush to jump to our own ending, I fear regret now more than ever.

Hope this letter can lighten up your day. After all, that was my sole intention. Catch you up next letter. I will hunt down some good news by then.

Dance me through the panic till I'm gathered safely in
Lift me like an olive branch and be my homeward dove
Dance me to the end of love.
- Leonard Cohen -

Your Anthony, forever and always.

Chapter 4: Scheming on Running Away

"So, what do you think? Do you think it'll work?" Ames asks, eagerly chewing her pencil. She covers the library table with a spread made of her overdue homework. Her math worksheet is still empty despite the three teenagers having been in the library for over two hours now. Dong stays silent, his eyes hyper-focusing on a math problem while his mind is repeating Amy's question over and over for a thousandth time.

"I don't know, Ames. I don't think my parents will allow me to have a sleepover. They were fighting yesterday. It will take at least one more week for them to even remember I exist." Dong sighs, erasing his answer on the worksheet.

"What does it matter? My mom can give your mom a call," Lizzie chimes in. "Oh fucking Hell, give me that poor thing, Ames. Do my essay instead." She snatches the worksheet from across the table and begins solving the derivatives problem.

"Your mom and my mom, huh? I'd love to see how things go down between them." Dong chuckles. "Remember the last time when your mom brought over homemade bread and they got into a big argument on child rearing?"

"Yeah. The Civil War of 2020. Lest we forget." Lizzie rolls

her eyes and jokingly raises her arms in a gesture of memorial.

The three of them laugh then hush each other when the school librarian looks up from her table and clicks her tongue. Far across the room, someone is building a house of cards just to see it fall.

"So, the party is this Friday. You must go." Ames stops bothering with her homework. She decides to leave the small problems up to God and turns to the bigger problem at hand that she can change with her own hand. "Listen, D-dog. What if this is the last chance—the only chance—for your life to be free?"

"When did I ever say that I'm not free?" Dong keeps on writing, purposefully ignoring Ames's words and feigning a calm presence. Inside him, an ocean twists and turns. A whirlwind of regrets and emotions rages on.

"I mean, is any one of us free? You are incredibly intelligent, D-dog, but you ask such silly questions." Ames looks at Dong's head.

She knows Dong well enough to prick at where it hurts, but she also knows the boy well enough to sense that he won't tend to his wounds. He'd rather let them fester and overpower him until he is but a tiny footprint on Earth. But Ames won't let him do that.

In the quietude of the slanting afternoon sunshine, Ames thinks about her father. He was timid and shy—the type of man who'd never cause anyone problems. His friends believed he was happy. They had no cause to doubt, until his death came upon him like the final tolling bell. She was nine years old. What sort of cruel fate could turn its hand when the clock struck midnight and take away the life of the only man who had cared enough to lessen his daughter's suffering, but not enough to think about the aftermath of his ending?

Until that point in time, Ames never believed in a suffering so mountainous that it could crush and curse the living out of someone else. And after that, time has continued pushing her back to that morning, when her mother knocked on her door, her eyes empty, whispering the news, "Ames, your father is—" Yes, she is never free, and she doubts she will ever be.

She lets her eyes wander about the school library. She used to daydream a lot, usually about being a badass princess who leads her own revolution and rescues her country from the dragon or simply being a badass doctor who can save her patients from the claws of death. But now she just lets it all go. After all, what can dreaming ever do? "None of us is really free, are we?" Ames mumbles under her breath, momentarily forgetting about Dong, about their plan to overtake every obstacle, about the final goal. About life. About her purpose here.

"Ames?" Dong waves his hands in front of Ames. His eyes are filled with worry. He knows better than to talk about freedom in front of her, but he lets the stupidity of his timidity conquer his mind. No words of apology are needed between the three of them. All they ever need to say to each other is, "Are you alright?"

"Yeah. I guess. Sort of." Ames jerks awake, trying to put a cheerful smile back on her face.

"I didn't say that we couldn't go with the plan. I'm just saying that there's no chance my mother will go along that easily." Dong twirls the pencil in his hand. For the first time since they got to the library two hours ago, he stops pretending that he is solving his homework.

"Look here you guys, you forget the most important factor

here." Lizzie slams the table, ignoring the hostile glare from the librarian and the hushes from the other students. The house of cards falls for the hundredth time.

"And what's that?" Dong asks, smiling all-knowingly at her dramatic act.

"That I'm the brain here. Well, Dong is the brain here when it comes to studying, solving problems, and writing essays. But in all other aspects, I'm the brain."

"Of course, you are," Ames mumbles. "It's easy to say so when you got an F on Shakespeare but an A on being a smartass."

"Yeah, but isn't that all the more reason why you should trust me with this adventure?"

"We want to get him out, not get him in jail." Ames rolls her eyes.

"And I said I could do it. Impossible Mission—Code Name: Jailbreaking. Isn't that fun?" Lizzie almost jumps from her seat with excitement, but she holds back under the gaze of the librarian, then whispers in a high pitch, "Isn't that exciting? You dig, huh? You all dig it?"

"You crazy ass," both Dong and Ames whisper back in unison. After a short moment of hesitation, Ames asks, "So, what's the plan?"

"The plan is... There is no plan. Just kidding, ow, Ames, stop kicking. The plan is my mom is going to have a showdown with Dong's mom. We'll need to cooperate on a little white lie: Ames's mom is on a need-to-know basis. We'll tell her that the three of us are at my house studying for the upcoming exam. In the worst-case scenario, she can be our last-standing ally. At least, she is more understanding than D-dog's mom. Dong's mom absolutely must not know about the operation. It's an us-against-the-world type of thing: We must stand as a united front and Dong's mom is the dragon we must fight with all our wits in order to free the princess, a.k.a. the A-plus student who knows nothing about life." Lizzie talks passionately while scribbling down the plan and doodling dragons and knights on the white page.

"What about the car drive? Is your mom still up to it?"

"Of course, my mom is still up to it. She's up to anything that can make her feel young again and this is the exact type of thing she'll dig."

"Can't believe the life you lead, Lizzie," Ames finally says, laughing. At this rate, they will get kicked out of the school library soon. The librarian is already standing up and heading toward their table.

"Yeah, me too, can't believe it." Dong shrugs his shoulders and turns back to the worksheets.

"Wait until you hear her teach us the '80's swearwords on our little road trip to the party," Lizzie flushes and mumbles in an exasperated tone. She is never embarrassed of her mom. Rather, she is proud that her mom always finds it in her busy schedule to shower her only daughter with so much love that Lizzie almost forgets she doesn't have a father.

"I don't know. That sounds fun to me," Dong says with a subtle hint of timidity mingled with jealousy. "I'm not allowed to swear at home. I learn swearwords plenty at school, but God forbid an allusion to swearing at home, in front of my mother."

"Think of it this way, D-dog, at least you have a father." Ames draws circles on Dong's notebook. "Neither of us have one. That must be nice."

"You wouldn't want a father like mine. Don't jump to such

happy conclusions too soon, it's not good for the heart." Dong chuckles. He is never afraid of showing his true self and speaking his truth in front of these two dear girls. Different as they are, it is a miracle that they found each other.

"Alright, two hours wasted in the library. Conclusion: We are all a miserable wretch. Ames and I don't have fathers. D-dog can't swear. My mom will teach us how to live in the '80s. Now, disperse. I need to be home for the beer cake."

"What will happen if you are not home?" Dong asks, poking his pencil at Lizzie's naturally curled hair that looks like locks of tangled web.

"Then my mom is not going to have a beer cake tonight. Off you guys go. The librarian is gonna turn into Medusa real soon." She waves her hands and shoos them away in her theatrical, exasperating way.

They all pack their stuff and head slowly out of the school library. None of them finishes their homework.

In his mind, Dong knows that he's going to spend a suspiciously long time in his room before dinner tonight. He hopes his mother will not notice, if she's even around to notice. His father is going to be at the factory tonight. Perhaps his mother will take on the night shift at the restaurant. That shift ends at two in the morning, or whenever the restaurant's last clients leave.

Dong is used to being alone in their cramped basement apartment in the home his family shares with two other families. They are his father's relatives, and partly due to seniority, partly due to the amount of investment in the house, the other families take the two upper floors. He has never gotten along with his cousins. They always say he dreams too big, and he always scorns them because their life consists of so little. It's a raging war whenever the three families get together for parties and anniversaries. His cousins' parents always brag about their children's income, whileDong's parents brag about how good his grades are in school or the scholarship he gets.

At those times, all Dong ever wishes for is to disappear and vanish into thin air. All those adults, and none of them interested in understanding what being a child means, despite once being children themselves.

His aunt would say, "Oh, so-and-so got a 50% raise in commission and bonuses. So-and-so is promoted to the team leader position." And his mother would say, while his father gulps down another beer, "That's admirable. Dong here is getting a full scholarship again. How many times is that now? Ten times, isn't it, Dong?' Fake laughter and strained smiles. Lies on their lips, scorn in their eyes. They breathe the living out of him. Every Goddamn time.

"D-dog? You okay?" Ames asks, her voice full of worry. Dong wakes up from his daydreaming.

The school bus slowly comes to a stop and Lizzie gets off reluctantly. Her eyes scan Dong's face for the last time, and she calls back to Ames, "Call me if anything happens. Wait, even if nothing happens, call me anyway." Then she jumps down and walks away.

"I'm alright. I'm just so tired." Dong rubs his eyes.

"That's why I always say that two hours in the library is too much. We only need, like, thirty minutes there. Anything more and I start to get sleepy. We need to breathe. We are not prisoners."

"I like studying, though. At least, that's the only thing I'm good at."

"Are you crazy?" Ames shouts, then lowers her voice at the

stare of the other passengers. "I know you, and you are good at plenty. And even if you *are* only good at studying, what do you take Lizzie and me for? Heck, without you, we'd probably just fuck it up with all our essays and fail all our tests. Don't underestimate yourself. Anyone can do that, but the last thing you should do is lower yourself and let them win."

"Even if the other party is my parents?" Dong smiles at her, defeated and surrendering.

"D-dog, you'll leave home when you go to university, yeah?" Ames asks absentmindedly, leaning back on her seat and putting an arm around Dong's shoulders.

"Perhaps. Perhaps not. It depends on what my parents want."

"Don't let them decide your life. For me, I won't leave my house. My mom needs someone to take care of her and the burden on her shoulders. But you should leave, or else that house would swallow you up, flesh and bones. This is me." Ames takes her backpack and, with the same reluctance as Lizzie, she says, "Call me if anything happens."

"You know I always do."

"Lizzie and I both know you. That's why we must repeat it so often. Bye."

She gets off the bus and walks through the gate of a one-story house. Along the path there is a little garden her mother tends to on her days off. Ames knows a lot about flowers and gardening; she says that she learns it from the best of them all: her mother. Dong watches her disappear into the arch entrance until her house becomes a tiny dot like a marker on a map.

The bus stops again. He heaves his sag of books and notepads on his shoulders, prepares his mental strength, and gets off the bus. As he unlocks the door, Dong sees that his mother has not chosen to work the night shift after all. But what he is not prepared for when he puts his shoes on the shoe rack and walks inside is the avalanche of insults being thrown at him and the phone at the same time:

"My son is not going to help your daughter study. It's her damn fault for failing, isn't it? Or is it yours? How did you raise her? No, no, I'm not calling her stupid, but she will drag my son's grades down. No, I won't agree with it." His mother slams the phone hard, then turns to him, her eyes red with anger. "Dong, did you ever get my permission to tutor those two stupid girls?"

Well, he thinks, *Here the nightmare goes again.* At that moment, Dong wishes she could absorb his entire being and return him to the nothingness where he had come from.

Chapter 5: The Liars Take It All

"Did you ever get my permission? Did you?" Dong's mom shouts across the kitchen as she works her way around the counter, preparing dinner for the whole family.

"No, I did not, Mom. But we just planned it today at lunch. I couldn't talk to you about it until I got home." Dong licks his lips, his hands clench into two sweaty fists, his fingernails break the skin of his palms. This is the first time he has ever lied to his mom, and eventually, his dad.

"Then why did that white woman say that you discussed this as a group three days ago? What are you trying to pull? Shouldn't I have been in the know those three days, huh, Dong? Shouldn't I?"

"No—I mean, yes, you should know. But three days ago, we only discussed it as a possibility. Then—"

"Then what? Even as a possibility, you should tell me first. Me, not that white woman's daughter."

"Lizzie and Ames are bad at English and Math, and exams are coming up, so I thought maybe I could revise while tutoring them," Dong says, his voice almost a whisper now. His mind screams, *Please say that it makes sense. Please believe in the lies I tell. Please let me have this one chance. Haven't you taken enough?*

"Dong, I always tell you that hanging around a wrong crowd can only make you go down. Don't disappoint your father and me further than this. I won't have any talk of this 'tutoring' any more, alright? Now go to your room. I will call you when dinner's ready."

"Mom," Dong says, trying his best to sound calm, but his mind is already a mess with shattered glass shards that cut deeper and deeper into his existence. "Do you even love me?"

"Of course, I love you. Why do you think I'm working twelve hours a day? I had so many roads ahead of me—so many—but I sacrificed them all for you. What's wrong with wanting you to be the person you should be with all those sacrifices? Don't let them whitewash you, Dong. Your father and I love you."

"I understand, Mom."

Dong nods, biting back a thousand screams, and drags his legs along the corridor to find the staircase down the basement. *The person you should become,* he muses, *And not the person you want to become.* He closes the door to his room, takes out his phone, and dials Lizzie's number. It takes a while longer than usual before he hears the chirping voice on the other line.

"Yo, guess it didn't go as planned, huh? Did you get an earful?"

"Worse. I got enough for a whole therapy session, if I could afford it and if Ma would even agree to let those white people treat me." Dong laughs in a quiet voice, fearing that his mom is standing on the other side of the door, listening in.

"Too bad, then. What should we do now?"

"I don't know. You are the brain, you tell me."

"Is there any way you can get out of the house without getting caught? Like, poof, Houdini-style."

"Are you joking? I'm in the basement. If not my mom, then one of my aunts or uncles would catch me."

"How about telling her that you are going to a—a test prep center to take mock exams?"

"Lizzie, you are supposed to be the brain."

"Yeah?"

"So, be the brain. Don't make up stupid lies that we all know will be detected as soon as we tell them."

"Oh, yeah? Then you be the brain, tell me, what's *your* plan?" Lizzie asks in a haughty voice.

"I don't know." Dong sighs. "I don't even know if this is worth it. This is even more tiresome than hiding a volume of Pablo Neruda's famous love poems under my pillow."

Lizzie laughs mirthfully into the phone. "Go with the mock exam story. I'll back you up."

"My mom knows your voice, and your mother's, too. We can't ask Ames's mom to do this."

"Everyone lies. And I never said that I was going to ask Ames's mother to help us lie. As you said, I'm the brain. You just tell the mock exam story. Leave the rest to me."

"Lizzie?"

"Yeah?"

"I can't believe the life you've led." Dong smiles, warmed with affection.

"Yeah, well I can't believe the life you've led, D-dog. See you tomorrow. Tell your mom the white woman's stupid daughter says, 'Hi,' and that she is not welcome in our house."

Lizzie hangs up with a curt grunt. Dong can almost see her face contorted with anger and her brows furrowed into a straight line on the other side of the phone. He leans against the door, trying to piece together the lies he needs to say, the evidence he needs to lay out, the trap he wants his mother to willingly step on. Then he can safely close the door of this house and leave everything behind to choose the life he wants to lead for just one fateful night. Suddenly, his mother is on the other side of the door, knocking vigorously.

"Are you in there, Dong? Dinner's ready. Get out and eat so I can go to my night shift," his mom shouts, trying to push the door open against his weight.

Dong stays silent, wishing she'll think that he's asleep and go away. He likes sitting in the dark and musing about how different things would be if just a simple atom in his life changed its course. Sometimes, he uses the spare darkness to mull over whether he wanted a different mom. He couldn't care less about his father. He's rarely home, and when he is, there's nothing but shouting, yelling, and insults thrown around, piercing his ears and stabbing his eyes. At those times, he wishes he was deaf and blind.

Outside, his mom yells again, "Open the door. Why is it locked? What are you up to? Dinner's ready." She pushes harder until the door cracks open and hits Dong's back. That is always her motto: If a door doesn't open for her, she will strike it down. It's a wonder to Dong how she hasn't burned a forest with her passion to fiercely kill everything that's living, including his father. Dong often wonders as he lies there in the dark, listening to the universe's breath, whether his mom loves anyone besides herself. She often reminds him that of all three of them, she is the one who sacrifices the most. And that's how he learned to hate that word "sacrifice," like a debt he needs to pay back; it is the prison he chooses to live inside. He breathes in the darkness amidst the thumping of the door against his back, his hand holding tightly on to the phone as his last remnant of sanity.

"Mom."

"Why did you lock the door?"

"I didn't lock it. I was just leaning on it to call Lizzie."

"I told you to keep the door open all the time. And don't call that girl. Dong, how many times do I have to tell you? Find intelligent people to befriend. Smart boys and girls with straight A's. Our ancestors always say that hanging around a black inkpot will only turn you darker. I say—"

She keeps pouring down words and Dong lets them float past him. He thinks about the lies he needs to tell, the story he'll make up. The house of cards he needs to build just to see it fall.

He clenches the phone. Lizzie and Ames's voices ring in his ears, *This is the last chance, D-dog. What if there is no other chance?* And despite not showing it to his friends, he always knows the threat, the fear, and the catastrophe of the phrase "There's no other chance." He faces his mom, his eyes trying to fight the tough battle of his generation against hers, his voice laying the first layer of the house of cards.

"Mom, I'm going to take a mock exam."

"What? You never discussed that with me."

It's funny how she uses the word "discuss," Dong thinks, since she always has to have the last word on all those discussions. "I have done some research about...about mock exams and there is a...a test prep center in Oakville that will organize one of those this Friday."

"Why are you stammering?" Dong's mom asks with suspicion dripping in every word.

"I mean, I didn't know if you'd agree, and I didn't discuss it with you first so I'm a bit ner—nervous."

"What's this mock exam about?"

"It's for Math and English."

"Math and English? And how long will it take?"

"The tests may take about two hours total?"

"Why are you asking me?"

"Sorry, Mom. It's going to take two hours. Or more."

"When will you go? And where is this school? Give me the address so I can find the way there. I will take you."

"No, no you don't need to take me. I'm going to take the bus there. It's easy to find. It's in Oakville. And I'm going there at seven p.m."

A long pause. The insufferable ticking sound of the clock on the wall. The beads of sweat on his back. Dong can't bear it anymore. As the truth is ready to burst from him, his mom asks,"What's the name of the school?"

"I—I don't remember."

Dong slowly lays down another card and the house of cards is swaying. His mom looks at him, her eyes trying to find the black spot of lies between Dong's averted gaze and the stammering words that mean nothing to her but the world to him.

"How come you don't remember the school's name if you're going there?"

"I just...you make me panic."

"Why? Am I scaring you? I just want to know the school's name. What's so difficult about that?"

"The school's name is—wait a bit, please, it's on my table." Dong quickly walks away from the door and heads toward his desk.

In his mind, Dong screams Lizzie's name and curses her for making him do something he's never done. But before his curses finish, his mom pushes him away and walks briskly to the desk, her eyes screening everything on there for the word "school." He grows nervous as every second goes by with his mom standing still in front of his desk. Dong is waiting for the house of cards to fall.

"I don't see no school here." And the first layer of cards is slowly shattering.

"I'm sure it's there somewhere," Dong stammers, his invisible hands reaching out to catch the falling cards and trying to put them on again. "I can call the school if you'd like."

"What are you trying to pull, Dong?" his mom says sternly, her hands on her hips, her lips set into a straight line. This is her way of saying, "You are testing my patience."

At that moment, Dong questions himself, *Yeah, what am I trying to pull?* What is he trying to pull when this plan is fated to fail right from the start? What is he trying to pull when he doesn't even know if this one chance can help him get the life he wants? What exactly is he trying to pull when he already knows that it is far too late? His whole body shakes with a rage he cannot place. His mind grows hazy; his first tear falls.

"Why are you crying? What did I do? You are a grown man, don't pull that sissy act on me now. Your father's going to give you a beating when he gets home. Now, answer me, what are you trying to pull?"

"Mom, I—" Dong is considering telling her the truth when the home phone suddenly starts ringing.

"You wait here." His mom glares at him while walking upstairs to get the phone. Dong takes a deep breath to calm his racing heart then he quickly dials Lizzie's number.

"Yo, what's up, D-dog?"

"I can't do it, Lizzie. I can't do it. She found out. Why did

35

I even try? I already knew—" Dong breathes hard into the phone, trying to get everything off his chest in one second because every second is precious to him now.

"Woah, calm down," Lizzie says. Her voice sounds like she's chewing something. "Now, what I need you to do is to show your mom the link I just sent you, then tell her that the school has a Vietnamese representative who's willing to discuss things with her anytime, then give her the number I included in the text. Let me take care of the rest."

"Lizzie, what are you trying to pull?" Dong asks, absent-mindedly repeating the same question his mom asked him a few minutes ago. Perhaps he's trying to confirm something he's not yet aware of himself. Perhaps he wants someone to tell him that despite everything, he can pull this off—whatever this is. Perhaps he just wants someone to pat his head and tell him that everything is going to be okay.

"What am I trying to pull, huh? I'm trying to pull the same exact thing as you."

"To be free?"

"To be young." Lizzie laughs. Her laughter echoes in Dong's ears. "It seems we are a bit different, then. Do as you are told, Dong." Lizzie pronounces his name in her clumsy way, then her voice grows serious. "May the liars take it all."

He hangs up at the exact moment his mom barges into the room. The text is ready. The website is open. The phone number is saved on his phone. Dong says with an ardent determination, betting against all that is lost and all that could ever be:

"Mom, I found the school's name."

Chapter 6: Letter #3

Simon, Simon, Simon,

I whisper your name in the sweet agony of the sleepless night, and with every note, I can taste the bittersweet poison of your existence, pouring into me, until I am no longer a free entity.

Simon, did you know that autumn here in Mississauga is very beautiful? Our neighbors recommended a nice park for my family to visit when we had time and all they heard from my mother was the sound of the curtains closing. Simon, why is it so hard to be living?

I know my mother is afraid. I know she had a hard life. She dropped the degrees, the certificates, and all the fancy shit back home to come here, looking for freedom, but now, freedom sounds more like death. Who'd have thought that a bachelor's degree in economics would prove to be less important than used toilet paper? I saw her burn everything to light up our small barbeque set. Her face showed no regrets, but if we were to believe the facial masks everyone puts in front of us, what kind of pathetic life would that be? Living based on lies or living to feel life—which do you prefer?

Simon, I don't feel well. I never do. I run high fevers of passionate yearning and I jump head-first into the nearest abyss without even considering the consequences and the aftermath. I cross the street without watching the light because no matter what, I'm just living to count the days. My life revolves around two months: October and May. The day you came into my life, and the other when you went away. Simon, a sage used to preach to his brethren that the more people leave your life, the more you'll forgive yourself. You don't know on what ground you'll need that forgiveness, but you will learn, until one day, the act of them leaving you feels like but a prayer on the softest footstep.

Simon, I wish I could weep. My tears are dried. What else do I have besides trying and trying only to see that the summit is but another torture? You are nowhere nearer, and I am nowhere closer. Between us is an ocean, and someday, we'll see it fall apart.

Simon, do you know that if the axis of the Earth was just one millimeter away from its current position, all of us would be dead? But I don't want to talk about that. Instead, let me talk about autumn in Mississauga. I biked around Erindale Park. The fallen leaves were crushed underneath my tires, and while everyone was mesmerized by the dead of the living, I couldn't help my feeling of disgust. A nausea took control of me, and now all I have left is apathy. It was like a movie scene: I was watching all of them dancing in the moonlight while isolating myself in a glacier jailhouse. I was waiting for my own spring. Two more years and I shall be at the entrance of university. Two more years, and I'll know the taste of freedom. Some say it's salty, some say it's sweet, others say it's that old trick—you are only craving it because everyone else is craving it. Simon, do you ever wonder why we are taught to fight for our freedom but the moment we raise our voices, we discover that freedom is not what we are fighting for? Do you ever wonder for whose sake it is that we rage those wars?

Simon, I'm sleepy all the time, but I don't sleep. Neither do I dream. Rarely do I live. I'm floating between the person I should be and the person I want to be. Simon, do you think it's selfish of me to be who I am? Is there as much sin in living as there is sin in dying?

Simon, Simon, Simon, the night is still, and I can hear the wind whispering your name ever so lightly against the rustling leaves. I did say that if I were to meet you again, we would jump on the first train and get out of here. I save some money from my part-time job. You surely have a small sum—or nothing at all, it doesn't matter. And we will get out of this stifling rat race. We will leave the GTAs behind, jump on the first train to Montreal, stopping at every stop to earn more money, and watch ourselves grow. The show will go on after us, the same way it went on before us. And thus, my Alexandra, why is it so hard to be living?

Your Anthony.

Chapter 7: I Know Where You Slept That Night

Ms. Hoa Nguyen, Dong's mom, is a stout woman and much stronger than her grave face lets on. With an almost non-existent husband, Ms. Hoa always carries on her shoulders a boulder of responsibilities that would last her a lifetime. She entertains herself with the thought that when she lies there dying, everyone will bellow a devastating cry for the jobs she left behind and she will be the one with the last laugh. Who can blame her? She's had enough. So, as a way of escaping this Hell-bound, forever-winter country, she allows herself the right to bestow miseries on the people closest to her. How else can she live in her own sorrow if everyone else is happy?

Such is Ms. Hoa's thought whenever her husband comes home, drunkenly starting his usual ruckus: throwing things, insulting her, screaming, chasing her around the basement apartment to land blow after blow on her. But Ms. Hoa never wishes to escape. She knows she can't solve anything if the only action she takes is running away at the soonest moment. No, far more reasonable than escaping, she wants him dead. How many nights like tonight, when she lies beside him, watching him breathing, has she imagined to herself how his throat will break under her arms and how he will suffer from suffocating, begging, pleading with her to let him live. It's not easy to keep such thoughts from overflowing her brain and turning themselves into a reality she can't undo. Ms. Hoa puts down her phone, closes her eyes, and tries to avert her mind from the dangerous path it is going down.

She is thinking about Dong.

The call this evening was strange. On the other side of the home phone, the woman talked a lot, and after fifteen minutes, she hung up curtly without waiting for Ms. Hoa to raise any objection. Not that she could speak the language perfectly, but she'd still prefer it if she could have the last word. A few curse words would do a nice job. But that's not the point. She recalls Dong's strange behavior after the call. He showed her the school's name, the website, the phone number of the Vietnamese representative and whatnot. But it sounded like a trap.

Ms. Hoa has lived long enough to recognize the nice facade of a trap when she sees one. Dong was standing there, wrenching his hands, switching his legs, stammering in broken sentences about how the teachers referred him to this school. *Poor boy,* Ms. Hoa muses. *He's never known how to lie.* Because Ms. Hoa didn't raise a liar. She chose a liar as a husband just so that she'd always know how worthless a liar is, and she swore to herself on the day of Dong's birth that no matter what, the boy would never go down that sickening path, strewn with thorns and mocking laughter from outsiders. He would grow up to be greater than whatever Ms. Hoa could have been. He was her hope, her life force, her source of happiness. He was her own existence. His is the only life she lives—because her life died a long time ago, the moment she stepped on the

41

asphalt road of this vast country.

And yet, he lied to me.

Ms. Hoa knows something is amiss. She noticed it the day Dong came back home from his friend Simon's home. It was a nice evening in May, and she was preparing for the night shift at the restaurant, when Dong rushed in. His face was flushed. His tears were flowing non-stop, like a broken faucet. He even ignored her presence—a thing he'd never done before because she'd raised him to be better than giving in to emotions and sentiments. Dong went straight to his room, and she could hear his sobbing. All she could think at that time was that she was running late. The owner of the restaurant might take these few minutes of comforting her son out of her paycheck. And Dong needed money for his tutoring sessions, for his piano lessons, his clothes, his hair, his life. She lingered near Dong's room, then, bearing the knife in her heart, she left the boy alone and went to work.

But when Ms. Hoa opened the front door, Simon's mom was there.

"We need to have a talk," the woman said. Her face was stern with a repressed anger.

"What do you want? I have nothing to say," Ms. Hoa retorted.

"Your son laid a hand on my son. Jesus, Hoa, I thought we were friends."

Ms. Hoa understood what "laying a hand on somebody" meant, but part of her refused to see the factual statement Simon's mom made about her son. Somewhere within her, a voice screamed out, *"We were never friends. You leave your son in the dark; I bear mine with light. You only care about your own kind of people; I am always just a decoration to your little circle of housewives. Your sorrows lie in not having the things you want; mine lies in not having the life my son deserves. You and I are very different people. But look, why do we even share the same skeleton?"* But Ms. Hoa stayed silent. She pushed the woman out of the entryway and closed the door behind her, barring her uninvited entrance.

"Dong's asleep."

"After what he's done to my son, don't you think sleeping is a stupid punishment? What is wrong with you? My boy's only in grade nine."

"So is my boy. What do you think?" She scoffed. "They are in the same class. That's why this *thing* happened."

"But he—"

"Look, I don't care what your boy did or what my boy did. My people have this proverb: There's no smoke without a fire. So don't you go on blaming my son for what your son has a fifty percent share of blame. You call that punishment stupid? I will let you see how stupid a Vietnamese mom can be."

Ms. Hoa gritted her teeth. Her accent was strong, but her hands were stronger, and her English was powerful enough to silent the enemy. She threw herself at Simon's mom, pushed the woman to the ground, and both tumbled in the pathway, floundering to find a way to stand as the moral victor, as if the whole matter could be solved by deciding who was the stronger woman. Ms. Hoa held the other woman tightly, screaming her lungs into the Earth and the grass.

"Don't you dare accuse my son of that. Don't you dare. Let the boy live. Damn you. Let the boy live."

They struggled for a while on the driveway. Simon's mom tried to escape but Ms. Hoa kept holding her back—grabbing her ankles, her wrists, her blouse. Anything within reach was

Ms. Hoa's weapon. For the first time since Ms. Hoa came to this strange land, she tasted her first taste of freedom. It was bloody. It was hard to swallow. It was everything she'd lost and nothing like the picture people painted for her. It was Hell. And she was sure that she could drag the woman down with her to her own pit of freedom. Yes, let her suffer. Or, better yet, let them suffer. Anyone can be the sacrificial lamb—even Ms. Hoa—as long as Dong could continue walking, spreading his wings, and flying to the Heaven that all mortals yearn for.

That day, Ms. Hoa took her night shift off. After Simon's mom ran back home, she calmly fixed her hair, got into her car, and drove to the nearest Tim Hortons. She ordered a hot coffee, a bagel with butter, a donut, ten Timbits, and allowed herself to indulge in this new happiness. *So*, she thought to herself, *I still have a lot of fight left in me.*

She never told her husband about the fight. After a night of crying, her son stood up and walked outside like nothing had happened. Ms. Hoa knew that it wasn't an ending then— and time has proven her right—but she decided to let it all go because Dong never said anything to her. It was her duty to protect whatever was left in him to keep him happy. But at that moment, when she was indulging in the warm coffee and the sweet taste of the pastry, she never once thought about any of those heavy consequences.

And now Dong is lying to me.

Ms. Hoa turns to her side, away from her drunken husband's snoring. She wants to know what is so important to Dong that made him commit such an unforgivable act. She wonders where it all went wrong. In her mind, she plays the tape of memory repeatedly.

Dong in his baby clothes; his first day at primary school,

44

secondary school, and, most recently, high school. In between are the blank gaps for which she can't find any fitting puzzle pieces . She never sees him much; she is too busy with the whole house's burden on her shoulders. Turning over the pages of her scant memory, Ms. Hoa startles and sits up in her bed. How long has it been since the last time she saw Dong laugh? It's a mystery how his childhood has gone past her like a cart before the wheel, and she is left with nothing but this film reel of the things she has lost.

Ms. Hoa gets off the bed and walks toward Dong's bedroom. The light is out. The door stands ajar. She slowly steps inside the room and sits down on the bed. The boy's sleeping peacefully. His face is serene; he's smiling in his sleep. Ms. Hoa doesn't have the power to control what her son is dreaming but she is content with the thought that whatever it is, it must be a good omen. She strokes his hair, whispering, "What are you trying to hide from me?"

The boy turns in his twin bed and Ms. Hoa withdraws her hand, fearing he might wake up and see this gentle side of her. She's always believed—or rather, she was taught to believe—that a good child can only come out of a strict parent. But is that good logic? If it is, her son would not need to lie to her to get what he wants. She comforts herself with the thought that maybe tomorrow, Dong will tell her with a small guilty voice what he's been doing and why he tried to pull a blind over her eyes. She knows that it won't happen, but still, what does it cost a person to hope?

"Mom?" Dong's hoarse voice brings her back to the dark room.

"What?" she answers in her usual curt voice, but something breaks in her throat, and what comes out is an ocean of repressed tenderness. He is her only son. The hope of her life, the core of her existence. And yet—

"Why are you still up, Mom?"

"Nothing. Do I need your permission to stay up?"

"I'm sorry, Mom," Dong whispers quietly, then he sits up and looks at Ms. Hoa with half open eyes. "Are you worried about my grades? I will get straight A's again, don't worry."

Ms. Hoa turns her face away. She wants to tell him that it is okay, that he doesn't need to try so hard, that she only needs him to be happy. That she wants him to smile at her one more time, or many more times, the way he used to smile at her in his childhood. Used clothes and hand-me-down backpacks; days without heat and piled-up blankets on bare mattresses, but the two of them were blessed with laughter, and they were free, instead of separated by this labyrinth of misunderstanding and words not spoken in the mist of foggy deception. Ms. Hoa looks at Dong—he is no longer a baby.

She doesn't know why that fact takes so long to register in her mind. She knows he will grow up, and that means she's growing old, too. But why can't she let him go? Why can't she be content with the knowledge that he's perfectly capable of taking care of himself? All Ms. Hoa can think of, day and night, in the stuffy basement, in the nail salon, and in the kitchen of the restaurant, is how Dong will survive after she's dead. Would it be better if she had stayed in that country and raised him to speak Vietnamese instead of this strange language? Would it be better if she'd married a husband for love, not for a purpose that she now deeply regrets?

The phrase *Would it be better if...* echoes in Ms. Hoa's mind until all she sees is a blurry image of what her life could have been. But the chance is long gone, ever since the day she stepped off the plane. She forfeited everything just to see her child have a future she wished she had had. Perhaps that is where things went wrong. Perhaps Dong doesn't wish to be her wish fulfillment. But what else can she do? And what else does life require of her, so that she can have a moment like that again—the moment of content and happiness after she fought with Simon's mom and indulged herself in the luxury of coffee and pastry? A moment where she can taste the bitter taste of freedom?

"Mom?" Dong shakes her arm anxiously.

He is fully awake now. His mom's silhouette is carved on his retina, and for the first time, he suddenly feels the solitude in that bent back. Ms. Hoa's entire body is shaking with broken sobs. Dong quickly gets out of his blanket and scoots over to hug her. He is somewhat surprised by the bony frame of his mother. Her hair is a mess; the white streaks are more numerous than the youthful black ones, and Dong wonders how much youth is left within her. He feels the truth bursting at the seams, and he almost blurts it all out. But what good would it do to them both? Dong will lose everything, and his mom will bear all the pain. Between them is a sea of make-believe, curt answers to earnest questions. He cannot fix the entire universe with a single drop of truth.

"Mom," Dong whispers into his mother's hair, his voice breaking everywhere and breaking in between. "Mom, what's wrong?"

"Dong, you'll never lie to your mom, won't you?" Ms. Hoa asks, her hand holding on to Dong's tender embrace as if it will fall apart any moment.

"Why do you ask?" Dong swallows dryly, his heart in his throat.

"I don't know. I don't know anything anymore. I mean, Dong, you grew up so fast," Ms. Hoa says amidst the tears. "Too fast, for that matter."

Dong stays quiet, his hand on his mom's shoulders. *Is there any chance she knows already?* Dong thinks to himself, flabbergasted and confused. The fear runs through his blood and pumps his heart with adrenaline. He needs to do something, but he doesn't know what.

A voice in his head urges him to tell the truth. Perhaps in her vulnerable state, Ms. Hoa will agree to let him have this one chance—this one moment—to be free. But another voice tells him that won't happen. That his mom doesn't want him for who he is. That his mom prefers an ideal, not a son.

He doesn't want to hurt his mom, but he yearns for a taste of the freedom that Lizzie and Ames have. He yearns to live the life he wants, not the life other people want for him. He yearns to fly. He yearns to be loved. And what is wrong with those wishes? Dong shakes his head with a strong determination. No, he won't give in to these claws of darkness disguised as the sweet temptation of innocence.

"I won't lie to you, Mom," Dong says, swallowing the burning, salty taste of unforgivable guilt. "I never lie to you."

"Then that's alright. Hey, Dong, do you remember the night shortly before Simon's family moved to Oakville?" Ms. Hoa suddenly asks, as if the intuition of a mother wakes up and rings an alarm.

"What about it, Mom?"

"I know what happened that night" Ms. Hoa turns back to face her son, her eyes filled with water, but the tears refuse to surrender to the pain she carries. "I know where you went that night."

Dong jerks back. His eyes betray him with a glimpse of repentance, but his face is set with determination, and his lips tighten into a straight line. "I don't know what you are talking about, Mom."

"Then perhaps I was dreaming. I was dreaming of my son having an intimate relationship with another boy. I was dreaming of my son coming home, sobbing and crying, wishing he was dead. I was dreaming of that boy's mother coming to our house, accusing you of infamy. All of that was my dream only. And where is my reality?" Ms. Hoa weeps, and her pain echoes around the dark room.

"Mom, it's not what you think." Dong tries to hold back his emotions. His mom's words bring destruction to his entire world. He had been happily dreaming about meeting Simon, and he never noticed that the grass beneath his feet had turned into thorns.

"Because Dong, I said it, and I will say it again, as often as I can, as long as I live, that is no way to live. That is not the right way to become the right person. That is not the cross you should have to bear. Dong, don't be gay."

The room turns silent, the air stops breathing, the notebooks and textbooks on the table stop rustling. Everything in the universe stands still for a second to listen to despair dropping its final notes of the great requiem. Dong inhales sharply, ready to bite, but he closes his eyes and reminds himself, *Mom sacrificed everything, and she is sacrificing still. Mom has sacrificed. Mom has sacrificed.* He lulls himself out of his anger until there is nothing left of him as a son, and only an ideal exists.

"I'm not gay," Dong says, his voice quivering, mourning for the person he lost the moment those words escaped his mouth.

"Good. Then you should stay that way. You should be happy. Goodnight, son."

Ms. Hoa stands up and walks out of the room, leaving Dong sitting still on the bed—his mind stops working, his heart is shattering in the still night—and if she stays by the door like she did the day Simon's mom come over, she would almost hear her son weeping for the life he gave away. But instead, she walks back to her room, climbs into her bed, and lies there fully awake all night. *He will understand,* she comforts herself. *He will understand. No child of mine should have to suffer. I have suffered enough and have prayed enough. No Gods have the right to make my child suffer. They have taken enough, now let me be the one to do the taking.*

Ms. Hoa thinks about her past and her present. She has never cared much for the future; no one can own it, and no one can control that monster. She thinks she's paid a fair price to come this far, and all she wishes for, all this time, is the freedom she felt in that little coffee shop, when all the world went on living while she stood on the sideline for a moment, surviving.

Chapter 8: I Got to Get Away from Here

Dong sits still on his bed long after his mom leaves the room. The clock on his nightstand shows the time 1:30. He looks at the red LED light, thinking, *I have to wake up early tomorrow. There's Math class, and the test, I promised Mom I would do well on the test. And I—.* Suddenly, an overwhelming feeling of defeat fills Dong's heart and he's suffocating in a vast abyss of indifference. He couldn't care less about the test, much less about the final grades and the university of his choice—his mom's choice, to be exact. He thinks about how she had asked her nail salon colleagues and her Vietnamese friends about the best university. He was there; he knew how desperate she was to know which place to set her son in, to settle him on the highest mountain. To be proud. To be respected and acknowledged. He watched her small figure bustling about the house and her workplace every day, and somewhere deep inside his heart, the prickly thorns of guilt had slowly grown into a field. He wants to make her happy, and more than that, he wants her to get back the life she traded to secure this life for him. But he never asked her to sacrifice that much for him. And she always tells him that it is not his fault, it is just how Vietnamese mothers want it to

51

be. They keep chasing after the shadow of what is best for the other person and killing themselves amid an illusion of the ever-escaping, never-within-reach happiness.

Dong lets his arms fall loosely by his sides. His entire being is weighed down by the responsibilities he is asked to carry but must be thankful for being handed down. A rage rises within him. Why must he be the condemned one? Why must he bear this grudging love within him, while others are free to live how they want? Look at Ames. Look at Lizzie. They never have test prep centers. They never have straight-A reports. They never need to aim for the top university in the entire country. And Dong knows they are happy.

He lets out a sob. It's been so long since the last time he cried his heart out. No one ever listens, and no one cares. He lets the darkness embrace him in a futile attempt to feel the warmth of some human touch. "Simon," he whispers, "why must it be so hard?" He remembers listening to Leonard Cohen's song, "Joan of Arc." Simon was leaning back on his chair, his eyes closed. The light of early August was shining through his room's windows. He was singing, breathing life into the verses, bringing back the legend of old...

"Now the flames they followed Joan of Arc
as she came riding through the dark
No moon to keep her armour bright
No man to get her through this very smoky night."

"It's strange how you only have taste for the saddest songs." Dong laughed, his chin propped up on his hands, his eyes sparkling. There was a glimpse of joy and childhood glee in his voice. His heart was in front of him, strumming the guitar Simon picked up in a garage sale not too long ago, singing with a hoarse voice that was just barely broken by puberty. He was stepping on the first stone to

adulthood. He was almost free.

"I like the old guy's voice. He made everything sound sweet and golden." Simon strummed away the rest of the song. He noticed Dong's gaze and reciprocated with an adoring smile. Dong had these gentle eyes that were like no others. Dark as the night and warm as the August light. Once in a blue moon, if he were attentive enough, Dong would let Simon see this twinkling star rising timidly in the depth of those immense quiet night skies. And that would be what helped him through the day. That would be what helped him through everything in life, if only he could be by his sweet side until the Earth exploded, or until humans had finally learned to love each other.

"But you only choose his saddest songs. Remember the time you let me listen to that song you like, 'Alexandra Leaving'? I did some research on the song. It is a very sad story, and it is based on a very sad poem, too. Don't be so close to sadness, it will draw you in. By the time you notice, there will be no way out." Dong sat up on the bed, dangling his feet. "I don't want you to feel sadness."

"And why is that?" Simon asked, his voice full of mischievousness. He still had that youthful, boyish character which he refused to grow out of. It was his second skin.

"I don't know. I just want the people I love to be happy," Dong said, his voice growing smaller. "I guess I was brought up that way."

"The people you love?" Simon repeated the phrase, more in a hopeful tone than a surprised one. "So, I am one of the people you love?"

"Yeah. You are my best friend," Dong said tentatively. His heart was beating so loud he was confused why Simon didn't hear the rhythm of his passion and desire. It was reverberating around the room like the songs they shared with each other in the innocence of what they had lost.

53

"I don't know if I'm happy with that."

"Why?"

"I don't know, D-dog," Simon said, calling Dong by the nickname he gave him, his voice now tender and soft. "I guess one of these days, rather than being one of the people you love, I want to be the only one person. The one who you'll miss on every summer night. The one you can't wait until morning to meet. The one you'll run to when you are in trouble. The one who is your everything. I want to be your world."

Dong was stunned by Simon's straightforwardness. He thought he had grown used to how the boy always came forward with what he desired so blatantly. He still remembered the day Simon kept holding the teddy bear in his hands until they turned purple, despite being told by the teacher to let other kids play with it. Simon never let go of what he wanted. And Dong was envious of that willpower. That same Simon was saying that he wanted Dong to be his world. Dong jumped on that train, only too quickly, too greedily. Deep inside his heart, he knew that it was his turn to hold on to the teddy bear. He inched closer to Simon; his back was leaning against Simon's legs. He would sit leaning like that forever, if only this world were a bit gentler.

"You are already my world," Dong mumbled.

"But that is not true." Simon put the guitar down beside him. "Your world is your mother. Your world is her happiness. Your world is being the person everyone expects you to be. You are as strong as the last hope. And as weak as it is, too. Do you know what will happen when the last hope fails us?"

"What?"

"We will all perish."

"And you don't want to perish."

Simon bent down and cupped Dong's chubby cheeks in his hands, *his eyes searching for the things he treasured most. "I'd rather perish, so long as you'd be happy. And it'd be a cherry on top if you being happy means that you'd love me."*

"Really?"

"Spare a thought for me. In your most desperate time, spare a thought for me."

Simon ruffled Dong's hair and let him go. Neither of them knew at that time what a storm they had to face, what force they needed to go against, what distance they had to traverse, only for that sentence to be true: "In my most desperate time, I'll spare a thought for you."

"I saw her wince, I saw her cry

I saw the glory in her eye.

Myself, I long for love and light

But must it come so cruel, and oh so bright?"

Leonard Cohen's voice whispers into the chasm of sadness in Dong's ears. He sits there, holding his legs, his chin on his knees. For a moment, he doesn't know what he was born for or what he should be doing with the life that was forcefully put into his hands, chained as it was, but it still demanded to be lived through. He thinks about calling Ames or Lizzie, but it's too late.

No one is listening to the beating of his heart. The light of August had departed since that day, and though many Augusts have come and gone, Dong can no longer find the strength to hold on to this life of his. What he needs is a lot greater than love, and a lot lesser than faith. Who else will stay by his side the day he decides to take the final jump? He searches for the bottom of the void in his heart. His feet almost trip down the ragged edges.

The darkness is all he sees, and the darkness envelops him

in the pitiable solitude of a body that is too young to contain itself in whole. He grows cold. The warmth he yearns for is not his to choose, not his to own, not his to swallow and feel himself burned alive. He longs for the touch of a hand, the fingers dancing on his forehead, the palm roughly ruffling his hair. He wants to see that smile, to hear that tender voice, to bask in that foregone summer. He was everything then, and he is nothing now. Dong suddenly understands what people talk about when they talk of "being alone." He feels like he is the only person living in this entire world, and he is floating around in the dark galaxy, watching the Earth from above, crying for the loss of humanity. Dong steps off the bed, feeling the coldness of the tiles seep through his feet and reach everywhere inside his body. He wipes his eyes, fully awake. Then he quickly sits down at his desk, pulls out a notepad, and writes neatly on a piece of lined paper:

Dear Simon,

I've got to get away from here. Any place is better. If I don't, I will only perish this way. And you don't want me to perish. Simon, I also don't want to perish. If you still spare a thought for me, write me back. Remember that song we often listened to on the school bus? If you have a fast car, let us get out of here.

Your Anthony

Dong folds the short letter into four and puts it inside a small envelope. The dawn comes along with the sound of his alarm clock. He hasn't slept at all the entire night, but he doesn't feel tired. Instead, his heart is more alive than ever. He bets his entire life on this tiny letter. The melodies of those faraway songs ring in his ears. Perhaps the end is near; perhaps he will have his own happy conclusion. Perhaps the storm is only as strong as the fear of it. When he leaves for school, he drops the letter into the postal box and jumps on the school bus. Friday night is almost here.

What he doesn't expect are his mom's actions. She skips a day at work, drives to the address he gave her the night before, and stands there watching the empty parking lot. Ms. Hoa lets the cold hand of winter blow over her. For the first time since Dong was born, she feels entirely lost. She doesn't know where she should go, what else she should do, or what other sacrifices life demands from her. She stands there, leaning on her used Toyota. The sudden feeling of being forsaken swallows her whole being. Ms. Hoa laughs in short breaks, then she falls to the cement ground, crying. She punches the hard ground, trying to find something to keep her from falling apart.

She knows she needs to be strong, but her legs refuse to assume the stand of the victor. A part of her still wants to believe that there is a school. That the address her son gave her was a false one. Perhaps he was also fooled by the simple website. Perhaps he was tricked into it somehow by those two girlfriends of his. She thinks of a thousand possibilities, trying to find among them a feasible excuse that will make the suffering tolerable enough for her to forgive and forget everything. None of them gives her any comfort.

She inhales the cold January wind.. Everyone is laughing, acting out the role of the protagonist in their own life, while she's here, forever a side character of her son's theatre. Ms. Hoa tries to stand up. She opens the car door, sits at the steering wheel, stares at the vastness of this foreign place, and drives away. She doesn't have a destination in mind. She's just trying to get out of this labyrinth, set up by the bitter lies of her son. She thinks of her country, of the bustling city, flooded with neon lights and crowded traffic. Of her old job at the large bank, of the people she grew up with, of the language she spoke so well because she'd learned to love it before she even knew how to form the first syllable. Of her mother and the sheer strength that she had managed to gather to raise her and her siblings without the help of a male figure.

Growing up, she never thought a man was a necessity. He would be something to fill in the blank—a decoration, almost. She wonders whether she'd been raised differently, if her life would be on a better path. But her mind refuses to believe in that flimsy, phony notion. How can a child not love her mother, the woman who brought her life?

Ms. Hoa stops at a strange coffee shop amidst the squares of condos and townhouses. She thinks about how people keep building things up just to tear them down. She orders an iced coffee with her curt English and sits on the patio, watching everything go on as she's stuck there, in the same position as her mother, only with a different location.

Her freedom is gone. It was a fleeting dream, and no matter what other people might say about it, to her, it was once beautiful. Her life could have been everything she wanted it to be, and she doesn't consider acting to change it; she is content with the thought. She decides that she will watch Dong closely. Friday night, Oakville, a secret place. Those are the three clues she has, and they all scream bad omens. Ms. Hoa sits as the light of day changes its shade to a marble purple, then she stands up, gets in her car, and drives home. The evening trails behind her; another day is ending.

Dong waits patiently yet tensely during the school day on Wednesday. If Simon responded right away, he could have a response tonight. He has no cause to hope for so much, but he can't resist the sweet temptation of that devil. *There's no way he won't reply,* Dong keeps thinking to himself. *There's no way my Alexandra will abandon his Anthony.* But the legend of old has always told him differently—that Anthony is always forsaken by his Alexandra, that he will always be there in that God-abandoned castle, watching the trail of people leaving, all alone, until he is the only person living in a desert of stone temples where no God reigns. When he gets home from school, no one is home, and he's far too used to that for his own good. Then his uncle comes down and calls out to him.

"Your letters. Give them to your mom. Now don't go nosing around before your mom checks them, alright?"

"Sure. I will give them to her."

Because Friday is in two days and I may have lost the last bet, Dong thinks as he absentmindedly peruses the flyers and newspaper. Then a small square envelope catches his eye. It lies there, quiet in its beauty and holiness. The alphabetical letters carve a sweet pain in Dong's heart: "For my Anthony." He runs to his room, almost tearing the envelope to pieces. Inside it is a phone number. He grasps his phone, dials the number. His hands are trembling with excitement. He can feel his breathing stop for a second. He is lost in a trance of imagination until a warm voice rings in his ear:

"I bet you thought I'd finished leaving, Anthony."

Dong falls to the floor, crying. A song by The National is still on, and the lyrics ring out: "It takes an ocean not to break." The light on that August day is shining, and despite all that has happened, there are reasons for him to go on hoping.

Chapter 9: The Pain You Never Knew

Simon sits at his desk, pretending to be studying while fiddling with the bundle of unanswered letters in the drawer. They are accumulating at a risky rate, and by "a risky rate," he means that one of these days, when his heart finally wins this battle of decaying reasons, he will jump on the first bus to Mississauga and find out what it means to live.

He opens them one by one and lays them on top of each other. They make a nice tower of his burning love. "Dear Simon," they all start, and with every word, the letters spill out a storm of unchecked passion until they flood his room with the wildest dreams and the almost unreachable person of that foregone summer. Perhaps this is what it means to go on hoping even when the last train has left the station. All that remains is the lonely shadow of a traveler, leaning against the pillar, waiting. And he is waiting for that one phone call miles away, a sign of that promise neither of them had spoken about yet neither of them would forget.

Simon reads each letter in no particular order. He prefers to imagine Dong's life in that chaotic storm of words and letters. "Dear Simon," one letter reads, "Today mom is doing her night shift again and I feel so alone in the darkness." Or another letter dated ten days before that one: "Dear Simon, my exams are near, and I have no hope of getting an A again, but I will try." And the one sent one year after that one: "Dear Simon, I walked through the mall, and the Christmas lights are on but why does it feel this sad? It's like I don't belong here. No one ever belongs here."

Simon has read them all and memorized each letter. He can recite them with his eyes closed, and by doing so, he can also hear Dong's voice in his head, ever so dear, ever so near, and yet, he is never here. Simon lets out a heavy sigh. He moves to the windows where the telescope his stepmom bought him for his seventeenth birthday stands and he looks at the stars raining on the darkening sky.

He loves looking at the starry night whenever the urge to see Dong comes too close to bursting. He has accumulated almost nine hundred photos of the starry sky in his phone. Nine hundred nights of longing, yearning for a chance to see Dong again. It soothes his heart when he thinks that in the basement apartment of that house in Mississauga, Dong is living under the same Heaven as he is. They are breathing the same air, thinking of the same things, listening to the same genres of music, and perhaps, on a lucky night, they will put the same song on repeat. The thought burns him up and keeps him alive.

Simon's parents divorced each other not too long after his family moved to Oakville three years ago. His mother blamed his father for not being a good male role model. His father blamed her for not being there enough. Neither of them accepted the fact that Simon was, at that time, all that he would ever be, and he was longing, on those hopeless nights where the sound of his parents' arguments was louder than his living, for someone to accept him. He didn't wish for much; he only wanted a reason to believe that he could be loved without needing to fit the mold that people pushed him toward.

He was not Dong. He would not sacrifice himself for others' happiness. He knew that he'd kill himself before attaining that goal; he'd watched Dong die every day in that household, and he wanted a way out. If possible, he wanted to save them from being the scapegoats of their parents' ideals. He wanted life. He wanted love. He wanted freedom. And his parents realized soon after the move that there was no way to change him.

Gradually, they grew tired of arguing, and finally, they grew tired of seeing each other's face. It was a matter of who would give up first, and his father raised the white flag. His mom moved out of the house after that. It was not a messy divorce—it was strictly business, and he was thankful it was over before Dong's first letter arrived. He'd have gone crazy in that fighting cage if he had to juggle the insults his parents were yelling at each other every night and the wish to be in the same room with Dong, listening to the '80s songs, strumming on his guitar, and just letting everything go.

He has never known such pain as loving someone this much, and his heart is breaking, tearing apart each morning he wakes up. It is true he *could* go on without Dong; he has been doing so for three years now. No one is going to die just because the one they love is not there. But he couldn't call this Hell living. He is only there on the surface, barely existing. He talks, but his words have no meaning. He laughs, but there is no laughter in his eyes. Wearing a mask to make people love him is easy. Humans can be deceived with sweet words and charming beauty. The only thing that keeps him alive is the thought that on this vast Earth, there is a chance for people with love in their heart to find each other again.

And just when he was ready to surrender himself to the waves of life, Dong's latest letter came in the mail. "Dear Simon," it said, "I've got to get away from here. Any place is better." And that was all he ever needed to leave. Simon grasped that piece of paper like a drowning man holding on to a lifeline. He decided that he needed to see Dong. He spent all this time running away from his fears—of being abandoned, of being left stranded on a foreign shore, where no one would love him anymore, of being hurt. What if Dong never wanted to take him back? He'd tried so hard to repress this water fountain. He'd been patient, despite the cuts Dong's letters gave him; each letter slashed through the old wounds, and he lay there, bleeding on the pavement, his blood fueling the love he thought he'd never be able to have.

But Dong never gave up. Between the two of them, Dong had proven to be the braver one. Of course, how could Dong not be, when he was the one who never shied away from sacrificing and bearing the pain? Simon thought about his life. He was tired of being a runaway. He gathered his courage and responded to Dong's letter right away. On the white piece of paper, he wrote only a single line: his phone number. He bet his life against the world and the cruel hands of adults who thought they could decide the fate of beasts and children.

And his bet proves to him that he was right all along—that it is never in love's nature to cave under pressure. Tonight, as Simon finishes folding the letters and puts them back into the lock box again, his phone rings. The wait is over; the winner is decided. A strange number. His hands are trembling. In that moment of anxious waiting, Simon thinks he has lived a lifetime within seconds. Suddenly, the voice on the other line brings him back to Earth: "Hello?" Simon smiles at the tiny trembles in Dong's voice.

"I bet you thought I'd finished leaving, Anthony." His tears flow, finally making up for the years of wandering in the unknown landscape of sadness and despair.

"And I thought I'd watched you leave that day." Dong chuckles. There is something new in his voice. Something bright. Something like a boulder has been lifted. Something like Atlas when he decided to stand straight and place the Earth under his feet, finally free. Something like hope.

"Why are you calling?"

"Why did you send me your number?" Dong asks, curious and incredulous at the obvious question.

"How do you know it is me?" Simon teases, surprised by his tone. He thought he had forgotten how to joke around a long time ago.

"Because there's no one else who would send me a written letter. Because I had bet my life on that piece of paper. And because only you would call yourself my Anthony."

"Then you already know why I sent you my number."

"Yeah," Dong says, his voice filled with a hint of laughter and youthful mischievousness. "I suppose I do."

They let the silence sink down the ocean of longing. The stars are twinkling—some of them are dying, some of them are living. The Earth continues its trajectory around the sun, and perhaps in that moment, the two of them can believe that Atlas is real, that he is carrying this planet on his shoulders to protect all the lovers and all the sinners. Simon can almost hear Dong's heartbeat through the phone—the small palpitation of lips touching skin, of fingers dancing on bare chest and naked waist. He is floating in the sea of memory, stuck between the place he can never return and the place he yearns to be but knows not how to reach. Simon lets out a sign, and he can hear Dong's quiet gasp on the other side of the phone.

"What is it?"

"No, it's just a bit weird," Dong says, embarrassed. "I thought I'd have a lot more to say to you than just being here, you know, breathing."

"Me too," Simon says with a laugh. "I'd imagined seeing you again, hearing your voice, talking to you about everything and nothing at all. And here I am, not able to find a single word."

"Well, do you want me to hang up?" Dong says jokingly.

"No, stay." Simon switches the phone to his right side. "I have paid tribute to the stars every day for the last three years to have this moment. Let me believe that it is real."

"You are a liar."

"No, I am not. But you can call me one if you believe I should be. Bestow the misery on me," Simon says in a sickeningly sweet voice, and he can imagine Dong frowning. Dong always hated his way of heavy expression and his abuse of words.

But Simon knows in his heart that to Dong, he is forever an exception. A special existence he carries within him like a newborn child, with the same protectiveness and reverence. Between them is a vicious torrent, and both are standing there, watching the immense longing through the years stream through the cracks of the dam until everything is broken and torn apart.

"Sweet talker," Dong says, after the pregnant silence. "If you'd spared a thought for me, you'd have written me a letter. Where were you when I needed you most?"

"I'm not a liar." Simon inhales sharply, readying himself for the price he must pay for the path he chose. "I was simply a coward."

"A coward with a pen and a strong determination is more dangerous than a hero with towering confidence."

"You have every right to be angry."

"But I'm not," Dong says, laughing. "And that's why I hate myself so. I could never be angry at you. I even forgive the pain you caused only because you sent me a measly phone number written hastily on a piece of paper. I'm a hopeless, pathetic drunkard in this garden of love."

"I guess we make a good pair, then," Simon replies. He looks at the stars outside and for the first time, he can appreciate their beauty in full. "A coward and a hopeless, pathetic drunkard."

Dong laughs; his laughter is contagious. Simon suddenly feels a seed being sown inside of him, and with each bell of laughter, the flowers bloom into a field, stretching beyond the darkness, until it reaches the edge of the world. He chuckles, imagining Dong standing in front of him, his slender profile shining under the August sun, his hand catching his hat in the wind, his smile overpowering everything that ever was and will ever be.

Dong has grown into Simon's existence, and he grows ever larger, until Simon is but a skin covering the forest fire that is Dong's happiness. Simon smiles at the thought. It is not so bad if his existence is reduced to that. On the other side of the phone, Dong is asking something, but Simon is too busy holding his own happiness in his hands. He has to ask Dong to repeat the question again much to his embarrassment.

"What is it that you just said?"

"I asked if you were going to the party this Friday?" Dong is still laughing. He has always found Simon's sudden burst of absentmindedness enchanting.

"I will be there. But the party will be pretty boring," Simon says, bitterly reminded of the "friends" he's made and the pretentious conversations they have. "Honestly, I don't want to be there."

"Then why do you bother going?"

"Isn't it obvious? Because someone is popular," Simon replies, feigning a haughtiness he knows Dong despises.

"And that someone is…?" Dong teases back.

Simon hears the harmless ridicule in Dong's mocking voice, still barely able to hide the laughter that is ever ready to jump out any moment like an overly excited kitten. He knows the boy will not let it go if he continues the confident and arrogant act of being Simon at school.

"Can't you let me be cool in front of you for a second?" He blushes.

"But you are always cool," Dong says, hurriedly withdrawing the teasing voice. "And I am never that."

"You *are* cool," Simon says, his hands on his desk, his face leaning impossibly closer to the phone, until he and the phone become one. "You are cool, and sweet, and soft as cotton candy. I can swallow you whole, you know, and you will melt on the tip of my tongue."

"You perv."

Simon laughs. He can't resist teasing the boy until Dong is speechless, cowering in a corner, covering his ears, all of him red like an overly ripe tomato.

"Why do you ask? Are you going to be there? Tell me you are going to be there."

"I plan to. My friends and I are pulling this stunt so I can be there, but I don't know if it will work." Dong bites his nails;

his voice hesitates on the thinning phone connection.

"What stunt? Also, what friends?" Simon becomes alert, his ears straining.

"Ames and Lizzie. You don't know them; they are my best friends in school. We study together sometimes, or rather, I teach them. And here's the stunt: I lied to my mother, saying that I will be at a test prep center for a mock exam on Friday. Lizzie's mom will take us to the party and back, and that gives me about two hours to see you."

"But I don't want you to simply be there."

"What do you want, then?"

Simon swallows. He knows this is a test. A trick question to which every answer is right and wrong at the same time. A complex Schrödinger's cat situation. But he puts his heart on the line anyway. "I want you to stay. Forever."

Dong is silent. Simon's life is hung on a thin thread, and with every passing second, he can feel his heart racing, screaming, until for a single moment, it stops beating. On the other side, Dong whispers timidly, almost inaudibly, like a swift breeze in summer, "I also want to stay. Forever, if I may."

Simon jumps up, almost screaming. He walks back and forth in his darkened room to calm his nerves. He wants to cry, and he wants to laugh at the same time. All the emotions that a human can think of bloom within him at the same moment. His voice trembling with a frightening kind of hope and wistful thinking, he asks, "Hey, do you want to skip the party?"

"And do what? I have to be home at nine. No, I *must* be home at nine. My mom won't agree to it otherwise."

"I never said that you have to cross the line and stay out late." Simon rushes out the words, his voice still trembling. "I only want you to stay at my place instead."

"What about the party?"

"What party? Let's just pretend that you are a stranger, and I am your host. I extend you an invitation to stay at my castle, forever. We will continue dancing in the hall and laughing till dawn comes and breaks our dream apart. Let's just pretend, D-dog, for one night, that we are free and happy."

"Two hours at your place?"

"Forever," Simon says, "at my place."

"I want to, but Ames and Lizzie—"

"If you really want to, there will be no buts" Simon pleads, his voice growing urgent with each passing second. "Say you want to, say you will be with me, say you will stay."

Dong ponders the demand. He imagines Simon on the other end of the phone, in a quiet house in Oakville, standing nervously in the dark, his palms sweaty, waiting. And that image is all it takes for Dong to answer, almost too quickly for his own good. "Yes!" he screams fervently. "Yes, yes, yes. I will be with you. I can stay until dawn. Simon, please say that nothing will break us."

"Of course," Simon says, his voice dripping with the sweetest potion. Both are ready to swallow the poison. "Nothing will break us. I will say it a thousand times if you want. I will record it and send it to you so you will have it carved in stone. I'm ready to stand there on Judgment Day to defend it to you. Nothing will break us."

"Okay." Dong sobs, his voice muffled. "Okay, I will believe it. Simon?"

"Yes?"

"Sing a song for me. I haven't heard your singing for so long I almost forgot how to be happy."

Simon puts the phone down and reaches for his guitar. He knows he cannot play for long; that his father, who's sleeping at the end of the hall, will come over in his drowsy state and take away the noisy instrument. But he gives it all away for the chance of singing to this boy, only because the boy said that without his voice, he had almost forgotten how to be happy. The strings quiver, and his voice rings into the receiver in a whisper:

"It's true that all the men you knew were dealers
Who said they were through with dealing
Every time you gave them shelter
I know that kind of man
It's hard to hold the hand of anyone
Who is reaching for the sky just to surrender
Who is reaching for the sky just to surrender"

The night fades away into darkness. The light of day shines through the cracks in the curtain. Simon waits for his father's footsteps, which are slowly approaching. On the other end of the phone, Dong's even breathing calms him. He puts the guitar away, feeling himself drifting into a quiet slumber. The last quiet sleep before the storm.

Chapter 10: The Last Night Before the Storm

Dong eats his breakfast in a hurry. To him, every second from now until tomorrow night is filled with treasures, and he is hunting them down, tracking them to their hiding place, until the one treasure is found. He doesn't notice the intense look on his mom's face, nor does he pay any attention to his father's grumbling and complaints.

He walks to the school bus, almost jumping with every step. Behind him, Ms. Hoa keeps on watching his back until long after the school bus has departed. Her eyes are keen, the dark irises straining with a strong determination. For the first time since she first stepped onto this foreign land, she is betting her life on something: a mission. For different reasons, and without the other knowing them, both Dong and his mom are awaiting the coming of tomorrow night in a nervous state. Dong is excited, while his mom is ready to hunt for her prey.

Dong greets Lizzie and Ames in the hallway. He whistles a tune while putting his stuff into the locker. The girls stare at him, amused and confused at the same time.

"What's gotten into you this morning?" Lizzie asks on their way to homeroom.

"Nothing."

"Well, that 'nothing' must be something pretty amazing because you haven't stopped smiling and jumping since the moment you got to school. Come on, spill the tea." Ames pokes Dong from behind as her eyes follow Dong's shy gaze and the red color that is spreading quickly from his neck to his face.

"Well, you see, tomorrow night—"

"Yeah, your mom finally agreed to it? To the 'test prep center,' I mean?" Lizzie interjects in a hurry.

"My mom hasn't decided yet."

"Then why are you so happy? Nothing is set in stone yet."

"Because I have decided. She might not have her decision yet, but I already have mine."

"And that decision is…?"

"I am going to Oakville tomorrow night."

"Oh my, are you running away? Tell me you are running away. That would be one Hell of a story to tell your mother." Lizzie squeals with delight.

"I don't know. I might run away. I might come back home at nine. I will decide when I'm on the road."

"D-dog, what's happening to you? Did an alien come by and kidnap you last night? Wait, are you still D-dog? Or are you a mysterious extraterrestrial being?" Ames bars her chest in faked fright. She is laughing, but her eyes are darkened, and her voice betrays a hint of worry, and subtly, envy crawls into the forefront.

"No, not an alien. But I suppose I did get kidnapped for a moment. Then I returned just in time for school." Dong laughs, still unaware of his friends' concerned looks.

"What is it?"

"I was a drunkard in the garden of love, and there, I met a

coward."

"Is this a sickening love story?" Lizzie screams. "Who is it? Is it the boy we talked about on Saturday? Oh, please tell me it's Simon. It will be the sweetest candy for me to chew on today before the English test."

"Yeah," Dong says, his eyes trying to find something to hold on to lest he lets himself fall too deep into the void beneath his feet. He is walking on hope alone. "It's Simon. I called."

"Shut up. Looks like miracles *are* still a thing in life." Lizzie grabs Ames's arm and squeezes it until the girl screams. "So you're going to be at his house tomorrow night?"

"At least, that's what I want to do. No, it's what I *must* do."

"So you guys will skip the party?" Ames asks, stroking her arm where Lizzie's bear-like grip left a red mark. She is smiling, but her eyes are gloomy with a never-before-seen malice. A monster is perched on her shoulders. Something has changed, but none of them is the wiser.

"Yes. He said he'd rather skip it and be with me."

"You don't say. Tell us everything. Don't spare any detail. What did you say? And what did he reply? Where did you guys talk? When? How? Oh my God, I can't—I just can't bear this suspense," Lizzie almost screams in her excitement. She changes from squeezing Ames's arm to slapping the poor girl's back until Ames yanks herself away from the grip in a curt motion. But Lizzie ignores her unusual attitude in a fit of happiness.

"He sent me a phone number and I called him last night. We talked until dawn. We drew plans and whatnot. It's all in the air, and I'm still high from it."

"And you will stay with him? Imagine that. You, the law-abiding, always-obeying guy, sneaking out of the house, staying at your boyfriend's place. Is it only me or is it screaming 'fuck the whole world'?" Lizzie hangs on to Dong, her face touching his, her eyes sparkling. It seems she is living and basking herself in this dazzling story even more than what Dong is experiencing himself. "Isn't it much, much too exciting?"

"Language, Lizzie," Dong says, blushing. "Plus, I am not going to run away forever. I'll just break the law this one time. It seems my mom doesn't know about the whole plan. I will push her a bit, and if she still doesn't agree, I will find a way out. I need to see him. After so much happened between us, I'd regret not seeing now more than ever. And I don't think there's any law that can come between two humans—between us. The cracks in our armor will let the light shine through. And I believe the Gods will be lenient to the lovers."

"Calm down. We are not opposing it. But you will only have two hours with him, right? Your curfew is nine," Ames mulls over Dong's monologue. Dong usually never talks much, and the fact that he is speaking not to her or to Lizzie, but to himself in a frenzy of words and ideals, makes her sense that a storm is brewing within him. Different from Lizzie's excitement, Ames fears that the storm will destroy Dong's last shred of reason. He will be killed, metaphorically, by his own passion. She should be worried, but a cruel joy blooms in her heart instead. "Don't tell me you are going to stay at his house until dawn."

"Whatever. Two hours or more, we can spend our eternity in that short duration. I don't care for the consequences, Ames." Dong turns to the girl, his eyes glazed over. "I want to be with him. I can't fight against what the heart dictates. And my heart is a dictatorship; it won't let the mind control."

"D-dog, please—" Ames begins to stop him, but Lizzie jumps in almost instantaneously.

"Of course, you should go after what your heart wants. You've been hiding for so long, it's time to be found." The girl pats Dong's shoulders and squeezes herself between him and Ames, practically stopping Ames from speaking her doubts. "You go on and stay at his home. We will cover the rest of it."

"Wait, we?" Ames says incredulously, but her question is nowhere as loud as Dong's fervent dream and the fever caused by the highest force on Earth: the fever of love, the kind of love that only comes once in a lifetime.

Ames knows Dong is smart, but the smarter someone is, the easier for them to fall into the trap. And Ames wishes she could reason with Dong before everything falls to pieces. She sees the future looming in front of her like a phantom resurrected from the savage realm called reality, and she yearns to stop it from actualizing itself. More than anything else, Ames doesn't want Dong to be hurt. But how can she get through to him, when even Lizzie is on his side? Her mind is torn in two. She wants Dong to be happy, but at what cost?

Half of her mind is angry at Lizzie for the almost overeager encouragement; the one who will bear the consequences will be Dong, not them. What could they—two teenage girls—do to protect Dong from the whole world when the Earth falls on him and shatters every one of his dreams? She wishes they could talk it through. Dong is always reasonable, and perhaps he'll see things in black and white if they are persistent enough. But before she can voice her opinion, Lizzie pushes him inside their homeroom. Both girls sit at their usual desk, two rows behind Dong. Ames takes the opportunity and whispers to Lizzie as their homeroom teacher talks about the coming events, "We should stop Dong."

"Why?" Lizzie asks, seeming not to care.

"You know why. His mom will kill him if she finds out."

"What if she already knows?" Lizzie turns her gaze to Ames. The sparkle of spontaneous fun and the eagerness are gone from her hazel eyes. "Whether she knows about it or not, it doesn't matter. Dong wants to go there, so let him go."

"Lizzie." Ames senses the fear rising in her. Something tells her that Lizzie has a plan carved out for Dong, and it scares her because she knows that this plan will either be the thunderbolt that strikes down the Babel tower, or the great flood that swipes out every existence on Earth. She swallows her worries, but they are still present in her shaky voice when she continues speaking. "Lizzie, you don't mean to help Dong run away from his family, do you? Be sensible."

"I am always sensible." Lizzie turns away, biting her lower lip. "And I believe that there's no reason why a person cannot choose his own happiness."

"But Dong is choosing his ending." Ames tugs on Lizzie's sleeve, her voice trembling in its quietness. "Dong doesn't know what he is getting himself into."

"Well, Ames, if Dong doesn't know it, what would give us the right to decide it for him?" Lizzie retorts curtly, her voice betraying a hint of suppressed annoyance. "Ames, I thought you knew better than that."

Stunned and speechless, Ames looks inside herself and finds the monster staring back at her with its vicious green eyes. *Jealousy, bring the love back to me,* she thinks. "I'm afraid. Not for me, but for him," she says, not feeling the sincerity in her words.

"Well, life's too short for that. Choose to be something else."

"And what if—"

"You can ask yourself a thousand what ifs, Ames," Lizzie replies, growing impatient as the clock is ticking away. "But they will not solve anything. They hang in the air, look you straight in the eyes, and they haunt you, because you never give yourself the chance to prove that you can win. And even when you lose, when you cannot reach the finish line, when you fall and cannot stand up, it will ease your mind to know that you jumped instead of sitting on the sideline, waiting for someone to save you like a Goddamn fairy tale princess. No, Ames, I believe Dong can have the happiness he deserves, not the happiness your what ifs will bring, with his mom as their dictator."

"But Lizzie, I—"

"Ames." Lizzie's voice becomes serious. Her eyes turn grave. Her facial expression is stern. She speaks with a force of will, a never-before-seen determination. "Have you ever seen Dong smiling and laughing that freely?"

Ames is astounded. She ponders the question. It takes her back to the first time Lizzie and Ames caught Dong secretly crying in a corner of the school's staircase. She still remembers that scene vividly, as if it happened just yesterday.

Dong was crouching, his head burrowed between his knees. His cries were muffled, but the sobs were audible if they strained their ears hard enough. His shoulders were trembling and his entire body was heaving. The light got in through the windows and it was shining on him, crowning like a fallen angel. A beloved child of God, forsaken only too soon, only too cruel. It looked to her that he had borne the weight of all living humans on his back, and he was crying for their pain and suffering. She looked at him then, and wondered, *How can the Creator build such a tiny body and stuff it with nothing but bleeding wounds?*

Their friendship story wouldn't have happened if Ames kept standing there and staring at that poignant, yet beautiful image. Lizzie was the one who walked up to him, shook his shoulders, and asked him what had happened. Between them, Lizzie has always been the more vocal one. She is good at attracting people's attention and she always finds her way around the most stubborn, unyielding silences.

Ames's mind wanders through the memory forest and finds the path the three of them have walked through. It was never an easy path; they had to trample on thorns and splinters until everything in them was cracked open and they could see that the blood running through their bodies was the same shade of red. Amidst the foggy remembrance, Ames realizes that Lizzie is right. During the time they have been friends, Ames had never seen Dong smiling and laughing so freely as he is doing now.

Even when the homeroom session starts, Dong cannot suppress his small chuckles. He is giddy, and he moves around in his seat, excited and eager for whatever may come his way. For the first time, Ames thinks, she can see for herself that Dong has his own hopes. That he believes in the goodness of life, whatever that goodness is defined as. That he also dreams, like all teenage boys and girls. That his life now revolves around more than just numbers and grades and the larger-than-life expectations he carries. That he has finally let the weight down. She bites her lips. *This is wrong*, a part of her thinks. But who is she to stop the boy from getting that happiness he had long given up on? Who is she to kill the small spark of fire in this cold, cruel winter night?

She knows it is wrong. She can foresee the avalanche as Dong slowly slides down the slope. But a part of her still wants to bet on hope, on life, on love, on whatever makes all of them human. Perhaps, in her deepest conscience, she wants to believe that her Creator cannot be any crueler than that day when she saw the boy on the staircase, forsaken, stranded, even though he was surrounded by an ocean. Perhaps Ames still wants to believe in that fundamental goodness, despite all the cautions and the warnings that are flashing through her mind. She tugs on Lizzie's sleeve, whispering, "Alright. I will join the game."

"This is not a game, Ames." Lizzie chuckles, returning to her usual cheery self. "If you want to be in it, you must be ready for sticks and stones."

"What would it take to make it happen?" Ames asks, trusting that Lizzie will get what she means.

"I don't know," Lizzie says absentmindedly, watching Dong's back as he writes down the announcement diligently in his notebook. "Not yet. It might take all of Babylon at this stage."

"I'm surprised you know about Babylon." Ames rolls her eyes, but she is assured now that both are thinking of the same ending.

"I'm glad D-dog has a person who will be there for him when his Babel tower falls."

"And it will fall, won't it?" Ames asks, her hands clenching unconsciously.

"It will, but hey, what's life for anyway?"

Lizzie laughs. Her hazel eyes are sparkling in the sunlight. Ames looks at her childlike features and cannot help but think that despite being the smartest one among the three of them, Dong could never compete against Lizzie's wisdom. None of them can. "Lizzie," she says, her voice subdued and calm, "you truly are the smartest one among us."

Lizzie's face lights up at the compliment. She turns to the blackboard and jots down a few important dates. They can copy the rest from Dong's notes later. Ames taps her pen impatiently on her notebook, waiting for the homeroom session to be over. She needs to ask Dong a few things, and she also needs them to plan a safe way out. Ames is never comfortable with going to war without an exit strategy. All the while, the monster inside her keeps laughing, repeating the same question that's been in her mind since Dong told her about Simon and the call. Why does everything good happen for him and not her? She shakes her head, trying to shove the monster away, but it keeps persisting, rooting in its place, clawing at her heart.

Dong deserves goodness. She soothes her mind with the thought, but it is no consolation. Biting the end of her pencil, she thinks about her mom, about her future, about taking the stage of the world at large. She knows it would take a special kind of talent, a bucket of luck, to be the leading role, and she is never that, or anything a passerby in the audience will remember. Would it hurt if she could also be special to someone? Would it hurt if her mom could care for her as much as Dong's mom did? She mulls the questions repeatedly until the word "hurt" is carved deeply in the wrinkles of her brain. Bile rises in her throat. The pain is so lonely it makes her want to weep.

The three friends are all immersed in different planes of thought. None of them know that the storm is so close. That the first thunderbolt is resounding and reverberating in the afternoon English class. That for the first time in Dong's student life, he'll receive a D on a test. And that the despair that Dong will be forced to slowly swallow until he can spit it out into letters and spell it with a tongue foreign to himself will come much later than any of them could foresee.

Chapter 11: The Day All is Gone

Ms. Hoa sits at the table, reading the Vietnamese newspaper. Her eyes glide over every word without a single meaning registering in her mind. She is thinking about tonight. The secret that Dong is trying so hard to keep, even if it means sacrificing her trust, betraying her love. She looks quickly at the clock. A few more minutes and the boy will be home.

He had asked her for a reply to "the test prep center" thing repeatedly since the day he first asked and she couldn't think of a reason to reject. Plus, with that defiant look in his eyes, Ms. Hoa knew that no matter what her reply was, Dong would go to the test prep center thing anyway. She had lost the battle long before the war was waged. Now her only strategy is to prey on his every move, ready to jump at his first careless mistake.

Ms. Hoa crumbles the newspaper in her hand, waiting for Dong's footsteps on the staircase. She has decided that she will give the boy one final chance to tell her the truth. It's not the lie she is angry at, no. Ms. Hoa closes her eyes, trying to suppress a sob that is threatening to escape any moment. She is angry at the fact that her son, who has never lied to her, is now lying with the determination of the most professional, pathological liar. It is not so much the act, but the seething, tethering betrayal behind it that is gnawing at her heart and boiling it until nothing is left but an empty hole, bleeding into everything.

Ms. Hoa is chewing on her pain until she hears the first thud on the staircase. She stands up quickly, unknowingly pushing the chair behind her. Then she thinks about her position in the battlefield, and she stands there, mulling over the steps she should take and the traps she should set. Every step along the way, she calculates and ponders over the future that is always beyond her reach yet eternally her greatest obsession. She subsists on the phantom of things not yet here and refuses to acknowledge the existence of the things living in front of her.

She has paid too dear a price, Ms. Hoa thinks. Too many sacrifices have been made along the way for her to give up and surrender. And what would happen then? What would happen if she surrenders? It doesn't ease her pain, and it certainly doesn't erase hurt she feels. The only thing it will help is the conscience of the guilty party. But in this battlefield, Ms. Hoa has long forgotten who the guilty party is. She feels that she has the rights, but her son is the one who holds the power to decide her final judgment. *Look at me*, thinks Ms. Hoa. *Look at what this life has turned me into.* She laughs bitterly and falls back in her chair. At that moment, Dong walks in. The smile is frozen on his face. The eyes betray a hint of gleeful giddiness and irrepressible joy.

"Hi Mom," Dong says, halting in his steps. His voice becomes one of the timid and shy boy again.

"Dong, sit down," Ms. Hoa says, emotionless and cold. She gathers all her will to force the hurt and the love that are overwhelming her heart to stay inside her ribcage. She can't afford to lose more than this.

"Yes, Mom."

"About tonight's arrangement—"

"Oh, about that. You don't have to worry about taking me to the test prep center. I will—I have some friends who will pick me up at six-thirty."

"Did I ever teach you to interrupt me when I speak?"

"No, Mom," Dong says, cowering, trying to hide his eagerness, but his constantly switching legs betray his ever-growing excitement. In his mind, Simon's words and his sweet voice reign over everything, making him their loyal subject. Basking in the high of it all, he forgets his mom's possible rejection that is hanging on his neck, the chance of failure whence the whole thing is exposed, and even the proper act—the dutiful mask—that has long been ingrained in his being.

"As I was saying," Ms. Hoa continues, her eyes following his movements warily, "I need to know more about this whole test prep center thing. You mentioned that the mock exam is at seven?"

"Yes, Mom."

"And it will end at nine?"

"Yes, Mom."

"Dong, I have never heard of a test prep center operating at those hours before," Ms. Hoa says, deciding to attack indirectly at the rear.

"Yes, Mom. I mean..." Dong quickly raises the shield and closes the defense gate. "They offer it for free, so I guess I don't have any choice in the timeframe." He grows cautious, chewing every word slowly. "You can check the website again if you still have doubts. There's also a representative who speaks Vietnamese if you want to ask about the program."

"Is that true?" Ms. Hoa asks. Her voice is shaking with anger and sorrow, but Dong is too far off in his own world to notice any difference in his mother's features, nor does he notice how Ms. Hoa's hands are clenching so tight that her fingernails are printing on her palms. She repeats her question, not knowing what she's hoping to get and what she's expecting to receive: "Is everything true?"

Dong looks at her, half wanting to tell her everything as he was taught to do so since the day he learned how to walk, half fearing that she will take this chance away from him and he will lose the life he wants. He keeps screaming internally, *Why can't I have the life I deserve?* But he suppresses it. He tries to think of his mother's hardship, of the constant night shifts she takes on to save enough money for him to go to college, of the nail salon where she earns money to pay off his father's gambling debt and fund his drinking habit. Of the sacrifices. But it grows harder and harder as his train of thought slowly continues down the spiral until it reaches his fundamental question: *Yes, but what about me?*

He looks at his mother, his mouth half open, ready to tell another lie. But his eyes meet hers. The wrinkles on her face, the crow's-feet on the corners of her eyes, the water that is waiting to overflow. The look of something stranger than anything he has ever seen in his mother stops his words. For the first time since his friends planned the getaway plan, he hesitates. If he tells her the truth, what will become of him? What benefit will the truth bring? The damage has already been done.

Dong's stomach churns. He feels a sense of nausea threatening to overflow. He bites back his words, his promises, his thoughts that everything will be alright as long as there is love, his belief that as long as he keeps on hoping, the world will be gentler to him, to every human in return. After all, how much does it cost to hold on to hope?

Dong shakes the spiraling thought away. Simon is right. He can't force himself to stay inside the perfect shell that he created for himself to appease others' demands. His true self is tearing at the seams, screaming, bellowing, begging to be born, to be living, to exist. Dong lowers his head in total defeat. He knows, no matter what he chooses, he will be on the losing side. There are no winners, and there is no glory to claim, either. He quickly makes his decision and stares right through his mom with the strongest determination known to mankind: the determination to be free.

"Yes, Mom. Everything is true."

Ms. Hoa looks into his fierce eyes. That stare is too foreign. That gaze is too insolent. He is no longer the son she cherished in her bosom. She keeps thinking that just yesterday, he was still a newborn babe suckling at her breast. But standing before her now is a stranger. A boy who fights against *her*, the mother who gave him life. She doesn't feel the pain as much as she thought. Or maybe the pain hasn't registered in her yet. Maybe those words are still floating in the air. And she is waiting for Dong's affirmation of the lie to hit her brain and take the fatal blow to her heart until she truly knows what it means to lose everything.

Ms. Hoa tries to remain calm, but her arms are shaking. Her body is trembling, not with anger, but with desperation—she has come to terms with her loss. Her sudden realization makes her eyes water, but she has long been an expert at holding back the tears. She is far too used to crying alone in the darkness, when nobody can see her humiliation. She is far too proud for her own good, and her strength sometimes cannot carry the weight of her will.

Dong continues staring at her, waiting for her admittance that he is the victor, though the price of that glory is much greater than what they both bargained for. Ms. Hoa falls onto the chair. A sudden tiredness consumes her existence. She grows small in the warm yellow light of the dining room. The gray hair on the top of her head shines blatantly under Dong's eyes. Her shoulders hunch over. Her head draws into her neck. She assumes the most vulnerable posture—the posture of a soldier who has witnessed his ideals being shattered to the ground, while he remains the only survivor of his war troops. With an almost inaudible voice, she says, "Alright, then."

"Yes, Mom?"

"I said alright. You can go."

"Really, Mom?" Dong asks, not so much in surprise as in fear. He is scared by the gift that is being bestowed on him by some unknown force, some Higher Being. No, his mom cannot accept it this easily. She usually never lets such a thing go by without asking him a thousand questions. Dong repeats the question, half awaiting the affirmation of the positive answer, half fearing that his mom will withdraw her agreement at any moment. "Do you mean that I can go to the mock exam?"

"Unless you don't want to go." Ms. Hoa looks at him, her eyes pleading, holding on to the last straw of hope. "Unless there's something you want me to know."

Dong is taken aback. But he can't withdraw now. He has won, though he has yet to know the cost he would pay for this victory. He has only tasted the slightest bitterness of his guilty conscience, and in his youthful vigor, he thought that was all there would ever be. He looks at his mom and firmly says one more time, "There's nothing for you to worry about. I never tell you lies. Everything is true."

And with those words, Ms. Hoa surrenders. With those same words, Dong sets himself a fate he cannot retract, a life he cannot win back, and a price far too expensive than he can afford. *But,* Dong thinks to himself, *I bet it all for this moment, and I will gladly accept the consequences.*

Ms. Hoa busies herself with the newspaper, turning page after page without reading any of the words. She speaks to Dong without looking at him, almost as if she is in a dream, a dark fantasy filled with premonitions for an ending she knows she has to face but is not ready to accept. "Alright, then. Good luck with the mock exam. I expect you to be home at nine."

"Are you going to your night shift today, Mom?" Dong asks, briefly suppressing his joy. He doesn't pay enough attention to the white knuckles on Ms. Hoa's hands as she grips the newspaper to the point of tearing it up.

"Yes. I have a night shift today. What about it?"

"Nothing in particular. Don't push yourself too hard, Mom." Dong fumbles for the right words as he puts away his backpack and tries to hide his phone as he texts Lizzie a simple "Okay."

Ms. Hoa's gaze fixes on his back. She thinks about all the time that has passed as she watched him grow up. How to turn it back to the beginning, and how can she fix the things that she did wrong? She keeps thinking it is all her fault. From the drunken and unemployed husband to the son who is lying to her now, it is all her fault. If she could go back, she thinks she'd choose to stay. No matter how tempting the freedom of this foreign country is, no matter how much money is presented in front of her eyes like the shiny toys and the sparkling costumes on Lunar New Year's Eve, she'd choose to stay.

Perhaps she'd find consolation in the poverty of her state. Or perhaps she'd become rich and revered in her field. She graduated from a local university with a degree in economics. She could have been a manager, or at worst, she could have worked as a bank teller until the end of her days. But anything would be better than this current situation, in which her degree is only a piece of crumbled up paper and all that knowledge only sketches new pains as she works on a client's nails or as she washes the soap bubble away from the dishes.

So this is the life she has chosen, the choice she has sacrificed her fortune for, only to realize it was fool's gold. Ms. Hoa thinks about the promises her husband made the day he proposed to bring her to this country. He had promised her a new fate, almost too perfect and too astounding to be true. A display of peppermint candies, warm fireplaces, and family pictures on the piano and the mantelpiece. She fell for the dream of seeing her children grow up to be happy, to be enveloped and protected in a sense of fairness that her country couldn't give her as she grew up.

She used to console herself with the thought that her child would grow to be free. The best education and the best health care system. And what is she now? A failed mother who cannot gain the trust of her only son. A failed woman, who cannot win back the life that is rightfully hers. She struggles to fight back the tears. She thinks to herself, almost in a superstitious way, that she can still fix everything somehow. That if she opens her eyes tomorrow, life will be back to how it was before this lie that Dong told her.

Ms. Hoa shuts her eyes, inhales sharply, and walks back to her room to change. She has to be at the restaurant in thirty minutes. She cannot afford to lose the money that is keeping her dreams alive. *Yes,* Ms. Hoa thinks to herself, *I have dreams. I have wishes. I have things I want to be when everything else is over and I can finally lie asleep on my hard bed. But it seems they take more than staying alive and facing the stones to turn them into reality.* Ms. Hoa looks back at the path she has been on, strewn with thorns and blood drops that look like roses. She closes the door behind her, falls to the cold, tiled floor, and cries. Her sobs escape in broken pieces of glass falling onto hard earth.

In the dining room of the basement apartment, Dong is pacing back and forth, waiting for Lizzie to call him. The table is set with a few dishes. His mom always spends the little time that she has before going to work making him dinner. She never cares whether his father has enough to eat or not. She'd rather not talk to, hear, or see his father. All of Dong's life, from the time he first gained awareness until now, Dong could see that his mom's existence only revolved around him. He is the sun of his mom's universe. *But,* Dong thinks to himself, *the sun will die. The light will fade out any moment.*

Since the first time Ms. Hoa brought him to the nail salon, Dong has wanted her to have her own source of happiness. Something that will scream less than a perfect son. Something that is hers and not his to decide. Something that smells less like acetone and dish soap and more like powdery perfume with luxurious meals. He removes the plastic wrapping of the sautéed vegetables and takes a small bite. He finds it tasteless. Another bout of nausea churns his stomach.

He doesn't think that he can eat any of the dishes his mom prepared. He knows it is not right. None of his actions are right. The lies he told. The noose around his neck. The gallows he is standing on. The scaffold is there, waiting in his

90

mom's room, amidst the frozen ocean and the cold sleepless nights. He remembers Joan of Arc. Perhaps, like in Leonard Cohen's song, tonight he can witness a love that will burn so cruel and so bright that he will be blinded by its shining existence.

He unwraps another plate. It is his favorite dish, braised fish. His mom has carefully picked the bones out and the simmering fillet is boring eyes into his conscience. He decides not to eat the dish and wraps it up again. He cannot face the table full of delicious food—the symbol of his mom's love and hope for him—right at the crucial moment when he is trying to knock the walls down and leave the prison he had long been taught to believe in as salvation. He turns away from the table.

The dining room is looking at him, a heavy consternation shining blatantly in its blackness. This is the place his mom has chosen to constrain her life. Her whole day can be spent in this kitchen, with pots and pans as her close friends and her confidantes. Dong always wakes up to his mom's clattering and puttering around the kitchen, and when he walks to the dining room, everything is on the table, ready for him to consume, while his mom is driving across town to her workplace.

Then the night will come, when, much like how it is now, his mom will bring dinner out, asking him a question or two about his day, then leaving for her night shift. They never actually talk much. Two separate lives, connected by the thin thread of great expectations. Dong picks up a slice of bread, puts a slice of cheese and spreads a thin layer of salted butter on it, and slowly chews the cold meal. Something inside him is urging him to abandon this ridiculous plan and confess everything to his mom before the last light of day goes out. But right at that tormenting moment between being perfect and being human, his phone buzzes. A text from Simon: "I hope you are not thinking of staying behind, Anthony."

Dong hesitates, then he texts back: "How do you know?"

"Just a hunch."

"But Alexandra is the one who's leaving."

"And won't you leave with me, Anthony?"

"The Gods have abandoned Anthony."

"And would you allow the Gods to abandon me, too?"

Dong ponders the question. His heart is beating to the rhythm of a passion he has never felt within him before. He texts back: "No, I will fight against the Gods and all that could be to save my Alexandra."

"Good. Because this time, Alexandra is not leaving."

He smiles at the phone as if this is his last hope. Another ring, and he sees that Lizzie is calling him.

"Hey," he whispers, half afraid that his mother might hear, half excited that Lizzie will be here soon and he's half an hour away from seeing his Alexandra.

"Hey, D-dog, what's up?"

"Nothing." He chuckles nervously. "When will you be here?"

"So the lie is not busted?" Lizzie's voice breaks intermittently with the sound of chewing. It sounds like she is eating her dinner while talking with him. She is far too calm for a situation that will change his fate now and forever. But Dong cannot pay attention to that reality. Lizzie has always been the one in control of their group of friends. He thinks of their conversation the other day and smiles. Lizzie is right; she is always the brain.

"The lie is not busted," Dong whispers into the phone. "At

least, not yet. She doesn't suspect it but she expects me to be home at nine."

"Jeez. That leaves little time for you and your Romeo, doesn't it?"

"I'm amazed you pay enough attention in class to even know the name Romeo."

"I pay attention to bits and pieces. Anyway, I'll be there in about ten. But here's the thing, we don't want your mom and my mom to see each other. That's, like, creating a suitable condition for another Civil War."

"Right."

"So I was thinking that you might have to walk a few steps away from your home."

"Right."

"So how about we park around the corner of the block and pick you up at the nearest stop sign?"

"Sounds good to me. I don't mind walking. But I don't think there will be any problem. My mom is going to her night shift in about a minute. She hates being late. Her pay will be deducted otherwise. How about you wait another five minutes or so before coming here?"

"That would leave you about...?"

"About one hour with my Simon. I mean, my Alexandra."

"Do we need a code name for your boyfriend now? One hour doesn't sound like enough, unless you are fine with it."

"I am not fine with it." Dong groans into the speaker. "But I don't want my mom to have any more reasons to be suspicious. I'm in a pinch here."

"That's why I told you to walk a few steps away from your house. Now, do you want to see the boy or not?"

"I want to, but—"

"Then it's settled. You should not let anyone impose their happiness on yours, D-dog. What do you think you are doing? You are killing your life the way you are living."

Dong swallows. Lizzie's words always have such unimaginable power on him at the most crucial moments. In that fleeting second, he suddenly forgets the guilt and the remorse that was haunting him, his mom's dishes, her tiredness when she speaks, and the small conversations they have in the little time they share before going to sleep. He says with a strong determination, "Pick me up in ten. I'm ready."

He hangs up. In the promised freedom of the night, Dong fails to hear Ms. Hoa's cries behind her bedroom's closed door. Her tears are breaking the ocean between the life she wants him to have and the life he is choosing to embark on as the curtain of darkness slowly falls.

Chapter 12: I Watch You Every Day

Dong listens to the sounds coming from Ms. Hoa's room. After hearing the rustling of her clothes and her soft footsteps, he knocks gently on the door. Lizzie texted that she is outside, around the corner. He needs to go now. His mom answers from the other side of the door.

"What is it?"

"My car is here. I'm going now. Do you need my help with anything before I leave?"

"No. Everything is alright. Go."

In his palpitating happiness and the promises of the world where anything can happen, Dong cannot hear the silent defeat in his mom's voice. He walks up the stairs, almost runs through the entrance, and jumps out of the door in an excitement he has never known before. He whistles all the songs in his memory—one song is mixed with another, and no tune is the correct one, but he couldn't care less. He is young and free.

The whole sky opens itself before him, full of unknown trips and adventures. He thinks about the things he can take, the things that are rightfully his if only he'd reach out his hand, and in that moment, he forgets about the consequences, the desperation, and the seething conscience that is trying so hard to get him back into his mom's bosom. He forgets the safety net his mom had built for him, the love she'd spent her whole life devoting only to him. The guilt speaks to him in brief bursts as he runs to Lizzie's car, but how far can he go on fear alone? Deep inside his heart, Dong justifies himself with the statement, *I also want to live.*

Lizzie's mom's car is an old Toyota. The paint is chipped at some places. The exterior is dusted over with the mud from the winter. It seems that much like her daughter, Lizzie's mom, Ms. Dolores, doesn't care much for her exterior, nor does she care how other people think of it and of her. She is behind the steering wheel, waving at Dong excitedly.

Ms. Dolores is a woman in her late forties, but she is as young as the day she decided to have Lizzie and raise the girl all on her own. Her sheer willpower radiates from her posture, with her strong, well-defined, tanned arms and torso. Her face is beaming with joy. She is the type of person who will laugh disaster in the face and take it head-on without wearing any protective gear or heeding any caution.

Dong has always felt safer in her presence, and a part of him has never forgiven himself for that. He'll never forget the day his mother and Lizzie's mom broke into a big argument over the right way to raise a child, or the day his group of friends calls "The Civil War." Lizzie had told her mom about the strict curfew and the so-called great expectations Dong's mom had enforced on him since forever, and how Dong had "pathetically cried like the failure that he was and always will be" when Lizzie and Ames found him. That story enraged Ms. Dolores to no end. She thought of Ms. Hoa's action as child abuse, and she had no problem telling Ms. Hoa straight to her face how she was killing the boy with her actions.

No loving mother would do that to their children, and to Ms. Dolores, Ms. Hoa was only raising Dong to get back the life she had lost. To this, Ms. Hoa had only laughed contemptuously, and as a retort, she had told Ms. Dolores how her beloved daughter was no better than her nosy mother, and that the best Lizzie could get out of such a disgrace of a mother was a subpar education. "Look at the grade report she got," Dong's mom had said, her disdain in full view. "How many D's are in there? And what kind of future will she get with those? My son will be a doctor. At the worst of it, he'll still be able to use his degree to earn a luxurious style of living, while your daughter will be stuck here in this town, scraping dishes to earn her wage. And maybe—think about it—maybe by that time, she will learn to resent her mother. Have you ever thought about it? Or does all you think of, night and day, consist only of how to live your life while leaving your daughter's future behind?"

Ms. Dolores was enraged at Dong's mom for those words, uttered in the height of her anger and echoed in the abyss of her desperation. To Ms. Dolores, Lizzie's happiness reigns over everything else. It is true that she is scraping by, that she works as a full-time nurse with little time for her family, and most likely she won't be able to send Lizzie to a top university, but Lizzie was taught from an early age that she should prioritize her joy over other people's expectations. And Ms. Dolores is proud of how her daughter has turned out. She has grown to be a strong girl who has her own opinions and world views. And most importantly, as she screamed to Dong's mom, "My daughter never has to cower in a dark corner of the school staircase—or any other staircase—to cry because she got a B in math."

On that day, Dong and Lizzie stood in his basement apartment's tiny kitchen, watching the two beloved women in their lives arguing over whose child was happier. And as if that was not crazy enough, Lizzie's mom asserted that Dong would be happier under her care, that she would take the boy under her wings any day only to free him from the prison Dong's mom had built for him to suffer inside. To this, Dong's mom had kept a threatening silence, then she had shoved both Lizzie and Ms. Dolores out of the house, cursing in Vietnamese and swearing that the next time she saw them in her house, there would be war.

"And it will not be a normal war," Ms. Hoa said hysterically. "I will do everything in my power—everything—to ensure that you and your dumb daughter regret the day until the end of your life." Of course, Ms. Hoa knew when she said those words that she had no such power. But her fury was a mountain; it turned her into a wounded savage beast, not because the words Ms. Dolores said were wrong, but because they had pierced through Ms. Hoa's heart at the tenderest spot. The beast in her had no other option but to claw and scratch at the enemies' faces until all that was left of them was the blood and flesh scattered under her feet.

She knew how hard it was to raise a child on her own. She knew the woman didn't have any fault. She knew it was wrong from the start, when she yelled about the grades and how Ms. Dolores was only preparing Lizzie for failure. She knew it all, yet the mother in her couldn't stop the hurt from spilling out of her guts and hitting the enemies everywhere. She was desperate for someone to share her pain, and she realized that no one would understand the way she was sacrificing everything in exchange for her son to have the life she never had. So Ms. Hoa ran away, and Ms. Dolores, despite not winning the battle, had won the war.

Fast forward to this fateful moment: Ms. Dolores is here, taking Dong under her wings as she had said. She smiles at Dong as he gets in the backseat.

"How's your dragon mother?" she asks, starting the engine and backing away onto the street.

"She's fine, thanks for asking," Dong replies timidly while fastening his seatbelt. Somewhere under six feet of brain and cognition, he feels the guilt start creeping along his spine, chastising him for loving this woman more than the woman who gave him his life.

"You know I don't mean that." Ms. Dolores laughs in her carefree way. "Lizzie said you must be home at nine, huh?" She turns to Lizzie who is sitting shotgun.

"Yes, ma'am. I can't be home later than nine."

"Does your mom ever realize that you are almost eighteen now?"

"No, ma'am, I think—"

"Oh stop it, D-dog," Lizzie groans in her seat. "My mom is not going to eat you alive. Just be yourself."

Dong smiles, thinking to himself, *But I don't know how. No one has ever wanted me to be myself before. No one has ever taught me to love the self I want to become. Except him. And even then, I am still afraid. If I allow him to peel the skin off, layer by layer, will he still love me as I stand there, naked and fragile, no longer the boy he knew when we sang the sweet songs of Leonard Cohen under the August light?*

"D-dog? Lost in thought again, huh?" Lizzie asks him, almost jocularly. "I know you want to meet your Romeo, but can you at least engage my mom and me in small talk?"

"I'm sorry. It's just—the nerves are wrecking me, I guess."

Dong smiles, feigning a joyful look. His mind is a dark and gruesome place. He decides not to fall into its wide-open arms again during this trip. It is always ready to bury him alive.

"As my mom was saying, is your dragon mom still as fearsome as ever? Based on the curfew, I presume she is the same, huh?"

"I don't think so. She's allowing me to go tonight. Something she never did in the past. She's always jumped whenever I asked to be somewhere out of her sight."

"And she almost refused the trip, didn't she?"

"Yes, but she agreed in the end. I wonder what made her change her mind," Dong says, slowly letting the hard reality sink in. He gets the sense that something is wrong, but he doesn't know what yet.

"Perhaps she believed in the reputation of the test prep center you are going to," Lizzie says with a laugh. "Man, I am glad we pulled off the website, and I am proud of my mom for the fabulous work she'd done to help us."

"Aw, I love you, too, sweetheart," Ms. Dolores coos with her sugary voice. "And Dong, don't worry. When I heard your story from Lizzie, I couldn't resist the urge of wanting to help you with everything I have. Every child should be happy and free," Ms. Dolores says thoughtfully. "I don't know why—and I can't fathom the reasons—your mother always insists on you being a person she constructs in her mind. It's dangerous, don't you think, Lizzie?"

"Yeah, she even called us dumb over the phone the other day when you asked for permission to drive Dong to Oakville. I mean, if she had seen the reasons and been more understanding, none of us would have to lie to her. She dug her own grave."

"Lizzie, please don't talk about my mom that way," Dong insists gravely. He can't get rid of the teetering guilt on his conscience. "She only wants the best for me."

"Dong, sweetheart, of course, all mothers want the best for their children. But think about it for a second: What's best for you might not be the same as what she thinks is best for you. The life your mom is living is not the life you are going to have. Even if she is trying to steer the car on the path that she would have chosen for herself, nothing guarantees that your life will be better than what she imagines it to be. We are humans, and as humans, we err on the side of being wrong far more often than right. So, choose the life you want, not the life other people want you to have. After all, the one who will bear the consequences is you. Not anyone else, only you," Ms. Dolores says.

The car sinks into thoughtful silence. Dong looks out the window as he mulls over the words. He knows she means well, but how can he live in any other way? It is ingrained within him that he must give back the life he owes to his mother, as she has given him her life. In his mind, it is a fair exchange. But something in him yearns for more, for the fire in the darkest winter night, for the breeze and whispers of the mulberry trees in the August light, for that guitar with the soft melody and the hoarse voice, almost grown up, almost free. Almost like a fairy tale—a story with a happy-ever-after ending.

Ms. Dolores stops in front of Ames's house. The girl gets into the backseat and finds her place next to Dong. Ames seems contemplative. She keeps her silence and only lets her worries out through a sharp inhale every now and then. Lizzie finally has enough of it and lets her steam blow.

"Oh my God, what is wrong with you guys? We are going

to a party, not a funeral. And even at funerals, I know some that are happier than this whole car."

"Lady, watch your tone." Ms. Dolores glances at her daughter with a stern warning.

"It's alright, Ms. Dolores," Ames says after a long silence. "It's just—my nerves are wrecking me, and I can't seem to calm down."

"Dong said the same thing a minute ago," Lizzie says in an angry tone. "What are you guys? Twins?"

"Lizzie, stop talking that way. Don't you feel worried?" Ames asks, her eyes imploring Lizzie to think over everything without her putting her demand into words. But Lizzie, always becoming dense at the right moment, ignores her dark look.

"What's there to be worried about?" she says. "The plan worked out, didn't it?"

"Yes, but don't you think it's weird how smooth everything is going? I can't believe D-dog's mom would suddenly change her mind in a whimsical moment and allow him to go to Oakville. Heck, the test prep center thing makes it even more suspicious. I don't believe she didn't doubt it. Or rather, how come a person like her, who's always so vigilant and wary of everything D-dog says and acts, didn't double-check the website or search the school's name? Don't you think it's super weird? I can't stop this hunch, this dark premonition. I think we should just all go back and pretend that nothing happens."

"No, you go back, Ames, if that's what you think." Lizzie turns around, her nostril flared up. Her anger is visible through her hazel eyes and her dark irises. "We talked over everything. We agreed that we would be in this together. What are you being such a coward for?"

"I am not a coward," Ames retorts. "I just don't want D-dog to suffer for the actions we make him commit."

"No one can force him to commit any action. He wants to go. He wants to be there. What else do you need to know to help him? I thought we'd talked this through, and you understood how important this meeting is for D-dog?"

"I understood it. But I—I am afraid. Not for me, but for him." Again, Ames feels the sincerity growing hollower in her caring words.

"I am not afraid."

Dong speaks up for the first time since the two girls started their bickering as if he weren't there. He is determined. His eyes shine brightly despite the darkening sky outside. His lips set in a straight line. His face radiates the dawn of hope. "I am not afraid," he repeats.

"Well, you should be," Ames says, taken aback by the sudden change in the boy's attitude. "You are at risk of losing everything. You might not be able to talk to us or go anywhere without your mom's supervision if this gets out. I thought you knew your mom well enough to foresee what actions she will take to prevent you from pulling such a stunt ever again."

"I know my mom well enough. And sure, I might not get the same privileges that I have now if word gets out. But I also know myself well enough to understand that there's only one chance. Ames, I know you are worried for my sake, and I am grateful for that, but think about it. What does it take to be free, if only for one day in my life?"

Ames stares at Dong, stunned. She is amazed by the boy's courage to take a step this far. She almost can't recognize Dong, the same timid boy she's always known, the boy who would break down if he got anything lower than an A on a test.

The boy whose aim is to become a doctor but whose dream is to become a poet. The boy who puts everyone's wishes above his. Her hands grip the hem of her skirt. She doesn't want him to change. She doesn't want him to be better than he is right now. If he is still sad and miserable, she can still—what—pity him in her loving embrace? Ames startles at her wild thought. What has she become in such a short period of time?

She thinks about the talk she had with Lizzie the other day, and how after their phone call, she had lain awake thinking about how the story would unfold. She thought she knew him well enough, but perhaps she underestimated a human's willpower.

Ms. Dolores looks at Ames through the rearview mirror and smiles her all-knowing smile. Youth, the good and the bad of it all. Of course, she thinks, Ames has every right to be afraid. The girl is soft-spoken, and in a way, she is similar to Dong. Though she doesn't have the same pressure of being a perfect child, Ames is also afraid of hurting her mom's feelings. And right now, she is projecting that love and fear onto Dong. Ms. Dolores thinks back on the time she learned of Lizzie's existence in her belly. She was frightened by the weird and sudden presence of another human being inside her. She never asked for it, and she'd thought that Lizzie was there to remind her of the life she had chosen for herself—a life where she was so much more than an unwanted daughter of an alcoholic mother.

Of course, at that time, she didn't consider Lizzie's existence a blessing. But now, as she looks at the beautiful young girl next to her, with her blonde hair, her sharp nose, her hazel eyes that are always bright with new adventurous ideas, and her wandering mind that is always ready to embark on journeys,

Ms. Dolores silently vows to herself that even if she were given the choice to go back in time, she'd still choose to have this girl.

It was a hard battle, raising the girl on her own without help from anyone. But she managed to bring the girl laughter every day, and by watching her grow, Ms. Dolores slowly learned to live a life full of love—something she never imagined she could have done before—and more importantly, she learned to forgive her mother. *No*, Ms. Dolores thinks to herself as she casts another quick glance at Ames's worried face. *It is right for them to be on this adventure. They might end up in different places by the end of it, but one thing is for sure: They won't regret a second of it.* And she says to Ames, "Don't worry, little sweetheart, I will watch over you guys. I'm the chaperone, am I not?"

"Yes, Ms. Dolores," Ames says, her voice still featuring a hint of hesitation.

"Aw, just Dolores is fine. I don't care that much for the title and the seniority. Be casual with me."

"Yes, Dolores," Ames replies, emboldened by Ms. Dolores's carefree attitude. It is true, she doesn't have to worry so much. There's an adult with them. And perhaps it is just her nerves. Perhaps luck is on their side. Ames sinks into the car seat, watching the scenery pass by. Her mind is not at ease, but she has settled for this little disquiet.

From his seat, Dong is looking straight forward. His eyes are keen. He is committing the landscape outside to his memory. From the barely budding trees to the barren fields of wheat and corn, he wants to remember them all. This is his chance to take in everything that life has to offer, and he greedily drinks every last drop of the elixir. As the car passes by the Ninth Line and reaches the corner of Trafalgar Road, Dong feels his body come alive, as if each part of his body is kindled, and the fire is spreading through his entire being.

He pulls out his phone, texting Simon: "I'm almost there." A few seconds pass by, and his phone chimes. On the screen, the text stares lovingly at him: "And I am always here." Dong smiles, hugging the phone to his chest. He wants to sing every love song he's ever heard. He wants to fly and soar up to the sky until the sun burns his wings, and he'd die the same way Icarus did, filled with passion and no regrets. Dong hums a little tune.

In his bliss, he never notices a familiar car in the rearview mirror. A black sedan, old and battered through many winters. The woman is tightly gripping the steering wheel, her hands all white knuckles. She is watching the old Toyota closely, inching forward in secrecy, wary of Ms. Dolores's careless way of driving. Her mind is all jumbled up. She drives over the speed limit a few times to chase after Ms. Dolores's car, her heart in a nest of fear. If she were caught by the traffic police, that would be the end. She doesn't have the money to pay for such nonsense as a speeding ticket.

That white woman, Ms. Hoa thinks to herself as she stops at the red light, one car behind Ms. Dolores's Toyota, *She dares to corrupt my son. No doubt it is the fabulous work of her useless daughter. No wonder she called me the other day asking permission to bring him to the test prep center. There's no test prep center for sure with that dumb daughter. I should have known—how long have I been feigning oblivion to their friendship? It only gets worse over time. What could possibly bring them to Oakville? What, indeed, could possibly bring him to lie to me?*

As she is thinking this, the light turns green. Ms. Dolores drives ahead, her car full of laughter and jokes between the three friends. She looks in her mirror for a fleeting second. Ms. Hoa's heart jumps; her paranoia tells her that Ms. Dolores's eyes met hers just then. But it seems that it is only her nerves.

Ms. Dolores drives on without a second glance at the black sedan. Behind her, Ms. Hoa follows closely and carefully, her face hidden by a mask. Amidst the chase,Dong is oblivious to everything. If there's one thing he is holding on to at that moment, it is not guilt. He has long forsaken it. All he has in his mind now is that smile, that voice, that warm embrace as he runs into Simon's arms. The world fades away into darkness.

Chapter 13: I Knew That It Was Wrong

Ms. Dolores leaves Dong at a stop sign on a tiny road leading to a row of houses, each one the exact carbon copy of another.

Dong finds his way to the house three doors down the empty road. The sky above him is a gradient of a purplish-pinkish hue. He can feel his heart yearning for something that is as beautiful as that sunset, or maybe more. He is greedy for what is to come, and in that moment, he has put every consequence before him—from the lies he told to the grand betrayal he schemed—down the dark oblivion of a forgotten abyss.

Dong knocks on the door as a new person—a human who is not quite himself, but at the same time, is a version as true to himself as possible. He waits anxiously for that tall figure, that toned body from playing basketball, to open the door and shelter him from the upcoming storm.

"Hey there, Anthony." Simon smiles at him and the Earth stops moving.

His eyes sparkle under the light of the nearby lamp post. The irises reflect the twinkle of the first stars in the evening sky. Simon reaches out for Dong's hand, his fingers twisting gently around Dong's wrist, tugging at his shirt sleeves, and guiding their way along until they intertwine themselves around each of Dong's fingers. Dong feels the warmth of his skin seeping through the tips of his fingers and suddenly, he has the urge to cry. He spent three years waiting, not knowing when his torment would end. Dong wipes his eyes, but there is no trace of tears. Simon looks quizzically at him. "What's wrong, puppy?"

"Nothing's wrong. It's just—I never imagined it to be like this, us meeting again, in Oakville, under a darkening sky." Dong chuckles. "It's scary. But a good kind of scary. I think I will learn to love it."

"And I hope you will." Simon laughs and pulls Dong in for a tight hug. "It's not what you had imagined, but is it everything you had wished for?"

"More than that." Dong's voice is muffled in Simon's chest. He closes his eyes, letting himself sink into the deep ocean of all the promises made and all the promises broken. "Much more than that."

Simon places a gentle kiss on Dong's forehead and ruffles the boy's hair. Dong has grown taller since the last time they met, but Simon has also grown. Everyone changes; nothing stays the same. It seems the only constant in both their lives is how they keep moving forward. Simon laughs at Dong's astonished face and leads him into the house.

The boy keeps looking around, half believing that he is living the truth, half thinking that everything is a complicated, intricate web of lies orchestrated by some powerful force beyond his control. Simon makes him sit down on the soft, brown leather sofa. He keeps standing up, and after a struggle, Dong agrees to his position on the right corner of the sofa, where he can watch Simon pacing back and forth in the kitchen, taking out drinks and snacks. He rests his chin on the sofa arm, his eyes half closed as he listens to the footsteps, and he thinks to himself, *So, this must be what they mean when they talk about bliss. The sound of footsteps on hardwood floor, the clinking of porcelain dishes and glasses, the rustling of snack bags; they all sound like bliss.* He is on the verge of sleeping when Simon reappears in the living room, saying jocularly,

"What's up, sleepy kitten? Like what you see?"

"No, God, no, when did you learn to talk like that?" Dong flushes crimson and jerks up into a straight sitting position.

"When did I learn to talk like what? I simply asked if you like the decoration of the house." Simon laughs at Dong's reaction. He loves teasing the boy, especially now, when he can see those almost too-innocent, too-sweet reactions in a person with a mindset of the Titans that once ruled over humans' existence. "What else did you suppose I was talking about?"

"I—I suppose nothing. Yes, I like what I see. It's a nice house." Dong fumbles with the bag of potato chips, trying his best to open it, but the bag keeps slipping through his fingers. He bends down to pick it up and mumbles, "And I like what I see when the door opens, too."

"What did you say?" Simon picks up a chip and dips it into the creamy onion sauce. It's been so long since the last time he felt what happiness is. He is not going to let this opportunity slip by him. He smiles, full of mischievousness, and scoots closer to Dong's back on the sofa, whispering into his ears, "What do you like when the door opens?"

"You are a fucking jerk." Dong jumps in surprise. His face is beet red. He twists the hem of his shirt into a bunch, staring at Simon in shameful embarrassment.

He cannot control himself whenever he is with this tall boy.

He is always at a disadvantage. From height to wit, from being the victor and the failure, from being the one in love and the one who's out of it, he is always on the side of the losing party. But Simon disagrees. To him, Dong is the bravest soldier he's ever met.

Perhaps it is the struggles Simon has seen him go through, perhaps it is the unyielding smile that Dong puts on his face like a war mask, or perhaps it is the sheer resilience that brings Dong here to him, standing straight, bearing the weight of the whole world on his shoulders. No matter what the reasons are, Simon finds that he falls deeper and deeper into the depths of his adoration for this boy in front of his eyes. He is so bright, so dazzling, that Simon almost fails to believe that he is real. Simon reaches for Dong's hand and drags him back to the leather sofa.

"You know I meant well," he says simply, pulling Dong closer to him and wrapping his arm around Dong's shoulders. The boy flinches under his touch but gives in eventually.

"Well, you know I am no good with jokes. Especially jokes like those."

"But that was not a joke. You know how much I wanted you to like me when you saw me again. You don't know how many times I've changed my shirt because whenever I thought of the possibility of you turning away when you saw me, I started sweating to death"

"You are lying," Dong mumbles, half believing his words, half expecting Simon to give him reasons—no matter how small—to trust everything he says without question.

"But it's the truth. I can show you the shirts," Simon says, laughing. Though he appears confident, his nervousness and anxiety betray him with the small trembling of his arm. Dong can feel the fingers involuntarily dancing on his shoulders. He looks at the boy next to him. Small beads of sweat are showing on his forehead. *It might be true,* Dong thinks to himself, and he hopes it is true. He turns away, flushing. The thought that his existence could mean so much to someone else fills him with a strange sense of happiness and contentment—a feeling he has never had before and is only too glad to see it bloom.

"I never said that I don't trust you, now, did I?" Dong says. His voice is almost inaudible. His hands keep twisting the hem of his shirt.

Simon sees through every one of his actions. He wants to squeeze Dong into a small fluffy ball and keep him by his side forever. The timid way Dong averts his eyes and focuses on the rug, his eyelashes trembling slightly, his cheeks a pale color of pink, his thin lips set into a straight line—all of them stir Simon's heart into a boiling cauldron until it melts into an ocean of burning lava. He ruffles Dong's hair, coughing a few times to suppress the urge to hug Dong until the boy is suffocated in his embrace.

"Well, I'm glad," Simon says.

"And I'm glad you are glad," Dong replies. His wit is out the window. He curses himself for being so obtuse and stupid. He has forgotten half of his vocabulary already. It is bad. And he knows that with Simon sitting so near to him, his warmth seeping into his skin, it will only get worse.

"What's with us?" Simon finally says, laughing, his head leaning on Dong's shoulder. "If we are going to waste this one hour on exchanging pleasantries, then it'll be a waste of your courage to lie to your mother, wouldn't it? Come on, do something."

"Do what?"

"Anything. In this space, now, you are free." Simon spreads his arms wide open. "Do whatever you want. Especially the things that scare you. I'm ready for your attacks."

"You don't know the meaning of half of the words you've said" Dong turns to face Simon, angered by his own fear and ineptitude. "It's always so easy for you—for anyone—to speak. Actions are harder."

"Then would you prefer it if I act first and leave the speaking for later?" Simon raises one eyebrow. His eyes show a keen sense of curiosity and ingenuity.

"I never said that," Dong protests, and in his mind, a thousand scenarios run past with the speed of light. He realizes, only too late, that he has dug his own grave.

"Well, then I am saying it. And not only am I saying it, but I will also act on my words. After all, you said that actions are harder, right? Then let me do the more difficult things."

"Stop it, you—"

Before Dong can finish his words, Simon starts inching slowly toward him with a fake threatening posture. Dong laughs and runs around the living room, trying to hide behind the sofa, underneath the coffee table, and cover himself with the thick teal curtains. Simon chases after him, roaring with laughter. He waits until Dong settles himself behind the curtain, chuckling with bliss, then he jumps at Dong, hugging both him and the curtain, swaying them back and forth. They become a giggling mess, each one's laughter contagious to the other. They fall to the floor and roll around on the rug until Dong almost hits his back against the sofa. Simon quickly reaches out his hand, pulling Dong closer to his body to prevent him from getting hurt.

Neither of them feels awkward about the closeness of the

two bodies, now colliding in an invisible distance. There is no gap, no room for anything to come in between. They can feel the skin of the other person quivering through their clothes. The boisterous laughter slowly dims to an awkward pause, and a heating silence commands. Dong can hear Simon's heart beating with a racing speed.

The ever-quickening thumping sound almost materializes itself and caresses Dong's earlobes. He burrows his face into Simon's chest as his nose sharply breathes in the scent of fabric softener and the woody aroma lingering on Simon's body. Simon holds him closer; his nose is on top of Dong's hair. The scent of spearmint suffocates him in a warm embrace. He has never felt such a sense of calm and safety. He breathes in the scent greedily. His hands squeeze Dong's arms until they leave behind a red mark. Dong trembles slightly at the force, but he stays still.

"So, what are we going to do now?" Dong whispers. His breath tickles Simon's skin.

"I don't know. You tell me."

"Can you let me go?"

"Impossible. After all"—Simon holds Dong closer, until their chests touch each other in a furious longing for the other's warmth and presence—"I didn't know you had grown this much. Your body fits perfectly in mine." Simon chuckles.

Dong can feel his hair rustling in warm, gentle fingers. He puts his arms around Simon. His cheek sticks to Simon's chest. His eyes close. In his mind, he is walking slowly on a darkening road until he goes back to the origin of beings, where he is immersed in the warmth of nothingness before everything comes into existence. They stay like that for fifteen minutes, thinking that they've spent an entire lifetime in that small window. Simon strokes Dong's back gently; his hand finds its way along Dong's spine. He likes the way the boy trembles with each movement and yet still tries to accept the new feeling that Simon gives each time he moves his hand. Simon asks, "Should I let you go?"

"No. I forbid you," Dong says. His voice is muffled in Simon's chest.

"Then tell me what I'm allowed to do," Simon says. His voice is hoarse. His breath lingers on Dong's forehead.

"I don't know what you are allowed to do. Acts are harder than words. You said you'd do the more difficult things."

"Then am I allowed to do whatever I want?"

"I don't know."

"Dong, I'll let you go. Because if things continue this way... "Simon pushes the boy from his chest. Dong's eyes are glazed over with a thin film of mist. "I don't know what I'll do. I don't know what I am capable of. I might be a beast. The worst beast you've ever met."

"But I know you."

"You knew me before. You don't know the me now." Simon ruffles Dong's hair, trying to bring back the innocent laughter they just had. "And the me now might scare you. And neither of us want that."

"But you also don't know the me now. Perhaps I want that beast. Perhaps I even love him." Dong looks up at Simon, his eyes in a daze. He is expecting something he does not yet know. It's a territory so strange, so cruel, and yet so dazzling to him that he can't help but want to sink himself into it.

"You don't know what you wish for," Simon says, feeling the danger creep up on him from behind. A voice echoes in his mind, *Take this chance, claim what is rightfully yours.* But that is the problem: Simon doesn't know if Dong's pure love is rightfully his. He is afraid of the unknown. What if he fails to protect the boy? What if this joy is only the frosting, and the cake beneath it is the pain? He is teetering between unleashing his inner demon and keeping Dong safe in his nest of innocence. His hesitation reflects in his dark brown eyes, and Dong can see it as clear as day.

"Well, you are right," Dong says with a firm voice. "Acts are always harder."

Then Dong pulls Simon close and gives him a gentle peck on the lips. And that is enough for the demon in Simon to wake up, roaring, fighting for his way out. Simon pulls Dong's head closer and kisses him with a feverish fervor.

He devours the soft lips, the breathless mouth, the timid tongue that is trying to hide from his chase, and the occasional gasps that barely escape before a new kiss comes back, stronger than ever. Simon pulls up Dong's shirt, sliding his hand on Dong's skin like a snake coiling around its treasure. Dong shies away from the first touch, then he abandons all his reasons and gives in to the warmth of the fingertips dancing on bare skin. He never knew that a person could feel so much pleasure that he would be willing to drown in it until the last drop of this golden elixir burns him to ashes. In this moment, he wants to tell Simon that he knows what he wishes for, and not only that, but he also knows that he will do anything to get that wish. His whole body has finally awoken after a long slumber. He eagerly awaits each kiss, each touch, each caress, as if he is a famished drunkard in the garden of love, waiting for the feast of unyielding passion to envelop him and swallow him whole.

Simon's kisses move to Dong's neck. His lips can feel the

boy's quickening pulse through the taut skin. He bites into the pale, yellow flesh and is happy to hear a surprise gasp from the boy beneath him. It's almost as if he is a wild lion, and Dong is the ever-elusive prey, outwitting him in every way, but always ready to surrender to his gentlest touch. He jumps at the first moment of Dong's careless mistake and swallows his prey in small bits and pieces until there's nothing left of the boy but a melting mess. Dong gazes at Simon, his eyes seeing, but his brain refusing to comprehend what is happening to them both. He reaches Simon's face, tracing every feature, every curve, every prominent point on that loving canvas. He feels thunder booming in his heart.

It is surreal how things have turned out, and Dong wishes they could lean on each other like this forever. Simon looks intently into Dong's eyes, finding his reflection in the dark irises shining through, overjoyed at the fact that a person can desire his existence so much. He jumps into that darkness without the slightest hesitation, happily drinking the darkness from Dong's loving embrace, willing to be the sacrifice for a fleeting moment of being needed, being alive. He kisses Dong's nape and traces the kisses along his shoulder. His hand clumsily trails along Dong's torso and firm waist. A heat is slowly building up between them, with the ragged breathing and the lost caresses on bare skin. Right when Simon starts to take off his shirt, the doorbell rings.

"Are you expecting someone?" Dong asks, still breathless from the too new, too dangerous passion.

"No. My parents are not supposed to be home this early. And I'm not expecting any other visitors this evening," Simon says, trying to recover his sense of reason. It seems his sanity is still finding its way back to his brain. His eyes are still hazy.

"Just ignore it."

"How can I ignore it? Someone is knocking at the door. You should go and check." Dong sits up and pushes determinedly at Simon's chest. The boy groans in frustration, and with visible regret and hesitation, he stands up and walks out the hallway to the door. Dong giggles at the sight as Simon looks back at him and throws him a kiss. But his face soon freezes as he recognizes the familiar voice outside:

"Hi. I am here to pick up my son."

It is his mom. Ms. Hoa is standing in the doorway, looking carefully at the tall, dark boy who is barring her way and stopping her from forcing her entry into the house. In her confused mind, she doesn't recognize the boy from her memory—the son of her neighbors many years ago. He looks at her menacingly, asking with a cautious voice, "Who is your son, ma'am?"

"You know quite well who my son is. He is the one in your house right now. Give him back to me," Ms. Hoa says. Her voice trembles with desperation. She is too immersed in her own pain and suffering to hide the pleading in her tone. "Give my son back to me."

"Ma'am, with all due respect, I don't know what you are talking about," Simon says adamantly, standing stock-still at the door, refusing to give in. He knows it will only lead to disaster if he moves an inch out of the entrance.

"You know what I am talking about. The Vietnamese boy you seduced is my son. Now, move."

"Ma'am, I can't just let you in my house."

"This is not your house. It's your parents'. And the boy inside this house is not yours. He's mine. Give him back to me."

"Ma'am, I—"

"I am a mother. And perhaps you will never understand the weight and the power that word carries, but the boy you are trying to hide from me is rightfully mine. Mine."

Ms. Hoa screams. Her anger is bursting at the seams. She cannot hold back the rising tsunami of desperation; the Earth underneath her feet is sinking. She is drowning, trying to wave her hands, begging for the help she knows will never come. She breaks down in tears, not caring that the person in front of her is a boy of seventeen years old. She keeps repeating, "Mine. Mine. Mine." But the boy refuses to move an inch.

Simon stands there, holding the door frame, determined not to let her in. He bites his lips, trying to think of a way out. If this woman is still here when his father comes home, that will be the end of their story, and who knows what lies beyond that ending? After all, there's never a true end and there's never a good beginning. He racks his brain, trying to find an excuse to get Ms. Hoa away from his house as quickly as possible, while praying in his heart that Dong will stay where he is in the living room and will not be so stupid as to go out and worsen the situation.

But Dong turns out to be exactly that: He is a stupid drunkard. A cowardly lover whose most heroic act was lying to his mom. And when he sees that the intricate castle of betrayal is falling apart, he chooses to run.

"Mom…" Dong suddenly appears behind the looming body of Simon, looking straight at his mom. No one knows what he is thinking at that moment, but all of them know the disaster is coming.

"I told you I knew where you were that night," Ms. Hoa

sobs.

She reaches out her hands and grasps Dong's arm firmly, trying to pull him out of the house. But Simon holds on to the other arm and tries to remove her claws. They are at a stalemate. Ms. Hoa pulls harder. "I knew it would come to this. You lied to me. You lied to your own mother. Did you ever consider, in that cruelly clever mind of yours, how much it would hurt me? You don't know, Dong, and you never will. You are not a mother. No, more than that, you are not me. You are not the one who laid down her life so that her son will never have the same suffering and the same hardship that she bore on her shoulders. I give you shelter, Dong. And look at what you are doing. You destroy me. You shatter everything I've built with only a few words. Are you happy now, seeing me so wrecked? What have I done to deserve this kind of treatment?"

Ms. Hoa claws at Dong's skin until it leaves red marks. Some of the neighbors are looking out their windows and wondering about the scene. Simon looks around him and decides he needs to get Ms. Hoa off his doorstep. He cannot risk having her here, hysterical and yelling, when his father and stepmom come home. *The plan had been perfect,* Simon thinks, *but the one factor I did not count on was the strength of Dong's mom.* The strength of a mother.

He keeps a hold on Dong. He cannot let the boy go back to that tortured basement apartment. He cannot leave Dong in darkness. But the darkness is so near, and though he is trying his best, he cannot save someone whose hope for salvation has long disappeared behind the closed walls of a darkened bedroom.

"Mom," Dong says softly at first, but his voice grows strong, "you are right. I am not you. And I can never be you, or anyone else, for that matter. But you don't see—no, you never see me for who I am. Mom, before being your son, I am also a human. Can't I have a bit of happiness?" Dong says, pleading, his eyes are tearing up. He is not scared; the tears are out of frustration. He's had enough of being blamed for everything that happens in his mom's life. And he's had enough of living another person's life. He says firmly, "I only wish for freedom. And Simon is my freedom."

Both Ms. Hoa and Simon look at Dong, their eyes wide open in surprise. Ms. Hoa finds Dong's words utterly ridiculous, and she doesn't know where the boy got that idea from. She grasps at every feasible reason in front of her, trying to find a way out of the maze Dong has put her in. Hanging on the door frame, Simon looks intently at Dong. His eyes sparkle; he can't hide the pride he feels in his heart for the boy.

Apparently, Simon was wrong. In those three years of being apart, Dong has not only grown taller, but he has also grown in bravery. A bravery that has been hardened and refined in the fierce fire of the oven. He watches Dong in silence as the boy fights for his rights. This is his first time rebelling against the force of the generational curse. The curse that has been passed down to his mom since the time the Supreme Mother gave birth to one hundred eggs—one hundred Vietnamese children. The curse that doesn't allow her to be happy. The curse that forces her to choose a path with thorns and broken glass with the hope that her son will have the best life he can ever dream of, without a guarantee that the path she sacrificed herself for is the same path that will bring her son happiness. The curse that breaks everything and heals nothing.

Simon gently pulls the boy back into his arms, while Ms.

Hoa lets him go. She is stupefied, lost in the labyrinth of thoughts and beliefs that she has created for herself since she set foot in this country with the paper husband. She cannot believe what she heard. "My dreams ," she mumbles, her eyes growing wild. "What about my dreams?"

"But those dreams aren't mine," Dong shouts, his bravery feasting on his mom's sudden weakness.

"So, you chose him over me. You chose this thing"—Ms. Hoa waves her hand in a wide circle—"This thing—"

"I did not choose him." Dong firmly holds Simon's arm. "I choose my freedom. It just so happens that he is my freedom."

Simon looks at him incredulously. He is not the same person Simon remembers. The timid boy, who listens to everyone, who would rather smile and accept the fate handed to him, no matter how unfair, because he always believes that it is his duty. That boy now says that Simon is his freedom. And what is Simon doing? All he's done since the start of this battle was wallow in his own suffering, holding on to a past that had long been fading and refusing to participate in anything that cost him more than reaching his hand out to take what is rightfully his.

Simon turns to look at Ms. Hoa, and his words escape him with a firm conviction. "And he is my heart."

Ms. Hoa looks at the two boys standing there, hand in hand. She suddenly feels exhausted, as if the force that had been holding her up behind the steering wheel all the way from Mississauga to Oakville has decided to let her go. She falters back onto the steps, laughing. Anyone passing by this scene would call her a mad woman. No one would know that she is grieving the life she has lost. And it's not her life, she thinks in that moment of wild laughter and heaving breaths. It's Dong's life. Or rather, the life she always imagined Dong would have on her sleepless nights, tired, with every joint in her body aching from washing mountain after mountain of dishes.

"Freedom," she says, her voice breaking between the laughter. "Freedom, you say?" She finds the whole thing ridiculous, a bad acrobatic act of a sad clown aiming to incite laughter from a poor audience. She looks at Dong, and the boy finds the lurking monster inside her depthless irises frightening as he trembles at her grunted words. "And who do you suppose will give me my freedom?"

The three of them stand there. No one thinks of speaking, and none of them can find a solution—a way out of the labyrinth. Each of them is at a different corner of the maze, trying their best to get their words through the thick cemented walls, hoping all the while that they will reach the others. But all they hear is gibberish. The words are jumbled up, twisting, coiling around the different meanings, and when they finally reach their ears, all they can feel is sharp glass stabbing into their scarred, bleeding backs.

"I never asked you to sacrifice your freedom for me," Dong says, his voice now weaker than before.

Much like his mom, he feels exhausted. The will to fight is still there, lingering around his words, but he doesn't find the same conviction in them anymore. Is this a wrong choice, after all? Should he have stayed back home, like the perfect son that she expects him to be, and bore the world on his shoulders until the end of his days? Should he have opted for the same curse his mother has and accepted that he would always live others' lives, forgetting that his life is there, on the sideline, watching him walk with shackles on his ankles, begging him to choose it instead?

"But whose sacrifice did it take for you to grow up, lacking nothing and having everything served to you on a silver plate?" Ms. Hoa asks, her voice seething with a vengeance she never knew she had in her.

He surrenders. He can't find the strength in him anymore. Dong's mind seems to wander off in the night without knowing the ending or the path he is embarking on. "I could have sacrificed myself for you, too."

"And you choose not to. Because freedom is what you are after."

"Should I not have happiness then, Mom? Did you ever, in your whole life, since the time I was born, wish for me to be happy?"

"You'll be amazed to know that I did. I constantly do. I am on my knees begging God to give you the happiness that I don't have. I plead to Him to take my happiness and give it all to you. But Dong, not like this. The happiness you choose is cursed," Ms. Hoa says, her voice feeble, her sobs continuing to break in.

"No. My happiness is not cursed. Mom, have you ever had a happiness that is so dazzling, so bright, that it burns you alive, and despite the pain, you still gladly accept it as the greatest blessing life has to offer?" Ms. Hoa shakes her head, her eyes wide with fear of the words her son is speaking, but Dong continues, "That happiness is not a curse. It is freedom. It is love."

"No. I won't give you up. You are coming home with me. And you will give me your phone. You are grounded. I will not leave you out of my sight. Not anymore. You want freedom huh? Then I'll show you the price you must pay for it."

Ms. Hoa takes Dong's hand and yanks him forward. Simon

is taken by surprise and lets go of Dong's other hand. As Ms. Hoa drags Dong back to the battered black sedan, Simon runs after his heart until the boy is seated in the front with the seatbelt fastened, and he screams, "I will come for you. Action is always harder. And this time—"

Before he can finish his sentence, the car drives off. He stands there on the pebbled walkway, whispering in the wind, half praying, half pleading, "Let the more loving one be me."

Chapter 14: Letter #11

Dear Alexandra,

I watch the birds flying south every day, my Alexandra. They seem almost happy. I say "almost" because I know on their road, some of them will live until they feel the warm sun nestle them up, while the rest of them will die dreaming of it. I often look out the classroom windows and ask myself, "What would it take to be a bird?" Do you know the story about Icarus, who builds his own wings to be free? But he flew too close to the sun, my dear Alexandra. He never knew how much his freedom would cost. It seems that freedom always costs someone's life. In history class, my teacher tells us about all the wars that were ever had. They all died for freedom, although when their lives were extinguished, none of them had tasted freedom on their tongue.

But my dear Alexandra, that night, I tasted freedom on your lips. Even if it was only a fleeting second, I knew what happiness was. And I regret nothing. I am sitting at my desk. My only companion is the lamp. I told the lamp about you, and he urges me to write you this letter. I wonder if love will still be there when the last human leaves the Earth? And if it is, then why are the poor lovers tortured for the crimes they never commit? Is loving you a sin? But my Alexandra, you'd promised me that you wouldn't leave. I live on hopes and promises alone, and you can deduce from that sentence that my life now doesn't have any. Only you and the thought of you keep me alive. I'd die a thousand times over to see you again for just a second longer. But you don't need to know that.

My dear Alexandra, you told me that you weren't leaving. But you ended up leaving, didn't you? And I don't blame you; I'd rather go on believing the lie you fed me. It is so sweet, so sugary that I can get drunk on it for the rest of my life. So please, don't take this away from me.

Your Anthony.

Chapter 15: After the Storm

Ms. Hoa stops her car at the school gate and her eyes follow Dong's silhouette closely as the boy walks up the steps and goes inside the school building. She counts each footstep and keeps the time with her wristwatch. It is an understatement to say that Ms. Hoa is dictating the boy's life or controlling his existence with the absolute power vested in her, as it was in her mother, and the Supreme Mother of all Vietnamese mothers. It's been two weeks since the secret rendezvous of Dong and Simon. Three weeks since the scheming and the orchestration of the betrayal. Time has gone so agonizingly slowly that Dong cannot believe his eyes whenever he wakes up and crosses the dates off on his calendar—the only thing his mom allows him to keep in his room, along with his textbooks, notebooks, and the barest essentials to write.

Could it have been only three weeks since the start of everything? How can his life have changed so much after mere weeks? He can't wrap his head around how time functions. He knows the calculation—the math and the theory behind its existence. But that knowledge can only make his mom proud; it refuses to answer Dong's question. Dong lives in the clouds. The body that is waking up and going to school every day now is only a materialization of what he was before the storm. Dong's soul is no longer residing inside it.

He smiles, but his eyes are a bottomless abyss. He laughs at the jokes about his appearance, but his brain can't comprehend them. He goes through the days as if they are a haze—a dream he needs to keep on living in without any option to get out and wake up. Dong wonders where his reality lies—was it by Simon's side as they were rolling on the rug in the living room of that house in Oakville, or is it now, with his mom's existence hovering over him, haunting him with every step, clawing at his heart with guilt and contempt?

He walks in a trance to his homeroom and sits down in front of Lizzie and Ames. The two girls look at his back; their worry shows clearly in their eyes, but they are too scared to voice it. Lizzie's mom was furious when she heard the news. She never understood the motive behind Ms. Hoa's ferocious outburst. Lizzie and Ames were crying the whole way home, their hearts unable to bear the pain that Dong had to suffer from Ms. Hoa's verbal abuse.

"The boy is broken enough as is," Ms. Dolores said. "I don't understand how his mom even found out about this whole thing. And what I don't understand even more is how she can just drag him around as if he is her puppet."

Answering her was the sobbing and tears of the two girls. Ames tried to keep her composure, but she couldn't think of anything. She kept repeating the words Lizzie had said before the day they came to Oakville: "Have you ever seen Dong smiling and laughing that freely?" If only she had stopped him then—but what would give her the right? Sometimes, she wakes up in the middle of the night, frightened at the thought that maybe her jealousy was the jinx behind all of Dong's bad luck. Maybe her wish for Dong to be miserable was strong enough to materialize as a curse. She weeps into her pillow, devastated and exhausted by the monster she calls her mind.

On their way home that night, Lizzie was sitting beside her, biting her lips to prevent a cry from coming out, but tears were streaming down her face. She wasn't crying because she regretted her actions. She shed those tears for the plan she had failed to construct and the tiny happiness she could have given Dong in return for everything that the boy had done for her and Ames. Ms. Dolores looked at the two girls in her rearview mirror, an anger rising inside her. She could not let things end this way. It was never in her nature to agree to abusive behaviors, no matter where they came from. And it was even more hurtful to her to see her sweet girl reprimand herself for the abuse that Dong had received.

"What has the world come to?" Ms. Dolores asked herself on the drive home. "For children to suffer this much, and for nothing but only love?"

In their homeroom, Lizzie taps Dong on the shoulder. The boy turns around, emptiness clearly showing in his eyes. He replies, smiling automatically like a carefully programmed robot, "Yes?"

"Are you okay, D-dog?"

"Why do you ask? I'm perfectly fine."

"You don't look fine to me."

"What can I do? I try to look fine enough," Dong says, and his voice suddenly breaks. He stops and recovers his usual tone. "I look fine enough to everyone though."

"But everyone does not include Ames and me."

"You should try to be everyone," Dong says, a hint of pain showing through. "It will do you good. And it's fun, too."

"D-dog, you are ruining yourself." Lizzie stands up from her seat, shaking Dong as if to wake him from the nightmare he is living in, but Dong is already too deep in his sorrow. "Do you plan on living this way forever? Do you plan on giving up on having your own life? You are not your mother, and you have no reason to be the person she wishes to be. You are you. You have flaws, you have secrets you want to keep, you have dreams—no matter how silly they are. You have freedom. You have choices. Why do you let it all go?"

"I don't know," Dong answers, not really comprehending Lizzie's words. "I don't have the right to decide. She said I'd pay for my freedom. It was only half an hour of freedom, but it could last me a lifetime, Lizzie." Dong smiles at the memory. "It can satisfy me to live for a while yet."

"D-dog, you—"

But the homeroom teacher enters. They leave the conversation at that. Lizzie pretends to listen intently to the teacher's announcements, but her mind conjures up a thousand ways to fix this whole mess. She goes through her contacts one by one.

There's a girlfriend she knows who goes to the same school as Simon. Their relationship is not the best, but she can ask a favor from her if she begs hard enough. There's also the person who hosted the party. That boy sure was nice. He had walked Ames and her to the car and had even given her his number "in case we can meet again sometime."

She racks her brain, wondering who she should contact to get to Simon, that mysterious being who is friendly to everyone but close to no one. As the homeroom teacher finishes his schedule for the day, she bites her lips and decides to ask the boy who hosted the party about Simon. But when

131

she is in the hallway going to first period along with Ames and Dong by her side, a stranger's text appears on her phone. After reading the text, she urges the other two to go ahead without her. Lizzie skips class, goes to the nurse's office, claims to have a stomachache, and quietly calls the number.

"It's me."

"Yes, I know," a husky voice says in a soft whisper through the phone.

"How did you get my number?"

"I can get anything I want if I try hard enough."

"Damn you popular people. What do you want?"

"Listen, you were the one who planned my Anthony's escapade, weren't you?"

"Your Antho—who?"

"Dong."

"Ah, right. You are his Alexandra. Speaking of which, are you guys alright in the head? What kind of names are those?"

"Never mind that. I would like to ask you a favor."

"Good. I also want to ask you a favor."

On the other end of the phone, a threatening silence reigns. Lizzie swallows her heart as it jumps to her throat, waiting for the answer.

She thinks of Dong, of his listless eyes as he asked her if she was okay, of his way of caring for everybody—anybody—but himself. She is determined to get what she wants, no matter what. *This is not for me,* Lizzie thinks. *This is for Dong, and all the children who have to grow up in the prison built upon their parents' wishes and expectations, who have no dreams but must go on living.*

In a sense, she realizes, this actually *is* more for her than anyone else. She wants to be the reason for others' happiness.

Something is lurking inside her, and she doesn't know yet what it is. Something akin to aspiration, a dream, a desire to do something that will outlive her. Then the voice on the phone brings her back to Earth.

"I think your favor and mine coincide with each other."

"I think so, too."

"I want to see Dong."

"I want to help you to see Dong."

They announce their favors at the same time and laugh. The other voice says tenderly, "I figured the mastermind behind this whole business would be an intelligent person. And I'm glad I wasn't wrong."

"Not many people would call me 'intelligent' per se," Lizzie says. "I mean, you should have seen my report card."

"Well, all I can say is that being intelligent and being a successful person aren't necessarily the same thing. Look at me. Look at Dong. Would you consider us intelligent?"

"I suppose not, judging from the things you guys did and the maze you guys are stuck inside."

"Yeah. And everyone would call us successful." Lizzie can sense a smile in the voice. "We are only good at acting. But acting won't get you very far. It only ruins you in the end. After a long time, you won't know who you are anymore, or what you are living for. So, before that happens, I want to drop the act. It's high time for Alexandra to get back to his Anthony, damn the Gods and anybody in between."

"You've got yourself a deal."

"Thank you. Now, this is what I need you to do—"

"Nah, little boy," Lizzie says firmly. "If you want a favor from me, then it will be me dictating the rules. This is what I need you to do—"

Through the first two periods, Lizzie confines herself to the bed in the nurse's office, scheming, planning. And the voice is always there, listening patiently to her, confirming her plan, and adding his own solutions. Lizzie patiently goes through the smallest details: whose car they will use, what day of the week they choose, the time, the place, and, most important of all, the dragon they will fight to rescue the prince in the fortress of darkness. The voice chuckles now and then at her excited way of talking, her crude jokes about the helicopter parents his Anthony has. "I mean, can you believe it? He's only gotten straight A's since I met him. What more do they want from him?" Lizzie fumes.

The bell for third period rings and the nurse casts a few warning glances at her. She doesn't mind a student using her office now and then to ditch class; God knows she loves a wild youth. But three periods in a row is a bit much, and she won't allow the youth to take over the children's future. She taps a pen on the table impatiently. Lizzie's sick note is ready. The girl looks at her sheepishly and smiles her sweet apology, then whispers into the phone, "Listen, I have to go."

"Yeah, I don't think I can stay much longer either."

"No kidding. You are in school, right? Who's allowing you to use the phone in class?"

"Who says I'm in class? I'm in the nurse's office."

"F—I mean"—Lizzie looks at the teacher and quickly changes her tone—"You and Dong do make a nice couple."

"Of course," the voice says with a laugh. "Why else do you think I was willing to wait all these years?"

"I'll get to you later. Bye."

"Wait."

"What now?"

"Send my love to my Anthony. He needs it now more than ever."

Lizzie hesitates. She wants to tell the voice about the alarming state Dong has been in since the storm cast the gloomy sky over their wild days. She also wants to let the voice know that at this rate, his Anthony might not last that much longer. He is already losing his mind. All that is left of him is a body acting on strings. But she swallows the words and says instead, "Sure, I will let him know."

As soon as the words escape her mouth, she knows that it's a lie. She can't possibly give Dong hope where none may exist. Yet she wants to believe in her willpower. She wants to believe that love will cure everything. The voice seemed to detect the hint of uncertainty in her voice as she said those words, but it says, "I know," then it hangs up.

When Lizzie arrives at the English classroom for third period, the test results are already handed out. She takes up her seat next to Ames, and in her cheerful tone, tapping Dong's shoulder, she says, "Hey ge—"

But before she can finish her sentence, Ames holds her hand back and slightly shakes her head. Lizzie mouths her question, "What happened?"

"Dong got a D on his test."

"Wha—" Lizzie jumps from her seat, then, noticing the teacher's severe look, she sits down again and whispers, "Isn't that, like, impossible?"

"It's not impossible," Dong says, scaring the two girls with his calm voice. "It is simply a matter of illusions shattering. I thought I could have the moon, so I reached out for its reflection on the still lake, but it turned out the moon was not mine. Nothing is ever mine." Dong turns and smiles at the two girls. "I should have known better than to believe in happiness."

The two girls look at him, stunned. It is both amazing and frightening how a burning love can change a person.

Ames tries to find the right words to say, but Lizzie grabs her arm firmly, shaking her head. There is no right word to say to console a broken heart. She knows she can gather the broken pieces and try her best to glue them together, but the heart would still have cracks all over, allowing both the darkness and light to filter through. And what Lizzie wants to give him is a truly mended heart. It is in a human's nature to yearn for the light, but Lizzie doesn't want Dong to suffer the price of darkness. She writes on a small piece of paper, "Meet me after school at my house" and passes it to Ames. The girl reads it with a knowing look and nods her head firmly. They know that when the adults have failed to save the world, it is their turn to face the aftermath of the storm.

Chapter 16: At Lizzie's House

Ames rushes into Lizzie's house right after the bus drops them off. She is in a hurry to find out what Lizzie has to say about Dong's situation. A part of her is festering with guilt, and her heart yearns for the right answer to appease the boulder that is ready to fall off a cliff at any moment. But Lizzie seems uncertain. She takes her time in taking off her shoes, shuffling her bags, and she stands in the entrance as if waiting for something that Ames can't figure out.

"Well?" Ames stands in the hallway, looking at her dubiously. She is flushed with impatience and anger. Why did Lizzie ask her to come? She wants a clear answer. She thought that Lizzie could solve anything if the girl put her mind to it. But the way Lizzie is acting now, Ames wonders if maybe she was wrong. The two girls look at each other in awkward tension.

Lizzie looks down at her shoes on the rack, mumbling, "Well what?"

"You tell me. You told me to come. And here I am at your house, waiting for you to say something, but you keep shuffling your bag back and forth. If that is how you want to play this whole thing, I'm better off finding a solution on my own," Ames yells.

"It's because you haven't let me think."

"I thought you had plenty of time to think in the nurse's office and on the way home. Don't even think for one second that I didn't know what you were up to today."

"And what was I up to, if you are so clever?" This time, it is Lizzie's turn to get angry. She storms off to her room on the second floor, with Ames trailing behind her like a lost child.

"You must be concocting some plan or other. You were the mastermind behind this whole thing after all. And I told you this would happen before we went to Oakville. I told you it was wrong, but you didn't listen. Look at how things turned out. Are you happy now?"

"And are you happy to see D-dog so miserable all his life? Do you suppose that a life like that is worth living? You saw him in English today. We've seen him every day since we found him crying on the school staircase. Tell me, do you see a person there, or do you see a phantom of someone who's barely breathing? What is so bad about getting a D?"

"Of course, I am not happy!" Ames breaks down and cries, standing at the entrance of Lizzie's room. "I thought I would be. It's scaring me that I thought I would. I thought if he was miserable then I could be by his side forever, consoling him. I have no good things except D-dog. And look where that's gotten me. It is not my wish, but I don't know what to do. What can I do to help him survive this prison, when he is the one who's choosing to live inside it?"

"Ames…" Lizzie is too stunned to speak. "Ames, put that aside for a moment. That's where you are wrong. He never chose to live inside this prison. Simon told me so. He recounted the whole event to me. You are right, I did concoct a plan with Simon today. I believe we have an escape route."

138

Ames looks at Lizzie, trying to find her balance, then she decides to settle herself on the soft pillow by Lizzie's desk. She grabs the stuffed frog from Lizzie's pile of plushies as if to ground herself. There are so many things she wants to ask, and she can't find the right order to ask them. Should she start with how Lizzie managed to contact Simon? Or should she ask about what really happened that night between Simon and Dong? And what is this escape route Lizzie is talking about? The questions drown her in a tumultuous, stormy ocean, and she keeps her grip on the stuffed frog so tight that the poor thing becomes shapeless.

"Well? What do you want to know?" Lizzie asks.

She wants to have Ames as her aide-de-camp in this war, and she is not about to give up now, even when the D on Dong's test is making things more difficult than ever. She believes she can fight her way through the thistle and weed. Much more than that, she believes she has the same willpower her mom had when she decided to raise Lizzie all on her own. She knows the women in her family are built to win, and she won't let the victory in her grasp slip away through the cracks of her fingers. But an anxious voice speaks in her head: *Ames wishes for Dong to be miserable so she can feel good.* She tries to swat it away, yet it remains immovable.

Ames, on the other hand, is still hesitating. She wavers between her desire to help Dong and her fear that once things get better, she will be left all alone again.

What if Dong's mother raises Hell on him, and through no fault of his, makes him the sacrificial lamb for the things she wants? Ames can't help but remember Dong's face as they were leaving school today. His eyes were open, but they did not recognize anything. His face was calm, but beneath that calm and peace, Ames could detect a hint of sadness. Of course, no one likes the feeling of defeat. But Dong has been a defeatist all his life.

Ames wonders if one can settle for darkness when he has seen the light at last. She is scared, but what she is more afraid of is the glaring fact that if she leaves things as they are, she will live in regret for the rest of her life. It gnaws at her conscience when she knows that her actions can impact a person's life so much, and yet she is still refusing to walk on that path simply because she does not know where it will lead her. Sometimes, it frustrates her how much of a coward she is, especially when sitting opposite her is Lizzie, always so calm and composed, always full of the answers to life's sorrows.

"If you are not going to help, then you can leave my house now," Lizzie says sharply. She can detect the hesitation in Ames's face as the girl keeps chewing her lips and gripping the stuffed frog in her hands. She knows her words only increase the pain in Ames's gentle heart, but she can't afford to lose the war when the plan is already in action and the promised victory is so near to her that she can almost kiss it.

"I never said that I'm not going to help."

"Then why the long face?"

"It's just…what if the plan you talked about backfires? Have you ever thought about how it would be for D-dog if everything falls to pieces and shatters his life more than it already is?"

"I see." Lizzie leans on her bedframe, her blue eyes screwed up in a cruel glare. "I see. You are not thinking for D-dog. You are thinking for yourself. You are not afraid that his life will be wasted. You are afraid that you will be haunted with regret. No, Ames, I don't have a place for a coward in my plan. And if that plan backfires, I will be the one shouldering it with him."

Ames looks at her childhood best friend, her dark brows twisting in agony. She wants to say that she doesn't mean it that way—she doesn't have selfish intentions, and she is not a coward. She knows that Lizzie is already too deep in the swarm she had dug for herself. Ever the heroine. Ever the protector of light and goodness. She is the leading role. Ames quickly realizes the green-eyed monster as it rears its head inside her heart. Sure, let Lizzie get her way. No words from Ames could ground her back to the firm floor of the darkening forest anyway. Against her will, a cruel joy sparks within her soul. Let the tower fall. She won't bear any consequences after all.

She wishes she could go back in time and refrain the two of them from ever talking about the party. But she stops her train of spiraling dark thoughts and asks herself, *Why must I feel guilty about showing D-dog the photos of Simon? Am I really afraid? And for whom?* Lizzie's words stab her at her tenderest spot, and they ring in her mind in a tormented, incessant toll of bells: *"You are not afraid that his life will be wasted. You are afraid that you will be haunted with regret."* She continues chewing her lips. She can't find the right words to express her feelings, and in her confusion, she steps on a landmine as she asks, "Why would you go so far for D-dog?"

Lizzie stares at Ames, too stunned to speak. Then, she simply replies, "Because I am a human."

The two of them look away from each other, each lost in her own thoughts. Lizzie doubts that it was the right decision to bring Ames into all this talk. She can see that the girl is almost crazy with fear, anxiety, and even a rare jealousy. She knows Ames doesn't take rebellion well. Her bravest act was that day when they smuggled Dong to Oakville—to bring Juliet to Romeo. After that, she stepped back behind the curtain; to Ames, her role was done.

But Lizzie refuses to be a side character. To her, the stage is still bright, and as long as the lights are on, she will do anything to make the most of the play. Be it a warrior or a secret helper, she can be anyone the situation dictates. She refuses to give up her role to any other person who, she knows in her heart, will only cause more pain and suffering. After a long silence, Lizzie says softly, her mean demeanor vanished, "I never asked you to be in the plan. You are free to go as you please."

"But you will still carry on with your plan, won't you?" Ames asks sheepishly, her fingers fidgeting with the stuffed frog's long limbs.

"That goes without question."

"And you'd rather do it alone?"

"I'd rather have a companion." Lizzie smiles weakly. "But I don't want to hurt you, or see you drive yourself into a corner just because you can't bear the fact that I will be alone in my endeavor."

"I never said that I'd be happier that way."

"Then what *are* you saying?"

"Tell me your plan." Ames looks at Lizzie, her eyes suddenly focused and her gaze sharpened. She twists a lock of her naturally curly hair, half expecting something great, and half filled with fear of that greatness.

"So, here's the plan—"

"No, I changed my mind, tell me what happened that day in Oakville."

"What's there to tell? His mom barged into another person's

142

house and literally dragged Dong to her car, then drove him back to Mississauga in a fury. That's all I heard."

"Did Dong ever say he didn't want to stay?"

"What, you want some security?"

"No, I want to be sure that we are doing something good for him, not vice versa."

"No one can ever be sure that the things they're doing will end up being good for the other person, as you wisely put it. You and your frail vanity. Forget being a good person. Be the person you want to be. Morality is a grey area, in which anything can happen, and nothing will ever stray out of the lines."

"Are you trying to philosophize with me?" Ames looks at her best friend in bewilderment. This is the first time she's ever heard Lizzie speak about something so abstract, and she doubts the girl understands her words' meanings herself.

"I am not philosophizing anything. I just...do you ever wonder if what we did was wrong? Or selfish? That planning D-dog's escapade was our futile attempt at proving to the world that we are capable of anything?"

"I don't know," Ames says after a long time mulling over the question. "I simply thought he would be happy. D-dog was right after all. Nothing is ever that simple."

"Well, I have thought that. I wanted to prove to myself that I was capable of anything." Lizzie lies face down and sprawls out on the floor.

She looks like a lazy, old cat who is enjoying the last ray of sunlight of the day. "I guess I was angry with you because I can see my own failure. It is not your fault. Maybe some caution would do us good. We thought we were so wise, but we never understood how far D-dog's mom would go to cage him in her embrace. I mean, what did I think? I should have suspected something, especially since she agreed to D-dog's impossible hours. I mean, she never lets him out of the house after dusk. How could I not see it?" Lizzie's eyes glisten; her voice trembles.

In that single moment as the revelation descends upon her, she feels like the world has abandoned them all, and before them, there is only a barren desert. This time, it is her turn to hesitate. She was so excited to tell Ames about the plan with Simon, but now the words fail her.

The more they both think about that day, the more fearful they become. Out of all the what ifs they can think of, none of them feel like a happy ending. Ames pouts; her hopes begin to shatter one by one, and she is trying to pick up the pieces, holding on to Lizzie's sheer willpower. Both girls are silent, drowning in the static noise of their own thoughts. Then the door cracks slightly. Ms. Dolores sneaks her face in, asking cheerfully without noticing the depressing atmosphere in the room, "Hey girls, do you want some snacks? I have chocolate chip cookies, freshly out of the oven."

Lizzie looks at Ms. Dolores. A storm of feelings and emotions sweeps her heart away as she watches her mom's gentle smile and listens to her soft, tender voice. She never knew how happy and blessed she was until that moment, when she realizes that God has prepared her for all sorrows and suffering by letting Ms. Dolores be her sole parent—her mom. A woman who was so strong that she refused to follow what society dictated. A woman who was so tender that she was willing to give her daughter all the chances in life, while she herself withdrew to the backstage, watching the stage light shine on the little girl from the time she was a baby until now.

Lizzie thinks of her mom's busy shifts at the hospital, of her efforts to always be there on her birthday, Christmas, New Year, and every other holiday, with a gift in her hand. She looks at her mom's gentle face—not a trace of the hardship of fighting against the world so that her daughter could grow up to be anyone she wants to be—and she has the urge to cry. She has had so much love, enough for a lifetime. Ms. Dolores looks worried as the two girls remain silent, and Lizzie's eyes seem ready to shed tears at any moment. She quickly rushes into the room and settles down beside her treasured little girl, asking in a confused voice, "What's wrong? What happened?"

"Mom, it's just—I just can't believe how unhappy D-dog is." Lizzie burrows her face into her mom's warm bosom and sobs.

"Oh, it's alright, darling. We will help the boy in whatever way we can. You guys are so close to graduation already. The boy will be fine. He can go to a school far away from home. He can decide his own life, then," Ms. Dolores says soothingly, patting Lizzie's heaving back, but the girl only cries louder.

"He got a D in class today. I don't know, Mom, he looked so sad I thought he would leave this world for another one— somewhere he doesn't have to try so hard to be loved. He looked almost like he wasn't even here with us, like he was only passing through. I am so scared. And I figured out a plan with Simon, but what if it is only my ego talking? What if I can't bring him the happiness he deserves? He is so good to us. To think that the day he went to Oakville was the first time—and it might be the last time—I saw him laugh with such a childish glee in his voice. I can't bear it, but what can I do? How can I mend a broken heart?" Lizzie pours her heart out, and Ames is sitting there, watching her, wondering, *So, even the strongest among them fears the abyss.* She thinks of her situation, of her own mother, and she understands Lizzie's current outburst. She, too, wants D-dog to be happy.

Ms. Dolores looks at the two girls and her eyes shine with a sudden bloom of passion and enthusiasm that she thought had wilted away since the dusk of her youthful days. She cups Lizzie's face in her hands, asking her, "So, what did Simon propose?"

Both girls perk up. Ames is curious; that question is the reason she came to Lizzie's house in the first place. Ms. Dolores always has a way to get to the core of the problem. She coaxes Lizzie to tell the plan in the minutest details and nods agreeably to each sentence.

"In conclusion, he wants to see the boy, but he doesn't want to cause the boy any more anguish," Ms. Dolores mulls.

"Yes, Mom. He said he would settle for a chance meeting. A casual chat in a library or a walk in the park. He would agree to anything and—"

"Wait, I can see that a chance meeting will lessen that fierce woman's guard, but how can we get your friend out of the house?"

"I think I can persuade him to go for a walk near his house. There's a park in his complex."

"That's too risky. His mom can catch him anytime. Tell you what, the first thing you need to do is let Simon know that he needs to come to Mississauga right now. With that D, I don't think your friend is in a good state of mind, especially with his mom's obsession haunting him. Then, tell Dong to sneak out of the house when his mom goes to work. I presume she still has night shifts at a restaurant, right?"

Lizzie's eyes regain their sparkle. A fire suddenly kindles in her heart. She feels more alive now than ever. Finally, she can see the light at the end of the tunnel. She quickly reaches for her phone and puts it on speaker. She knows how stubborn Dong can be at times, and she believes that her mom can persuade him, no matter how hard he clings to the notion of accepting his defeat. But what pops in front of her only serves to scare her even more. It is a text from Dong. He writes: "I wanted to be saved. But what have I gotten myself into? I should have known from the start that dreams don't belong to people like me."

"Mom?" Lizzie cries, alarmed. Ames hurriedly scoots over to her side, and after reading the message, she begins to cry herself. Ms. Dolores takes the phone from Lizzie's hand and quickly dial Dong's number. A stern female voice answers, "Hello?"

"I am looking for Dong. Can you please put him on the phone?" Ms. Dolores tries to keep her calm.

"Dong is not here."

"Then you should be worried. Where is he now?"

"Why? What business do you have with him?"

"A very important business."

"Then run it by me first."

"Why? You are not him. This business ceased to concern you a long time ago."

"You insolent woman. You and your daughter put that pretty notion in his head. Now he's refusing to listen to me and has barricaded himself in his room. He even got a D on a test. Look at the mess you created in my life. You have no idea—"

But Ms. Dolores hangs up before Ms. Hoa can finish her hostile rant. She knows danger when she sees it, and her intuition as a mother has taught her many things. Among them is to recognize a child whose wish to live is outweighed by the desire to stop the suffering and the pain. She quickly stands up and rushes to the door, urging both Lizzie and Ames to follow her. Both girls grab their coats in confusion. Ames has not stopped crying, while Lizzie is already wiping her dried tears and putting all her hopes on her mother's superpowers. "Call Simon, put him on speaker," Ms. Dolores implores. Lizzie quickly redials the number in her contacts. A deep, husky voice answers with a hint of laughter, "Yo, how is it?"

"Simon? This is Lizzie's mother speaking."

The voice is silent for a split second, then it replies with sincere severity, "Hi ma'am. What can I help you with?"

"Are you free to drive to Mississauga right away? I will give you the address now."

"If the address is the same as three years ago, then you don't need to give me anything. Could you please let me know how severe the situation is?"

Ms. Dolores looks at Lizzie as if to confirm something. The girl knowingly nods as she settles herself in the shotgun seat.

"Yes, the address is the same. Code D: a failed test, helicopter parents, possibly major depression." Ms. Dolores puts the car in reverse and drives out of her lot as she speaks, then she speeds up along the street. It will take ten minutes to get from her house to Dong's. She is praying—hoping against hope—that the boy will still be there, alive and breathing, when she arrives. The voice breaks intermittently, mixed with the sound of things crashing against the walls, and finally, it says,"I'm on my way. I will be there in thirty minutes. Ma'am?"

"Yes?"

"Could you please, please, make sure he's safe?" The voice

148

breaks into small sobs, then quickly recovers itself, and begs Ms. Dolores again in a firmer tone, "I will bring him with me. As long as he lives, I will be there for him."

"Good. That's all I need to know. I will save the boy at all costs. You keep your word and I'll keep mine."

The phone hangs up. Under the darkening sky of a wintry day, with nothing but thunder and clouds ahead, two cars are running at full speed to the same destination.

A rare winter rain is splattering on the windshield. Ms. Dolores is trying to stay as calm as she possibly can. Beside her, Lizzie bites her lips to keep herself from the thoughts that are swarming her mind and clouding her judgment at a frightening speed. In the backseat, Ames bites her fingernails, overwrought with worries. She keeps repeating to herself, "All is well. All is well." Her nervous mind jumps at every stop sign, thinking that she is at Dong's house already. Her heart nearly stops with every crack of thunder.

On the road from Oakville to Mississauga, an old Honda is driving at ninety miles an hour. The boy behind the steering wheel stares ahead as the rain falls incessantly on the windshield. He hopes but dares not believe in his hopes. He prays, not for a miracle, but for the existence of God. He believes, but his faith is slowly fading away with each boom of thunder. Outside, the lightning bolts only signify a stormy sea ahead. Whether they can all land on a safe shore or not, none of them know.

Chapter 17: Letter #13

My dearest Alexandra, my most beloved, my forsaken love, my one despair, my only true hope, I have come to the end of my existence. I know you will call this a melodramatic statement. Or rather, I think that is what you would say. I am so deep in my head that sometimes I think I've had a glimpse of the end of the world. I live, but I am not here. I breathe, but the air is suffocating me. I can feel the burn in my throat, the hot coal on my tongue, the fire as they kindle up the wood as I stand there, prostrated on the crucifix, calling your name, shouting each syllable just for the night to swallow it all in her endless bosom. I've never known a freedom as boundless as the freedom I had when I whispered your name that night. Our breathing was one. Our skin glided on the other's; the heat of another human being made us go crazy with the desire to hold on to this life, no matter how cruel the world is to its children. And now that it is all over, what is the point of going on?

You are more than a reason to live, my Alexandra. You are the reason I started believing in dreams. I thought I had everything until you proved to me three years ago that what I've had, since the beginning of time, was a cage—a prison I was supposed to break free from, to rebel against, to simply be me. I lived in darkness for so long that I believed only darkness could save me. I walked on thorns and spikes for so long that I could not imagine a path without them. And then you came into my life. You showed me that darkness could not exist without light. You led me to the garden and showed me the roses rising above the thorns. You let me know that the spikes were there for a reason, and I had a choice to walk away from them. And I held on to you—my first hope, my last salvation. But you are leaving me, my Alexandra. All of this never should have happened. I sometimes entertain the thought of a life where I never met you. What would have become of me then? What would have become of Anthony if he had never had his Alexandra? The world would have moved on—when does it ever stop? But Anthony would have been blinded, and I would never have tasted the bittersweet taste of freedom. And I am grateful, in these last hours, that you were there. I am grateful for that eternity of happiness in a single laugh. I only wish that you could be here to witness the creature you created in me, but I have run out of luck. I traded it all to be with you for a fleeting moment.

Should I come back to this life on Earth again, I want you to greet me. Tell me how your life has been since the day I left. Tell me the happiness you had. And more importantly, laugh with me. I never believed that love would cure this sadness that we are all in, but laughter is all I need to have faith in life again.

Your Anthony.

Chapter 18: Show Me the Place

Ms. Dolores knocks vigorously on the door. Ms. Hoa comes out, full of anger. She is on the verge of cursing. "You—" she starts, but before she can finish her sentence, Simon cuts her off. He grabs her shoulders, shaking her stout body in a loud fury. "Where is he? Where did you hide him?"

Then, facing Ms. Hoa's stunned silence, Simon barges into the house, running at full speed to the basement, skipping the steps and almost rolling himself down the staircase. Ms. Hoa keeps her mouth gaping. She doesn't know what she has got herself into. She only knows that Dong has barricaded himself inside his room without permission, and he's failed a test. She was reprimanding him—as her mother did whenever she got bad grades—when Ms. Dolores called.

She hates the woman, and she wonders if perhaps Lizzie told her mother something. It is beyond her worst fears to imagine that someone outside her family might know about Dong's failure, so after the call, she reprimanded the boy some more through the closed door. The boy didn't answer, and try as she might, she couldn't pry open the door. The lock was not a problem; it felt as if the boy had used some heavy pieces of furniture to stop the door from opening fully. The only thing Ms. Hoa could glimpse through the crack was the total darkness of a room without light, without windows.

And then, this whole crowd barges in, crying, yelling to her face that she is a cruel mother. She cannot, for the life of her, figure out what the reason might be, so she fumes and fumes as she runs after Simon, the one person she never wants her son to see again. She had given Dong her old phone a while ago in case he needed to call her to get him from school early, and she had confiscated his phone on the night he sneaked away. To think despite benevolence and leniency, this is how he would betray her, Ms. Hoa can't help but feel a pang in her heart. The last thing on her mind, throughout this time, was his strange temperament as he got home, or the blank stare in his eyes as he handed her the test with the D on it. Neither did she think about the apathetic smile he showed her when he headed back to his room after her tidal rage of yelling and cursing.

But none of her thoughts, at this moment, can stop Simon from knocking on Dong's door. *Not this again,* Ms. Hoa thinks. *Not this nightmare, not another one coming all the way here to stain the honor of my family.* She quickly follows him and stands between him and the door.

"You are not welcome here," she says. "You need to go, now."

As much as Dong's temperament is the least of her worries, Ms. Hoa's words mean nothing to the panicked and the anxious Simon. He ignores, or rather, he seemingly doesn't heed her words. He screams at the top of his lungs, until his voice can fight its way through the wooden door and reach the stormy shore where his beloved is caged.

"Dong, open the door. I'm here. Your Alexandra is here." He shoves Ms. Hoa away as if she is nothing but a statue, an object

153

that is standing in his way—no more, no less. He forgets, in his fury, that Ms. Hoa is a human, and more than that, no matter what she did, she is a mother. She claws at him, trying to fight back his firm stance and his overbearing presence in her house. She can see the dark clouds gathering, although she does not know yet where these clouds are heading. "Dong, please," Simon pleads, on his knees, crying. "Dong, I need to show you something. Please have mercy on me. Can you forgive me for my silence? But how could I have chosen a different path? Do you know I've kept everything you sent me? Do you know I read through every letter until each one of them is crumbled and wrinkled up in a mess of laughter and tears? Do you know how much your Alexandra never wants to leave; how much he loves his Anthony? Dong, after hundreds of days, I finally had you in my arms last month. How could you deny me this little crumb of happiness, right when I could taste it for the first time?"

A little crack is opened. Simon can hear a small, tender sob through the thin opening—the abyss between his love and his loss. A letter slides through the door, then the door is closed again. Simon quickly grabs it as if it is the last drop of water on a deserted Earth after the apocalypse. He scans through it, then lets it fall to the pile of papers by his side. As if he is in a trance—consumed with a madness from a winter buried in an ancient tomb a long time ago—he sings,

"Show me the place
Help me roll away the stone
Show me the place
I can't move this thing alone
Show me the place
Where the word became a man

Show me the place
Where the suffering began"

The sobs are getting louder and louder as Simon's voice travels through a thousand oceans to mend a broken person. He grabs each little sob, trying to swim through the waves, until he can see the abandoned shore, where his lover lies, undone by the world he once believed in. Beside him, Ms. Dolores, Lizzie, and Ames stand in a close circle, daring not to move an inch. Lizzie's eyes are glistening with tears. Ms. Dolores thinks of getting Ms. Hoa away, but judging from the wretched look on her face, she decides to let the matter rest for a moment. Then a voice softly sings through the door, the syllables broken, but the will strong enough to mend them:

"The troubles came
I saved what I could save"

Simon continues the song:

"A thread of light
A particle, a wave"

And after a long silence, the two voices complete the bridge in unison:

"But there were chains
So I hastened to behave
There were chains
So I loved you like a slave"

Dong finally slowly reaches out his hand for the light of his life, just outside the door. Simon grasps the hand, firm and strong, capable of so much more than just giving up and giving in to the temptation of an ending to the sorrows that are ever so prominent. Simon feels the flower bloom in his heart.

A weight had pushed Dong to the edge of the abyss, and

looking at the schism underneath, he jumped without any hesitation. He thought he'd end up in Hell, so he was never ready for this Heaven. Simon pulls Dong out of the dark room. The boy lumps against him, his arms hanging loosely on either side of him. Dong does not cry; he has shed enough tears in the span of four hours. Rather, he only rests his head on Simon's shoulders, inhaling the warm scent of the sun—barely visible now in deep winter, but it is always there.

He suddenly feels sleepy. He wants to drown himself in the love of another human—something he has never had the chance to experience in his seventeen years of life. He is afraid that it is too late now to ask for so much. Simon gently strokes his back, keeping him close and sheltering him in his tight embrace. He never knew a life with a beating heart could be so precious—it is as if he is a sailor who has fallen from grace but has finally been able to touch the treasure at the heart of Poseidon and feel the golden thread of eternity slipping through his fingertips.

They keep their silence, but their love screams and echoes within the walls of the old prejudices and the bleeding wounds of a generation of women who had no one else to rely on but themselves. "Oh, what the Hell," Lizzie says as she finally breaks out and dashes toward the two boys, hugging them. Ames follows her footsteps and jumps in for the group hug. Ms. Dolores looks on in awe. She knows it takes a certain bravery to give up, but it always takes more than bravery to keep on going, no matter what the cost. Seeing her daughter's pride shining in her tears for the work she has done, the plan she conjured up, and the price she has paid, Ms. Dolores thinks she has raised her daughter in all the right ways.

She looks over at Ms. Hoa. The woman's face is contorted

into an ugly mask. Her wrinkles show on her skin; her eyes are dark and lusterless. She is no longer there—rather, it is her specter that Ms. Dolores is seeing. Ms. Hoa looks at her son, or rather, she looks past the limping boy nestled in the bosom of all his friends, and finds herself back in her home country, when she was still young and free. She looks past him to see herself growing up, her parents rarely home, her mother working from early morning to late at night, ensuring all the while that Ms. Hoa would have the best food. Her father is barely visible to her now. She only vaguely remembers that he was there on the rare occasion that he was not drunk with his friends from the construction company.

Yes, she looks past Dong to find herself, lost in a whirlwind of changes, because nothing stays the same and everything leaves. She runs across the fields of rice paddies with her younger self, laughing with her, feeling the wind in her hair, breathing in the scent of the newly cultivated fields and the baked earth after the rain, and she finds that she never had much to lose in the first place. Only herself and the memory of a faraway place that nobody in this household could love as much as her. Ms. Hoa smiles—the gentle smile of defeat.

She should have known she was not fit to raise a child. She is barely a grown adult herself. She feels that she'll remain that lost girl on the rice paddies forever. Ms. Hoa removes herself from the scene and floats back across the ocean, hoping that she will reach the shore of her mother's embrace. But all that she suffered, she suffered alone. She wants to spare the child her burdens. But whether it is a right decision or not, it is not in her power to judge. She walks out of the basement, crosses the threshold of the house she shares with her husband's brothers, and runs into the night with all the madness that has been built up within her since the first day she stepped on this foreign land.

As her footfall becomes heavier, Ms. Hoa asks herself in a high, feverish delirium, *Where are all the rice paddies? Where are they all gone?* Behind her, Ms. Dolores runs at full speed, calling her name, trying to stop her from crossing the street when the light is barely turning red. But Ms. Hoa cannot hear anything except the lullaby of her mother on that summer day when she was still young, and the world was still gentle to the children and the beasts.

But the young boys and girls in the house do not have time for this episode of madness. They have their own madness to take care of. Simon cups Dong's listless face in his hands, smiling calmly, his eyes unable to contain the sparkles of happiness that are shining through.

"What were you thinking? What did you plan to do with that nasty letter?"

"I thought no one would care either way," Dong replies, smiling softly at his own pathetic voice. "Not my mom. Not you. Not anyone. Because I am alone. I have been alone since I was born, and I will be alone when I leave this Earth." The boy trembles, then he quickly wipes away the tears, not wanting to show his weakness to his friends and his beloved.

"But we do care!" Lizzie shouts at him. "Did you seriously think that I would let that cryptic message you sent me go by unnoticed? Did you have the nerve to believe that we, of all people, would abandon you in your moment of need? Honey, it's in your head. You are just too deep in your head."

"And your mind has never been your friend," Simon says. "Don't be fooled by the illusion that it wants something good for you. It only cares for itself. You are so much more than a single thought." Simon strokes Dong's cheeks with his palms, as gentle and loving as he can.

For the thirty-minute drive here, he was haunted by the thought that his arrival would be too late. He asked himself a thousand times, *What if Dong is no longer here?* Each time, he gripped the bundle of letters, tied neatly with a white ribbon, in the hope that they would give him courage to survive the test of the world. He has never been the favorite child of God, so the thought of praying never crossed his mind.

Instead, he bet his life on the strength of the human in Dong. The invincible species that has survived all the bloody wars. So many lives have been lost for the species to go on living; how could Dong deny his only reason for existing? Did it never enter his mind that humans are fragile; that no matter how strong one is, they all fall in the end? Perhaps he did think of that, but just like how a devout never believes in any other deity but God in the human shape, Simon refuses to believe in the possible fall of the person he loves. The one person he owes everything. Simon thinks back of that dreadful drive, then he squeezes Dong once more in his embrace, laughing, tears streaming down his face. "Gosh, why are you so tiny?" In his mind, he muses in agony, *And why are you so strong? How did you hold on until I came to rescue you?*

Lizzie leans her head on Dong's shoulders while Ames scoots closer to the boys, her hand holding Dong's firmly. She says, "Do you know how long it takes for regret to form?"

The three teens look at her in bewilderment. She smiles, a smile almost too weary to be that of a young girl in her budding state of life. "It only takes a split of a second. But to fill that hole, you'll need more than a life. Isn't it funny how humans are built only to be destroyed?"

159

Lizzie wants to reply with something witty, but she thinks better of it and finally settles the matter with her roar of laughter. "It is. But we are not destroyed yet, are we? So, let's keep on living for a little while longer. And even if the world destroys us, who can say we have not led a fabulous life?"

"And when we die, we can have that famous inscription on our tombstone," Dong mumbles, nuzzling his face closer to Simon's neck.

"What's the famous inscription?" Lizzie asks, curling into a ball near the wall. Her eyes become animated again, her sense of vitality finally kicking back in.

"'There are no strong men, there are no beautiful women. At least, you can die knowing this and you will have the only possible victory.'"

"Where is that from?"

"Charles Bukowski," Dong says, his voice growing quieter until it becomes a whisper of safety and warmth. "The man who died with the words 'Don't try' engraved on his tombstone. But we can bask ourselves in his glory rather than fall into his self-deprecation."

"Aw, my little librarian," Simon laughs, and he falls to the floor with Dong still in his arms, with Lizzie and Ames lying on either side of them. "You are the smartest boy with the stupidest ideas."

"And I won't hold any grudge for that insolent statement," Dong murmurs, then in the silence that follows, he falls into a deep sleep. His chest rises and slowly calms to little movements of breathing. Beside him, the three young friends also surrender to the oncoming of the deep slumber. Simon breathes into his hair. "Whatever it is, let tomorrow take care

160

of it."

"No truer words have been spoken tonight." Lizzie yawns then reaches out her long arms to hug the two boys.

"Agreed," Ames says, then quietly leans on Dong.

Her dreams start flashing through her mind instantly and she is immediately taken back to her home, when her father was still there, and her family would find a way to enjoy the beauty of the seasons in Canada. Cherry picking, flower viewing in High Park, camping in the forest in the summer— all those scenarios come to her in the short expanse of a starry night. She doesn't care if the world is going to collapse tomorrow; all she has in her heart now is the warmth of the living, lying beside her. Nothing is too late.

But is it too late for Ms. Hoa? Outside, on the pavement of the intersection, Ms. Dolores tries her best to restrain Ms. Hoa from jumping into the oncoming traffic. Ms. Hoa screams and flails her arms around, trying with all her might to escape Ms. Dolores's tight embrace. The passersby look on with curiosity. Some cars honk as a form of asking if the two women need help, but Ms. Dolores smiles at them amicably and urges them to go their way. She does not believe that the presence of another unknown person would be beneficial to the already hysterical Ms. Hoa. The woman seemingly does not see, or is not aware of, her current surroundings. It is as if she is lost in her own dream, where no one can hurt her, and no higher being can punish her.

"Let me go. For fuck's sake, let me go," Ms. Hoa screams in Vietnamese.

Ms. Dolores can only infer the meaning of the phrases through peripheral circumstances. She tries to drag Ms. Hoa to the nearby fence, hoping that by getting her away from the streetside, Ms. Dolores can somehow save Ms. Hoa's life. It was her mistake to think that only the children needed saving. Hearing Ms. Hoa's heart-wrenching screams in the night, Ms. Dolores realizes, for the first time in her life, that adults who never had the chance to be children need just as much salvation as broken children. Ms. Hoa keeps pushing toward the street without a care for Ms. Dolores's tight grip. Then, by the sheer willpower that she used to face all the hurdles of life, Ms. Dolores throws both herself and Ms. Hoa to the pavement. In the surprise attack, Ms. Hoa loses her footing, then she burrows her face into the hard cemented ground and bellows her pain for the world to hear.

"You need to calm down," Ms. Dolores insists.

"Leave me alone," Ms. Hoa screams, still using her native tongue without realizing that the strange, blonde woman over her cannot understand a word she says.

"Listen, you need to calm down. No, don't act so violently. It would not help either of us. You know I am far stronger than you, and I am capable of taking you to the nearest hospital for a close watch. Your mind is tearing you to pieces. For God's sake, quit struggling."

Ms. Dolores tries to resuscitate the too-far-gone Ms. Hoa from her delirium. But Ms. Hoa fights against the force with all her might, until what is left of her is a mess of unbridled thoughts, spiraling downward until they reach the bottom of nothingness. She faints and her limbs hang loose, her eyes close. All her troubles disappear in front of her, like the life she has led up until now is a dream—a nightmare—and by falling asleep, she will come back to her real life. Her life of rice paddies, of lullaby singing in the midsummer rain. Her mother. Her grandmother. Her friends. Her native language, which always curdles on her tongue without the hope of reaching the ears of anyone who might care enough to see the beauty in the sunspot.

Ms. Dolores, seeing that the situation is finally out of her hands, decides to call an ambulance. The car drives through the night with the alarm ringing in the ears of the sleepy citizens. Ms. Dolores sits inside the fast-moving vehicle, thinking about the reason behind what just happened. They all thought that the one lying here would be Dong. None of them cared to spare a thought for this woman, who, underneath the startling white light of the car, seems to have every one of her sorrows carved on her face.

Ms. Dolores thinks, in the silence of the night, *Why did you come here if this country bears so much pain for you? Why did you have to sacrifice your safe haven for something you didn't even know was good or bad? And most importantly, why do you suffer for others to live?* Then she thinks about Dong. The boy had the unfortunate fate of growing up just like his mother, in both temperament and thought. Perhaps, Ms. Dolores mulls, he had thought that his disappearance would bring everyone happiness. But what is happiness? That would be for each of them to decide.

All the while, the four young friends are sleeping peacefully. In their sleep, they cannot hear the home phone ring. Ms. Dolores is calling to inform Dong about his mother's mental state. She tries the number again and again, but there is no answer. The husband is not home, and none of the other families want to involve themselves with a late-night call.

On the floor, Simon's phone keeps flashing quietly. His father and stepmother ring every ten minutes. He had driven away in a hurry without informing them both about his destination and his intention. They keep calling his cell until it is one in the morning. Then, in a grave silence, his father calls his ex-wife, thinking, hoping, that Simon might be with her. But the woman only listens silently to his carefully chosen words without affirming his hope. She lets him finish his story, and without any ceremonious tact, she speaks bluntly into the phone:

"I know where he is. But you have no right to interfere with his life. You made your choice all those years ago when you decided that I was a mad woman for wanting him to enlist in the army. I told you—countless times—that he was weak. He was a—"

"And I told you that I don't care," Mr. Wiseman says with firm conviction. "No matter what else he is, and whatever he might become later in life, he is, and forever will be, my son. My flesh and blood. Something you failed to understand then, and I doubt that you understand now. Where is he?"

On the other end of the phone, Ms. Prudence keeps her silence. The man can almost see her lips set into a line as she tries to contain her anger. Then, he hears an exasperated sigh as the woman spells out the address of their former neighbor. In a rush, both he and his wife run to their other car and speed their way to the city center of Mississauga, in nervousness and apprehension. Mrs. Wiseman holds her husband's hands firmly in hers, praying. Mr. Wiseman focuses on the road ahead to divert himself from dark thoughts.

And just like that, the world of adults is turning upside down as the children and the beasts settle into their comfortable sleep with cotton candy dreams and warm embraces.

Chapter 19: What Would It Take?

I n the emergency room, Ms. Hoa lies lifeless on the hard, white bed. A social worker is standing by her bedside, together with Ms. Dolores. But Ms. Hoa does not see them. Her eyes keep focusing on the stark white ceiling and the blinding lights of the hospital. *Everything here is spotless,* she thinks. *So spotless that one does not want to be here because one will dirty the surroundings with one's existence.*

Her tears keep flowing, but Ms. Dolores doubts that Ms. Hoa is aware of it. The social worker—a dark woman with a stout and firm stance—looks on with sympathy in her eyes. She has been standing here for an hour, but Ms. Hoa refuses to speak, and she can only get a small glimpse into everything that happened through Ms. Dolores's words, which she does not plan to fully trust until she can confirm with the patient. But her time with each patient is short. She can only do so much for them, and they need to help her. *No,* she thinks, *the patient needs to want to be saved.* Otherwise, her presence here will not change anything. She asks in a futile attempt, "Does she suffer from domestic violence?"

"I don't know," Ms. Dolores answers rather curtly. She is a nurse, and she knows what's best for the situation at hand, but this is not her hospital. "I requested a Vietnamese-speaking nurse an hour ago. How is that request going?"

"Ma'am, I don't deal with that issue. But I will try to get my Vietnamese-speaking colleagues to be here as soon as possible." The social worker squirms uneasily on her spot. She dearly wants to help, and this teething feeling of not being able to do anything makes her anxious.

"Shouldn't there be a Vietnamese-speaking nurse on standby at all times?" Ms. Dolores asks, knowing full well that it is not a standard protocol. They will be lucky if they can find a Vietnamese-speaking nurse at this hour.

"Ma'am, I know you are frustrated and want to help your friend. But you must help us help you. All I know for the time being is your friend is in a state of hysteria, and we need to identify the cause of her trauma."

"Well, if I knew the root of everything, this wouldn't be so hard, wouldn't it?" Ms. Dolores replies, then, realizing she is antagonizing the social worker in her worries, she apologizes. "I'm sorry. This night has been very hard for all of us. And I can't reach her family. I might have to try again when it's light out."

"Ma'am, if it's domestic violence—"

"I told you twice that it was not domestic violence. That woman can fight two men on her own," Ms. Dolores says in her curt way. She is still marveling at the fact that Ms. Hoa could scream that much and was still able to resist her hold. *Yes*, Ms. Dolores muses, *that woman can for sure fight two grown men on her own.*

What worries Ms. Dolores the most now is the safety of the children at Ms. Hoa's house. She can't reach any of them, and she has a strong gut feeling that Dong should be the first to know about this, rather than hearing about it from his father, his uncles, or any other person at his house. She tries the home phone number again, praying fervently this time that Dong will pick up. But it is already thirty minutes past one in the morning. She knows that Lizzie will be sleeping and snoring soundly at this hour, and she knows that the girl won't be the only one asleep.Lizzie has always had an annoying habit of making sure that everyone is sleeping before she tucks herself into a warm blanket.

She taps her foot impatiently, waiting for the rings to end. Then, with a heavy sigh, more from frustration than from anxiety, Ms. Dolores looks at Ms. Hoa's calm face. She can barely imagine how just a moment ago, this mad woman was trying to kill herself by jumping into oncoming traffic. *What is she trying to escape from?* Ms. Dolores can't help but wonder. *Why is life so hard on some individuals and far too easy for the rest? Is it true that those individuals are carrying the cross to the desert, up the thorny slope, so that the rest can live peacefully? If so, what does Ms. Hoa's cross look like?*

Far too often, the two women throw insults at each other instead of calmly listening to each other's words. Perhaps right from the start, their approach to this relationship has been wrong. And how can she fix it, this late in the game? Ms. Dolores looks at the social worker, who is on the verge of stepping out of the curtain. She has other patients to attend to. The couple next to Ms. Hoa's bed need her as the girl has suffered from a severe overdose of sleeping pills and the boy is tearing his hair up. Ms. Dolores asks in her final attempt to speed things up, "When will a Vietnamese-speaking nurse be here, please?"

The social worker looks at her with uncertainty. "I told you, ma'am, we are short staffed, and you might have to wait for another hour."

"You said that an hour ago."

"And you see how hard things are for us at this moment." The social worker fumes, then she suffuses her anger quickly. "Look, ma'am, I need to attend to the couple next to your friend's bed. They have it tough, and I need to calm the boyfriend down before he finally tears all his hair out. I will urge the nurse to be here soon, but I can't guarantee anything."

"I know," Ms. Dolores says, biting her lips in frustration. "I am a nurse myself."

"Then you should know how hard it is for all the staff in the emergency room," the social worker says and steps out, leaving Ms. Dolores alone with Ms. Hoa as she starts to doubt everything.

Was it a wrong thing, earlier, for her to go and help Dong in that way? But if she didn't intervene, the one lying here right now would have been the boy. It's a hard choice, and Ms. Dolores must make peace with the fact that she cannot foresee everything; she could not have predicted Ms. Hoa running wild on the street, just like she could not have foreseen the fragility in Dong's broken voice and tear-stained face. She doesn't think she did anything wrong. But perhaps Ms. Hoa thinks differently.

As so often happens, one is always a villain in someone else's story. She wonders if Ms. Hoa sees her as some dangerous extraterrestrial being who would kidnap her son someday and make her lose everything for the last time. She believes that Ms. Hoa loves Dong as much as she can, with that unyielding, undying love of a mother. But she can't fathom the reason behind Ms. Hoa's strict rules and insults, the high standards and the great expectations, the weight of the world that the woman is trying to fit inside that little frame of the young boy's body.

In a moment of clarity and honesty with herself, Ms. Dolores realizes that she is helping Dong the same way she hoped someone would have helped her all those years back then when she decided to have Lizzie all on her own. She wants the boy to know that no matter what happens, there will always be a place for him to lean on, to return, to catch him when he falls.

As she is pacing back and forth for the millionth time, the Vietnamese-speaking nurse who was so dearly needed an hour and a half ago draws the curtain and steps in.

"Hey, my name is Nancy. I will be your nurse in the meantime. What can I help you with?" The friendly nurse speaks in a fast and efficient tone, not forgetting to throw in a calming smile. All these steps Ms. Dolores knows too well, and yet, she still feels something so helpless hearing that tender voice and the caring attitude.

"I think she's still in shock. She's only spoken Vietnamese since the time she got in the ambulance."

"I see, so she used to speak English before then?"

"Not always, but she can express herself well in English. I mean, after the incident at her house, she's been speaking Vietnamese only."

"I see, and what was this incident about? From the look of it, I presume she did not fall or wound herself?" The nurse goes to Ms. Hoa's side and conducts the regular checking while keeping the conversation going with Ms. Dolores. "I see that her pulse is regular, her heart rate is stable, and her other indicators are also at a normal point. I'm going to give her fluid. In the meantime, please wait for a blood test and we can see what we can do with her hysteria."

"I think it is traumatic for her to be surrounded by foreign languages. Could you please stay by her side for a while until she regains consciousness?"

"Ma'am, are you her family?" the nurse asks sternly.

"I am not. I tried contacting her family but it seems no one is at home right now. But I am her friend, and I am a nurse in a hospital in Brampton. I can show you my ID if you want," Ms. Dolores hurriedly answers. She fears that any reluctance on her part would cause the nurse to be more suspicious about the whole situation.

"Ma'am, I am afraid you can't stay if you're not related to the patient. I'm very sorry but it seems you have to go. You can leave the patient's contact information with the reception, and I will see to it that they are informed by the morning."

"No," Ms. Dolores yells. Then, with a calmer voice but with no less urgency, she explains, "You see, the matter is very complicated. Her son just came out to her, and his boyfriend is staying with him now. She is traumatized—that is what I can see from her reaction to the whole thing. The only way to get her to calm down is to get to the root of her trauma. That is why I needed a Vietnamese-speaking nurse."

The nurse listens patiently. If she is nervous from Ms. Dolores's frantic explanation, her facial expression does not show it. She walks to Ms. Dolores's side and firmly takes her hands, pressing them hard. "Ma'am, I think you are too anxious to speak about the event calmly. The psychiatrist will be here in the morning, and I need to take down as much information as I can. But I am no help if the patient herself decides not to speak. For the meantime, could you wait outside until I call you? I think that will be the best course of action."

"But I can't leave her alone. Her son depends on me. Rather, her son depends on what I can bring home this morning."

"Ma'am, with all due respect, I understand your frustration. But you need to assess the situation calmly, and calmness is what you do not possess now."

"I—"

"Leave her there."

A weak voice speaks in Vietnamese from the white bed. Both the nurse and Ms. Dolores look at the person lying on the hard mattress, feeble and tiny, as if in her agony, Ms. Hoa is stripped completely of her flesh and blood, and what is left of her now is a bare, broken skeleton. She repeats, "Leave her there."

"Ma'am," Nancy says in Vietnamese, weighing her words carefully, "I'm afraid you are not in a good condition to have outside stimulus presented—"

"She is not an outside stimulus," Ms. Hoa says, her voice broken into tiny fragments between her breaths, her tears flowing freely without her even being aware of them. "In this moment, she is the only friend I will ever have."

Ms. Hoa tries to sit up and the nurse hurries to help her. Ms. Dolores, not understanding a word of the conversation, can only guess what Ms. Hoa needs from the determination in her eyes and the fierce fire in her ragged breathing.

"Dolores," Ms. Hoa says, slowly, intoning each word with a feeling Ms. Dolores has never seen in her before. "Dolores, why did you help my son betray me?"

"I'm sorry?" Ms. Dolores asks, though she is not sure that asking questions is the right decision. But how can she answer the question when she doesn't even understand a single word of it?

The nurse leaves the two women—much alike in their growing old and their struggle toward a life not of their own—as she softly whispers, "I will be right outside." There is something sacred in the air that she dares not disturb. Something akin to cold tears on a fiery heart. Ms. Dolores sits down by Ms. Hoa's side; her eyes glimmer with guilt, her head hangs low. She squeezes the firm hand of the immigrant woman, full of callouses from overworking at the dish-washing station, and speaks with a yielding conviction.

"I don't know what you are saying, and I don't think I can comprehend it, but speak it out, anyway, because…" Ms. Dolores looks up to find in Ms. Hoa's eyes the same fire that had burned in hers all those years ago when she thought she would lose her daughter to another person. She knows the pain of the flesh being torn and the bleeding of wounds on black and white paper. "Pain has no language."

Ms. Hoa, without fully understanding the words, continues speaking in Vietnamese. "Before this country, I was a good person. I even possessed a degree in economics. I thought it would only grow better. That my life would be filled with roses and champagne and parties through the night. Fake laughter, fake smiles. People take what is handed to them on a silver platter for granted, and the moment the thunder strikes down the tower of riches, they don't know who to turn to. They lose the ability to communicate. To speak. To feel the tears seeping through the words like an ocean that is about to break. I am also one of those people."

Ms. Dolores pours out a cup of water for the wretched woman on the white bed—an image so devastating in her mind's eye that it almost makes her laugh. She taps gently on the back of Ms. Hoa's hand as an encouragement for her to continue the story. At each pause, she nods her head. She doesn't know what is being said. All is seemingly lost between what is not understood and what is merely a mistake of a strange language, but Ms. Dolores knows.

Ms. Hoa goes on, "And then I met him. Love of my life. But it turned quickly into the pain of my life. I had Dong in my stomach before I knew what betrayal was. Oh Lord, the way that bastard gorged my heart out of my chest just to see me breathing my last. But I held on. I wanted Dong to have a better future than me. A future that does not smell of burned grass and baked earth and cow manure on a rainy day. So I agreed to abandon everything and left my home. I still remember my Ma standing in the doorway, looking at my back. Her eyes were so sad that you could almost see the devastation dancing in the sunlight. I haven't visited her for more than sixteen years. Almost as long as Dong's life. And now, when life has nothing left to surprise me, not even power, I want to see her. I want to hear her reproaching voice. I want to feel her arms around me. I want to be that baby daughter whose cries could only be appeased by her lullaby. But here we all are."

Ms. Hoa drinks the tepid water, and with trembling hands, she squeezes the white linen as if it is her lifeline. "This is not about me. I vowed that I would not talk about my sacrifices. I chose to lose so that my son could win. But win against what? All I ever conjure up is my own selfishness. The image I wanted to see has blinded me, and I wonder if I've ever seen him truly for who he is. It's funny. I want him to be happy, I truly do. But somewhere along the road between my dead-end jobs and his school, my definition of happiness and his definition of happiness have differed. He used to be this little obedient dove. So sweet you could almost taste his beaming smile on your tongue. I wonder where those smiles have gone. Was I wrong then, coming here? After all these years, I thought I have been a good mother. I act my role, wear my costume, speak my lines. And there he is, my son, standing in front of me, so tall I cannot reach. Almost a stranger. Do you know what the worst part is, Dolores?"

Ms. Dolores tilts her head, humming along, still not knowing what to say. In the avalanche of words, she tries to pick up the pieces of Ms. Hoa, who she thought she could never get along with. The pieces of a person from another continent, with her stout figure, her heavy accent, her crude speech and manner, and her relentless silence as she stands there, her feet firmly rooted in the foreign land as that same land's inhabitants are trying to tear her down.

She fights so well, and her head is so high, Ms. Dolores almost forgot that Ms. Hoa is another woman, just like her. Apart from the color of their skin and the difference in their languages, Ms. Hoa and Ms. Dolores are the same underneath. And though Ms. Dolores can't understand Ms. Hoa's life story as the poor woman keeps going on in her native language, there is one thing she is certain and one regret that is gnawing at her heart: She has hurt a woman who has been through the same fight as her. An act of betrayal to a kindred soul disguised as an altruistic intervention to appease her conscience. Ms. Dolores curses at herself. She is old enough to know better. And yet—

"Dolores, Dong never learns to call me Ma in Vietnamese."

Ms. Hoa breaks down, crying her heart out. She has confessed something that has always been a sharpness stabbing in her heart, making it bleed until she is reduced to nothing but a failure. The beauty of her language—the beauty of the word "mother" that danced on her tongue since the day she was a little girl—is lost on her only son. How are they supposed to understand each other when the only thing they speak is the broken grammar of a foreign monster, building up a barrier between the love she holds in her heart and the desire to cradle Dong in his arms?

Before this day, Ms. Hoa had been grasping at straws, thinking they were hope, knowing they were empty promises of a land that will only reward her if she conforms to the shape and the mold of what it defines as an immigrant. But Ms. Hoa doesn't want to be a definition in a dictionary. She wants to be free. Her eyes stare at the stark white curtain covering her bed, searching for something that is supposed to be there, but due to some sick twist of fate, it is too late in its arrival. Or worse, it has passed her by, judging by the state of her life that she no longer fits to receive its presence.

Oh, she had dreams. And now she is watching them shatter on the hospital floor with the occasional beeps from various machines as the background requiem. She looks to Ms. Dolores, her mind half realizing where she is, half wandering in the same landscape of her childhood. People are just trying to live. And this place is trying to save the lives that are losing their battle. But what about the dreams of a single mother who abandoned everything in exchange for a better life for her only son? Where are they now in this dark night that is turning into another day of monotonous, aimless living?

Ms. Dolores keeps tapping gently on the back of Ms. Hoa's hand, waiting for her to go on. But Ms. Hoa is done with her story. She slumps down, curls into herself, seeming like she is traveling somewhere else. Somewhere with no harsh winters, no back-breaking dead-end jobs, no mountains after mountains of dishes, just waiting for her to wash. No dying hopes. No dreams to waste.

Ms. Dolores sits there, waiting for what seems like hours in ten minutes. She opens her mouth, wanting to ask if Ms. Hoa has finally calmed down. Then she hesitates, wondering if Ms. Hoa is still in her trance of speaking only her native language. Ms. Dolores is frustrated with herself. For the first time in her life, she realizes the uselessness of the English language. The language everyone forces down immigrants' throat without a second thought about what it means to lose the tongue you've grown up with. She curses herself for being selfish, despite knowing that she had little choice in the matter. Between the potential suicide of a teenage boy and the unforeseen nervous breakdown of Ms. Hoa, Ms. Dolores had to save the life of the boy first. Goodness and evil—where does she draw the line? Ms. Dolores coughs a few times, drawing Ms. Hoa's attention, then says with a careful tenderness, "How are you feeling?"

Ms. Hoa watches the shift of emotions in Ms. Dolores's clear blue eyes. The woman is clearly fretting and on the verge of losing her mind over what she has done. And Ms. Hoa knows remorse when she sees it. She laughs harshly. "Like shit."

Ms. Dolores is stunted. This is the first time she's ever heard Ms. Hoa curse. She suddenly has the feeling of busting through a thousand brick walls, the next one more daunting than the last. Ms. Dolores laughs. "Yeah," she says, "I feel like that sometimes."

"Why are you here?" Ms. Hoa asks in a tired voice. "I

thought you were on the side of the children."

"Oh, forget the children." Ms. Dolores waves her hand dismissively. "The adults need saving, too."

"And you think you can save me?"

"Well, at least I can say that I tried."

"Trying, huh? That's the one thing my life never lacks."

"Yeah, mine, too." Ms. Dolores shakes her head, smiling. "Sometimes I'm so immersed in it that I forget others are also going through the same. Or worse. Hey, I'm sorry."

"For what?" Ms. Hoa asks, her eyes still a bit hollow, but they have regained the luster of her fierce living force.

"I don't know. I think it was wrong of me to intervene in how you raise your son. I'm a single mother, you know that. And I would be furious, too, if someone just barged into my life and dragged my daughter away from me. I mean, regardless of the purpose, the method I chose was out of line." Ms. Dolores picks her words carefully, then observes Ms. Hoa's reaction in her timid way. "Do you understand?"

"English? Yeah, I understand. Your apology? Not so much," Ms. Hoa turns her head away, her face trembling slightly. "You don't have to be sorry for saving my son's life."

"Hey, Hoa."

"What?"

"If you are up to it, maybe I can help you check out and we can grab breakfast at Tim's right around the corner. You can tell me more about your story—I'm sorry I couldn't understand a word of it. And maybe you can hear my side of the story. What do you think?" Ms. Dolores squeezes Ms. Hoa's hand, her smile warm, her face beaming with a joy that has been gone for far too long.

"What about my—? You know what, forget it, I deserve this.

177

Let's go. I'm sick of all this screaming and ether smell."

"Welcome to my life. And yes, you deserve a nicer breakfast than the low-fat yogurt and the stale bread from this hospital. Alright, stay still and leave the rest to me."

Both women laugh, gently at first, then their laughter roars out, reverberating through the emergency room's walls, surfing through the tossing and turning of the patients lying around, merging at the top of their lungs, and finding comfort in their own sufferings. The sufferings that are as far apart as the entire Pacific Ocean, and yet as close as the touch of a hand on a person's shoulder. Ms. Dolores looks at the wrinkles at the corner of Ms. Hoa's eyes as she laughs, thinking how she's seen this woman so many times, and yet, this is the first moment she's seeing Ms. Hoa as a person living her life. So joyful, so free, she almost reaches happiness.

But the question remains constant in Ms. Dolores's mind: *For how long can this fleeting, carefree happiness last? And what will happen after that?* The answer is fast approaching as Mr. Wiseman walks briskly up the front porch of Ms. Hoa's house and knocks rigorously on the wooden door, waking the sleeping children. Waking the beasts.

Chapter 20: You Want It Darker

Mr. Wiseman stands in front of the impassable wooden door of the townhouse in the first light of dawn, shifting his feet, thinking of the worst, convincing himself to believe in the best.

Mrs. Wiseman strokes her husband's arm, trying to calm him. Her mind keeps wandering between what might have happened in that dark house and her sleeping son currently at home. The boy will wake up soon. He needs breakfast before going to school. It could have been a perfectly normal morning in her perfectly normal life. Mrs. Wiseman bites her lips. She knows that she should love Simon as much as her own son. But a tiny part of her sometimes sparks up and tells her such nasty things.

Like tonight, when Mr. Wiseman sped through the lights, his mind focused on one thing only, the voice ringing in her head, telling her how nice it would be if Simon was not in the picture. The gruff teenage boy with his gloomy music and his locked room. They might share the same roof, but Simon isolates himself in his own galaxy. Mrs. Wiseman tries her best to be the mom that the boy deserves, but she can never be the mom that the boy wants. And every time Simon comes home in his silence, earphones on, heading straight to his room, it pains her acutely to know that the distance between them will keep growing until not a single word can be heard, even when he sits right next to her at the dinner table, sharing lukewarm laughter with a lethargic stare.

Mr. Wiseman knocks on the door for the third time, drawing Mrs. Wiseman's attention back to the dark reality. The door still refuses to open. Their hope is dying with every light that is shining through the leaves of the maple tree on the front porch. "Honey," Ms. Wiseman says, uneasy, "maybe you should try calling Simon again."

"Perhaps you're right." Mr. Wiseman sighs, pulling out his phone and dialing the same number that he's been calling the whole night. And again, the silence after the final beep is deafening.

Mr. Wiseman curses, almost throwing the phone on the ground. He kicks the decorating stones until one of them rolls off the steps, then leans on the rail, heaving. His son is missing, and he isn't even sure if this place is where he is. It has still not been 24 hours; that means he can't report this incident to the police yet. He racks his brain, thinking of all the places that Simon might frequent. The basketball court? Unlikely. The place is locked at night. Or the park near his school? No, the park is locked after ten p.m., and no one can get in without being caught by the neighborhood watch. Then where else? Where could he be besides this threatening townhouse and the nightmares it promises?

Mr. Wiseman grabs his hair. He realizes in the aching early hour that he knows nothing about his son's life since the day his ex-wife left. But is it his fault when the boy simply refuses to talk to him? Is it his fault that he found happiness in his wife? Is it his fault when he works from early morning to late at night to cover Simon's expensive private school tuition, the clothes he wears, the food he eats, the dinners at fancy restaurants? Mr. Wiseman can't think of a single thing Simon lacks in his life. But perhaps that is the distance between them: Simon doesn't need the things he can give, and what Simon needs, he doesn't pay enough attention to know.

He calls Simon's cellphone again, not expecting an answer. It's just that he doesn't know of anything better to do. And when that last glimmer of hope starts to dim in his eyes, someone picks up. "Hello," a boy's soft voice says, still sluggish with sleep. Mr. Wiseman feels a pang in his heart. This is not Simon's voice.

"Hello," he says, trying to calm his burning nerves. "Is this Simon?"

"Hm, Simon is sleeping. And you are?"

"I'm his father."

The other line goes eerily silent. Mr. Wiseman can hear the shuffling noise, the pattering footsteps on the tile floor, then the quiet thud of a door shutting. The soft voice resumes. "Okay? Where are you, Mr. Wiseman—?"

"I'm standing right in front of your house," Mr. Wiseman says. His hand balls up in a hard fist, trying to control a rising anger. "That is, assuming that you are Dong?"

"Ah, yes, I am. I'm sorry but Simon is sleeping—"

"You said that a moment ago. Can you open the door?"

"I'm sorry, sir. I can't. Simon will drive back home when he wakes up," the voice says, faltering.

"I don't care what he will do when he wakes up. I need to know that he is safe, so either you open the door, or I will call the police," Mr. Wiseman hisses. He couldn't care less that he is threatening a young boy who doesn't know any better.

181

"But I—"

A series of sounds echoes through the phone: girls' loud laughter, the sound of feet running around on the tile floor, the boy's quiet gasp, and finally, as if God has heard Mr. Wiseman's prayer, Simon's voice ringing out: "Hey, cutie pie. Who's calling?"

It is the sweetest voice he has ever heard from Simon. A voice the boy has never used in front of him or within his hearing distance. He can't help but feel frustrated, and the anger just keeps rising. The soft voice says quietly, "It's your father. He's here to pick you up." Another silence fills his ear, then he hears Simon's cold, piercing voice saying, "Hey."

"You disappeared in the middle of the night and drove here. Did you ever think about me, or about your mother? Did you ever think about how worried we would be? Simon, you are seventeen years old. You still need your guardians. What did you think I felt when I discovered that you were not in your room? Your mother said—" Mr. Wiseman pours out his anger while Mrs. Wiseman tries to hush him. A neighbor who is getting to his car is giving them a weird look and she is not comfortable with the whole situation. But that is the least of Mr. Wiseman's worries. Not when the answer he gets from Simon is a short laugh.

"So?"

"What do you mean? Open the door."

"It's not my house."

"Simon, this is your first warning."

"Interesting. Where is my last?"

"Simon."

"Never knew you could say my name so many times in such a short period. Father. If you still remember that you are my

182

father. Because I almost forget sometimes."

"What are you saying?" Mr. Wiseman is shaking uncontrollably.

This is not his Simon. Yes, the voice is the same, but his Simon is an obedient boy. He never talks back to his father, let alone provokes him in this ruthless manner. What happened in this one night? In a blink, Simon has gone so far that Mr. Wiseman can hardly see his back.

Mr. Wiseman repeats his question, distrusting his own ears. "Simon, is that how you treat your family?"

"Some family I have," Simon scoffs. "Never attend my recitals. Never come to my parent-teacher meetings. Never there to take photos when I win a basketball tournament, or when I'm on the dean's list. The reason? Busy. Yeah, I'd trade gold for this family."

"Is that what Dong tells you to say? Because—"

"Oh, so now you don't believe that I'm capable of feeling and thinking on my own?"

"Simon, you don't lack anything in my house. You study at the best private school. You always have the best clothes, the best food, the best devices—always the best. Am I wrong?"

"No, you are not wrong. I do always have the best," Simon says in his languid way, seemingly not knowing the pain of the words he chooses. "But father, I never said I want the best, did I? And the one thing you haven't done all these years is even stop to ask me what I want. People don't need much to be happy. You mistake money for happiness, and that's your way. Don't force me to go down the same path. I refuse to partake in this tragedy any longer."

Mr. Wiseman is speechless with fury. His sense of reason is trying its best to fight back the strong urge to kick down

183

the door and barge into this house that is imprisoning his son and turning him into a stranger. How can he be so wrong? He has built Simon up and prepared a path filled with roses and champagne for him, only for that boy to tell him over the cold line of a cellphone call that he refuses to partake in this "tragedy." What tragedy? In this moment of agony, his brain temporarily shuts off Simon's accusation that he is the father who's never there when Simon needs him most. But doesn't Simon understand? He is busy.

Mrs. Wiseman taps on his shoulder, whispering, "What is he saying?" Her eyes are filled with worry, none of which are about Simon. Her mind, after knowing that Simon is safely inside the house, focuses on her son back at home in Oakville. She should be there preparing him a warm breakfast. He's not used to hunger, and he will make a fuss if he wakes up without her there. But she can't express her wish to go home so soon—it almost seems heartless. Mr. Wiseman barely looks at her. His nerve pops up on his temple. He knocks on the door with a vigor strong enough to wake up the whole house. "Open up," he screams. "Open the door. I will call the police. You have kidnapped my son."

The door cracks slightly. The chain is still in place so Mr. Wiseman can't push it open further. A small head pops out through the tiny opening. It is Dong. He recognizes the boy from the first glance. Dong hasn't changed much since the day he last saw him all those years ago. The same small frame, the same timid eyes and soft-spoken manner. "Mr. Wiseman, it's been a long time."

"Where's Simon?" Mr. Wiseman swallows his rude words but he can't stop the hostility seeping through his voice.

"Mr. Wiseman, Simon says he will drive back later today.

He says he won't see you now, but he will talk to you once he is home."

"You know he is my son, and I have rights over him, don't you?"

"Yes, sir. But…" Dong lowers his head for a swift moment then lifts his face and looks straight into Mr. Wiseman's eyes with a fierceness that the man has never seen in anyone else before, and never will. "Simon saved my life. And this time, I swear I will save his."

Mr. Wiseman stares at the young boy in front of him, his gaze fierce with rage. But Dong is made from harder stuff than simple fear and wavering, despite his soft-spoken manner and his timidity. He is, after all, a Vietnamese, with a heart of iron and blood of lava. He doesn't yield before power larger than his own, and he never surrenders. Not when the stakes are high and the soldiers beside him are holding him in place, building him stronger from his broken place. The staring contest ends in a draw when neither refuses to turn away. Ms. Wiseman steps up, trying to make peace with the storm. "Hey kid, can we at least talk to Simon for a moment? I don't think he'll deny us that much. Maybe you don't know, but we are his—"

"Yes, madam, I know you are his parents." Dong bows his head politely. "But my answer remains the same. I'm sorry, this is Simon's will."

"No, that is not Simon's will," Mr. Wiseman shouts, flinging his hands, his spit flying. The calmness he's tried so hard to keep throughout the night is slipping. "It is yours. It is all because of you. You pit my own son against me. Against us. You—"

Mr. Wiseman charges into the door, and right before he can

nudge it open, a large hand slams it closed. The last thing he sees are Dong's astounded eyes, filled with a bewildered look that borders on pity.

He is barred from the world of his son; he has become a villain in his life story. A role he never accepted. Since when has he been this monstrous presence in the life of the boy he loves more than life itself? He punches the door in vain, bellows a hollow cry. He told his wife last night that Simon is his flesh and blood. Look where he is now, abandoned by that same flesh and blood he's trying his best to protect.

Mrs. Wiseman pats his shoulders, trying to find some comforting words to say. But she hates how her brain keeps nagging her about her precious little son, Nathan, who must be waking up and shouting her name by now in their sweet home. The scale in her heart has never been balanced since the beginning, and no matter how hard she tries, it has been leaning more and more toward Nathan as the years go by with Simon distancing himself behind a closed door and an indifferent heart. "Let's go home," Ms. Wiseman says impatiently. "Simon is not the only son you have, John. And Nathan needs both of us there."

As if someone pulls the strings taut on a broken puppet, Mr. Wiseman jerks up, staring at Mrs. Wiseman, a look of confusion in his eyes. "And it never crosses your mind that Simon might need both of us too?"

"No, well, I just mean—" Mrs. Wiseman stutters. She realizes her mistake only when her feet are inside the trap.

"Vivian, you are talking about my son. He was there before you and Nathan, and he will continue being there in my life. God, I never thought I would say this, but the boy is right. We are a family he'd trade a trove of gold for."

Mr. Wiseman stomps to his car, ignoring the desperate call of Mrs. Wiseman. He doesn't want to see his wrongdoings or the pain he's caused from the simple mistakes he thought that Simon would understand because he is old enough. But he let the most complicated mistake of all slip through his eyes in broad daylight: Simon is never old enough. All these years, Mr. Wiseman has kept piling boxes on the boy's shoulders. And all these years, Simon suffered in the only way he could: silence.

Behind the curtain, Dong watches the dusty Mercedes-Benze with its shiny brand logo back out of the driveway and speed through the foggy morning. It seems the car is trying to express the rage that its owner couldn't show in front of the seventeen-year-old boy. Dong bites his lips, wondering if he has done the right thing. He looks around the gaudy living room with the worn-out frilly sofa and the mismatched wallpaper, disconnecting somewhere between the walls and the door leading to the basement.

He doesn't have time to worry. His uncles and aunts will be home any moment from their night shifts, and his mother is nowhere to be seen. Somewhere between the dark night and the lucid nightmares, Dong thought he heard the phone ring. One time. Many times. But the warmth was too warm, and the embrace was too sweet. Dong was only as strong as the will to indulge in the gentle loving caress of Simon who kept stroking his hair, whispering in his raspy voice, "It is fine now."

Except that it isn't fine. His mom is not home yet, and Ms. Dolores is nowhere in sight.

Dong runs down the staircase leading to the basement, skipping steps. He arrives at the brightly lit dining room, out of breath, just as Lizzie and Ames are toasting bread. A piece of golden-brown buttered toast is hanging from Lizzie's mouth. Her eyes are wide open, questioning Dong without voicing it. Her cloud of curly hair is blooming on her head like a bouquet of warm sun rays. Ames picks up the newly toasted slices of bread and busies herself with a berry jam, singing a Taylor Swift song. Dong wants to tell them that there are a million things going wrong. That he is not sure he deserves this much happiness. That maybe he never deserved happiness in the beginning. That his mom has disappeared, and Lizzie's mother is nowhere to be seen. That he just chased Simon's parents away in the rudest, most insolent way—granted that Simon said he could do it—and he doesn't know where things will go.

But Dong just stands there, rooted firmly to the tiled floor, watching his life shatter on the ground, and in the faintest of hopes, he is waiting for the seeds to grow and the spring flowers to bloom. He looks to his room; anxiety fills his brain and courses through his veins.

In that moment when he is walking on the tightrope between the safe place of his home and the unknown future, Simon appears behind the closed door. "Hey," Simon says, flashing him a beaming smile, and that is all it takes to turn Dong's fears into vapor. He runs into Simon's arms, searching for the same warmth that kept him out of harm's way all night long. Simon squeezes his body into his, laughing all the while, completely different from the cold, distant person that he was when he talked to his parents. He plants a soft kiss on Dong's forehead and lets his lips linger on Dong's skin longer than he should, until Ames and Lizzie cough loudly and giggle like two mad people, drunken on the love of two other mad people.

"What's up?" Simon asks, touching his forehead to Dong's. His forefinger gently traces the curve of Dong's lips, slightly pushing on the soft flesh.

"Your parents just went home."

"Ah, great news, I guess." Simon gives him a peck. "A job well done, my dear miracle."

"I just—I don't feel too good about the whole thing. Your dad was very indignant, and rightfully so. And your stepmom, she seems—" Dong babbles.

"She doesn't care." Simon scratches his head and walks to the kitchen, picking up four slices of bread and popping two of them into the worn toaster under the scrutinizing stare of the two girls. "I bet she was too busy thinking about Nathan. That boy will throw a big tantrum if he doesn't see her there when he wakes up."

"But Simon, they are your parents," Dong says, raising his voice, then a thought crosses his mind, and he draws back into himself again. "Fuck, who am I to judge? I kind of did the same thing to hurt my mom."

"Dong, not all parents are good." Simon heaves a sigh. The slices of bread pop up with a quiet ding.

"And not all children are saintly angels, Simon." Dong skips to the kitchen table and grabs the buttered toast in Simon's hands. "And why the hard stare, Lizzie? Ames?"

"Mm-hm, nothing." Lizzie swallows her bread and continues with a sing-song voice, "Don't mind me, I'm just beaming about hearing D-dog swear for the first time. Not a censored word, but an actual curse word," she says with a laugh.

"And don't mind me either, I'm just"—Ames takes another big bite of toast and smiles with a mouth full of bread—

"enjoying the lovey-dovey fight."

"We are not fighting." Simon ruffles his hair in frustration. "It's just—my family situation is complicated, and I don't want to talk about it."

The boy leans on the kitchen counter, his hands supporting his frame, his head hanging. Dong feels like he should say something, but the words are stuck inside his brain in a chaotic rainstorm and his voice is failing him. He reaches out his hand, half wanting to pat Simon's shoulder, half longing to hold on to his firm, calloused fingers to save him from the spiraling darkness he is descending into. But he fears the cold rejection. The wall is there—the invisible border built upon the years they were apart and the love that was left unsaid. It seems that after all these years, the child within Dong has never had the chance to grow, while Simon has been running at full speed toward a goal that falls short of Dong's reach. The air is stifling with silence, and Dong can almost hear the sound of Simon's ragged breathing as he draws in a quiet sob. Simon wipes his eyes; the tears are dry. "So, anyways"—he turns back, beaming at Dong's uncertain gaze—"what else is new?"

"I don't know…" Dong wavers. "I'm worried about my mom. Ms. Dolores is not back yet. I thought I heard the phone ring a few times last night, but I'm not sure if it was all a dream."

"Does your mom have a phone with her?" Simon spreads a thick layer of butter on his toast and slabs a spoonful of berry jam on it. "We can try calling her."

"I don't think she has it. Lizzie, what about your mother?" Dong bites his nails. Simon reaches over and intertwines Dong's hand with his, softly squeezing the nimble fingers.

"I think she does. She never leaves her phone alone. But what's the worst thing that could have happened, huh? It's not

190

like your mom could have ended up in the ER." Lizzie laughs, then stops short upon seeing Dong's stern stare. She coughs awkwardly. "My bad, I will call her now."

Lizzie pulls out her cellphone and dials. All eyes are on her and the poor girl is trembling under the scrutiny of her friends. It doesn't help that Dong keeps muttering, "Push the call button," as if Lizzie doesn't know how the phone works. She shushes the boy, puts the phone on speaker mode, and lets the ring beat their hearts until they are bursting. A short click. The call ends to the astonished eyes of both Lizzie and Ames, and the hitched breath of Dong.

"What does it mean?" Dong musters his courage to croak. His legs are shaking without him knowing. Simon holds him up, his jaws tense.

"Well, I don't know. What do you think it means?" Lizzie retorts. The worries are now slowly getting to her. The reality of life is catching up to her.

"Do you have any other way of contacting her?" Ames poses.

"She only has one phone. Maybe I can send her a text, what do you guys think?" Lizzie starts texting before hearing an answer.

"What am I going to do? My aunts and uncles will be home soon, and my dad—well, let's not talk about him since he is invisible anyway. Things will not be good if they see you here without an adult in the house." Dong withdraws his hand impulsively, wanting to bite his nails again, but Simon grips him firm and hard. "What do I do? I've ruined everything with my selfishness again," he says, the desperation in his voice tearing at his friends' hearts.

Simon pulls him into a tight embrace, patting his head gently as Dong buries his face into the tall boy's chest with heaving sobs. Lizzie pores over her phone, trying to refresh the message app's screen every minute, waiting for her mother's text. Ames sits on the creaky chair by the dining table, overwhelmed by the sudden turn of events. She looks at the half-eaten toast, hesitating under the looming pressure of the suffocating basement. She feels a bit left out of the conversation.

Though she understands Dong's worries and anxieties, she can't help the surging warmth within her heart when a little voice tells her that her mom is waiting for her at her sweet home, with a hot plate of pancakes and a few jokes from last night's comedy show. The thought makes Ames want to run straight home—anything to escape this basement and the darkness of its promise. She feels bad, but it is not enough to make her stay. Ames shuffles her feet, weighing her words carefully. It's high time she leaves. She is a stranger in this world full of protagonists, and she is no actress. Just when she opens her mouth, Simon beats her to it.

"Dong, listen, I need to go home."

"What?" Dong stares at Simon, eyes wild with tears. "You're leaving?"

"Just for a short time." Simon brushes his cheeks. "I will find a way to come back here in the evening to check on you and see how things are. I can't miss school. I know this is not perfect, but there are things greater than us. And as much as I want to, I can't change that."

"But you promise you wouldn't leave," Dong says, but it seems like the words are floating right past him.

"I won't. It is only a temporary solution." Simon bends down until their eyes are on the same level. His eyes shine with endless kindness and gentle loving. "And you know that our problem is a permanent one."

"Yeah, D-dog, it won't be—" Lizzie stops short when her phone lights up. Ms. Dolores is calling back. "It's my mom."

"Well, put it on speaker." Ames quickly runs over, almost stumbling on a broken tile. "Ask her how things are."

Lizzie picks up the call with a trembling finger. Ms. Dolores's voice booms out with a roaring laughter and another woman's loud, harsh chuckle in the middle of a conversation, saying, "Wait, you didn't let me finish," and Ms. Dolores keeps repeating, "Hold on, hold on. Honey, sweetheart, how's everything?"

"Mom, where are you?"

"Well, I'm surprised you're only asking it now," Ms. Dolores says teasingly, and Lizzie can see her eyes rolling. "Ms. Hoa and I are having breakfast at Tim's near Trillium Hospital on Queensway. Let me tell you, it's just—"

"Wait, hold on, Mom, a hospital? What happened?"

"We spent a short staycation in the ICU and now we are just—"

"The ICU?" Dong shouts into the phone. "Where's my mom? How is she? What's wrong? I need to talk to her."

"It's alright, sweetie, it's alright." Ms. Dolores's voice remains calm amidst the raging storm. The background noise of the coffee shop interrupts her conversation with the teens, and she keeps pausing to agree with someone on something. "Your mom is fine. She's with me. She had a shock, and we got over it this morning. She is having breakfast and we'll be at your house in—how long, Hoa? Ten? Fifteen? We can get the boys and girls some muffins—alright, we'll be there in about twenty minutes depending on how long the line at the cashier is. Ciao. As I was saying—"

The phone hangs up before any of the teens can utter a single protest. Dong can't believe his ears. His mom is laughing with so much happiness he can hear the long-lost joy in her voice. She sounds like somebody else. Someone who is living a carefree life, hanging around with her friends. And Dong wishes he could be there to listen to his mom talking. He wants to hear her side of the story—the life she led before she became Ms. Hoa of today, the woman who always keeps her head low and focuses on the ground, making sure that she has one foot in front of the other—and maybe he can be more to her then than whatever he has been to her before. He can be the son she needs instead of the son she wants. He can curl up into her embrace, asking for a hug, begging for a kiss, and perhaps then, only then, he can learn to love her in the right way she deserves.

Simon traces circles on Dong's back, trying to calm him down. He realizes how useless he is when the trial comes beckoning, and he stands before the jury as he is: a teenage boy with so much to carry on his shoulders, holding the hand of another teenage boy who is too far gone in the mud of his own sorrow.

He wants to hug Dong and tells him that things will be alright, but the truth is staring him in the eyes: His father and stepmom are waiting for his confession at their home in Oakville, and his biological mom will raise hell once she gets the news of this event—which he doubts she already did. It is hard to focus on tempering the pain of another person when he is suffering from the same demon. There is one thing he knows: He won't give up. The only question in his mind right now is. "How much is the price?" *God*, Simon silently prays as he squeezes Dong's tremulous shoulders, *if you want it darker, please only turn down the light on me.*

As if God heard his prayer and decided to answer it in the wickedest way, the door of the basement clicks open. The teens listen with bated breath as the footsteps descend the deafeningly quiet staircase. The corridor light turns on, and there stands, as bright as Simon's fervent prayer could ever be, Dong's father, drunken and full of anger. "What is happening here? Where is your mom, Dong?" he thunders out.

Lord... Simon grits his teeth as he pushes Dong behind him. *So you really want it darker.*

Chapter 21: She is the Woman

The man stands before the children, tall as an insurmountable mountain, his presence looming like a shroud. The room is covered in his darkness and the strength to go on escapes their tiny bodies. The man will be there until the end of time, not moving, not changing his stance. His breath smells like alcohol that has gone bad for several days, or several months. His hands are shaking, and he is showing symptoms of withdrawal. His eyes bore holes into the young boy's body, his stare is that menacing. The man who is not needed but somehow always finds a way to be there, to sprout up from the Earth when everyone is at their worst. The man is Dong's father.

"Where's your mom, Dong?" the man repeats in Vietnamese, and Dong bites back a thousand words. He hasn't been home for a whole week. His mom has been working non-stop at minimum wage, and he takes it all to get wasted with his friends. And the man dares to stand there, asking, no, demanding for more. "Are you deaf? I'll ask you one final time, where is that woman?"

The man tries to walk. His legs stagger with each step forward and he almost falls to the ground a few times. But he persists. He holds on to the railing, the chairs, the walls, the table—anything that can hold him up—and yet, the Earth is pulling his body down. The man is a useless sack of meat who cannot live unless he leans on something, or someone, and sucks the existence out of them.

Dong reminds himself that he shouldn't fear the man. Why should he be frightened of a human who is just an empty shell? A hungry ghost. A lingering soul, finding its way back to the place it belongs. Dong knows this, but his hands are still shaking. His legs are trembling. His whole body remembers the pains and the bruises from the swooping leather belts and the sound of the dishes being thrown to the floor. Night after night, he lay in bed, muffling his cries, rubbing his bruises, telling himself things would be alright, when just outside the door, his world was falling apart. How can he forget the sadness and the desperation the sound a broken dish can bring? But the man wouldn't understand this. The man calls him a wuss. The man makes him. The man breaks him.

Dong pushes Simon's arm away, ignoring the other boy's astounded stare. He has been kneeling enough, and he refuses to be in misery any longer. "Mom's not here," he says in broken Vietnamese, the foreign tonality lacking the ability to show his anger. "She hasn't been home since last night."

"And you threw a party when your parents were away? The owner's not home so the cat steals the fish, huh?" The man doesn't stop. Dong maintains his stance, but his feet are sinking. The man reaches out his hands, and Dong forgets where he is, even the people who are standing behind him, propelling him forward. Dong forgets that he is no longer alone. He is far too used to the darkness of his locked room.

"Maybe if you'd come home more often, you'd know." Dong swallows. This is his fight, and he is determined to win.

"Who taught you to be so smart?" The man lifts Dong's collar, and the boy closes his eyes, expecting a slap, a punch, the usual course of action. The normality of pain. The normality of his life. But it doesn't come. He squints, and through the crack of his eyelids, he sees an unspeakable turn of events that silences him.

Simon is firmly grasping the shaking arm of the man. His vein is popping along his dark, glistening skin. Lizzie and Ames stand in front of him, sheltering him in their embrace.

The man flounders on his uneven footing, screaming, "You little fuckers—"

"And you won't touch any of those little fuckers," reverberates a strong voice through the walls of the stifling basement.

As the voice booms out, the man stops in his tracks. He freezes, and his arm hovers midair while his other arm twists around to grab Simon's collar. The man's menacing eyes turn soft, pleading, somewhat cowardice in their begging gaze. The man grows weak. The man finally falls on his knees, his hands crawling around. "Help, Hoa, give me some money."

Yes, as expected, the man is destroyed, because standing there in the doorway, larger than life, is a greater force than fate itself, the waterfall that will wear down the tallest mountain.

The man stands there in his naked apprehension, transformed into an invisible, malevolent being. He has an aim, and that aim is the woman's purse—or rather, the woman's money that she keeps hidden like a treasure, wrapped in many layers of nylon bags and papers. Anything that can stall his hunger for alcohol and keep his mind sane for one more moment. He reaches out his feeble hand, and Dong can't help but think of how this could be the salvation his teacher often talks about in class. But instead of God, the man is seeking money. The man is lost. The man is broken.

Ms. Hoa stands there with Ms. Dolores by her side, as glorious as victory itself. She seems like she has shed an old skin overnight, and now she has returned to the same stage, with a new costume, a new role, a new script to play. Her eyes shine like burning coal. Her mouth firmly sets in a straight line. She won't say anything unnecessary, and she means every word she utters thereafter. Ms. Dolores squeezes her shoulders slightly, encouraging her to go on. Ms. Hoa nods in grateful acknowledgement. She is fearless, not because she doesn't know the taste of fear, but because she knows that when she falls this time, someone will be there to pick her up.

"You won't touch my son, or his friends," Ms. Hoa says in Vietnamese. She walks toward Dong and stands in front of the huddled children; her stout figure covers them in a wholesome safety.

"What do you mean?" the man stutters, trying to figure out the shift in the situation.

"You won't touch Dong, or his friends, or me, or anything in this house," Ms. Hoa reiterates, her voice loud and booming. A storm is brewing.

"You useless woman—" The man unbuckles his belt and leaps forward. But to his surprise, Ms. Hoa grasps both of his shaking hands, unrelenting, with no intention to let go. The belt soon falls to the ground with an ear-cracking thud.

"And you won't hit any one of us. Yes, you are right, I was a useless woman," Ms. Hoa grits through her teeth, her nails digging into the man's wrist. "But I've learned that I can stand up. And I will. Let's get a divorce."

"What?"

"Mom!"

The man and Dong shout in unison, in surprise. But their voices can't reach Ms. Hoa's ears. She is standing on the top of her mountain, looking down at her life's suffering, smiling, thinking that she has had enough—that it is time she moves on. No one asked for her sacrifices, and she always thought that hurting herself for the sake of others was a form of love. But there are many forms of love. And maybe, just maybe, this time, she can learn to be the lover, instead of a sacrificing corpse.

"I mean it, let's get a divorce," Ms. Hoa repeats.

"You know that the deed of the house—"

"Hold your high horse," Ms. Hoa says, laughing with a tinge of cruel satisfaction. "I have a lawyer. Let's see what she says about the deed, the assets, and everything in between. I pay more for this household than you ever did, you filthy drunkard."

"Where did you even get a lawyer?" The man grows frightened. He looks around, and he sees her. The white woman. "So you side with them? You side with the white folks?"

"More than that," Ms. Hoa says with venom, "I'm friends with her. She is the only one who cares."

"I won't agree to a divorce," the man spits out.

"Let's see what the lawyer has to say about it. Dong, go pack up your things."

"Dong, you will go nowhere. I said I won't agree to a divorce."

"And I said let's see what the lawyer has to say about it. Dong, what are you waiting for? Go pack up your things."

Dong stands in the middle of the kitchen, his mind hazy.

What should he do? Why is his family suddenly falling apart? Sure, he did wish for something to change. But he wants to have a happier life, not—not this, whatever it is. He looks at Ms. Dolores, unsure of what he should feel toward the woman. Anger because she possibly convinced his mom to divorce his father? Happy because she saved his life? Grateful because at this moment, she is the only adult he can count on?

Dong is helpless in the whirlpool of emotions and thoughts in his brain. Was it Lizzie or Ames who said that his mind was not his best friend? He looks around at Simon, Lizzie, and Ames, and the three of them stare back at him with a questioning look. Dong realizes that he is the only one who understands what is happening in this stuffy basement. His parents are speaking in Vietnamese, and though they are close—though Simon kisses him tenderly and holds him tight in his sweet embrace, and though Lizzie and Ames run through the night to knock on his door and save his life— they are aliens to the language. They are strangers. Dong is unsteady on his feet. The insults that his father throws in his mom's face wheeze past his ears without fully registering in his mind. Ms. Hoa remains peacefully silent, allowing the words to be just that—words without meaning. She touches Dong's shoulders gently, turns his face to her, and looks him straight in the eyes, smiling. "Dong, pack your things, we'll get out of here. We'll live."

Dong startles. He feels like he just woke up from a very long dream. Ms. Hoa's words bring him back to the reality he is living in. Her smile softens his soul. Her Vietnamese accent is so familiar it reminds him that she is his own—his kind, his kin. He touches her roughened hands, unsure if she is real, if he is real. The love that he has been seeking has now been found. It is the warmth of these hands that he wished for, and it is the joyful, happy smile on her face that he has been living for. Somehow, amidst the storm of these chaotic years and the thundering broken dishes, Dong has forgotten the core of his being. He is a Vietnamese first. Always a Vietnamese.

"Mom," he utters—the one Vietnamese word that he thought he had forgotten long ago in those darkest of nights. Ms. Hoa stares at him, her eyes wide open, then she pulls him in closer and kisses his nape amidst the happy sobbing,

"Yes, dear, Mommy is here. Mommy will always be here."

Dong runs to his room and quickly puts some of his essential clothing and supplies into his backpack. Adrenaline is coursing through his veins. He doesn't know where he will go from here, where Ms. Hoa will take him, and whether it will be Heaven or Hell, but he knows this time, he will be safe. He charges into the kitchen. Ms. Hoa is staring at the man, not moving. She is patiently waiting for Dong. Ms. Dolores is discussing taking a day off school with Lizzie, Ames, and Simon. Simon now seems unwilling to leave, seeing as the situation is getting worse than he expected. Ames is hesitant. She doesn't mind taking a day off, but she doubts her mom will agree, and Ms. Dolores keeps assuring her that she will talk to her mom about the matter. The three of them look at Dong, a mix of worry, love, and confusion showing on their faces. But Dong is beaming. He knows he'll make it, no matter what it is. He takes Ms. Hoa's hand, smiling. "Mom."

"Let's go, the car is outside."

The children and the two women hurry out of the basement. Dong takes a final look at the man who he calls father. The man who he thought was insurmountable, whose presence was a shroud of darkness, of despair and fear, the man who he thought was undefeatable. Then Dong looks to his side. Ms. Hoa is holding his hand; her other hand is holding a bag of his belongings. *It is true,* Dong thinks, *what Mom says about Vietnamese women.* Dong has witnessed the truth of history. The woman comes, the woman conquers, the woman destroys. The man stands there, looming like a darkened future. But he can never foresee the end, where the woman always prevails.

Chapter 22: It's You and Me

"It's you and me from now on, Dong," Ms. Hoa says in her calm, serene voice as she backs the car out of the driveway and drives out of the neighborhood. Dong can only focus on the thought that he's going to miss a day of school, and this time, it is not because of an illness. He watches as his childhood home recedes into the groves of the maple trees and finally disappears after a corner, thinking, *This is the end.* Something in him fears what is going to happen next, but his heart is leaping out of his chest from joy.

No more broken dishes, no more shouting, no more arguments and curses thrown into the air as if he wasn't there. Behind Ms. Hoa's car, Ms. Dolores's old, white Toyota follows, then it is Simon in his dark blue Honda. Dong feels like they are leaving a life behind. A life that is not worth remembering, but within it are his memories, his burning love, his hopes, his dreams, mixing in a well of wishful thinking. And Dong prays to the unforgiving God that the life he is walking into will be better, then he closes the imaginary box of his wandering thoughts, turns back to his mom, and smiles cheerfully. "It's you and me, Mom."

His mom hums a familiar song. The tune is so well ingrained in his brain, it feels like this is the only song she has sung since the day he was born. But he doesn't know what its name is, and he never bothered to ask. He figured he wouldn't understand it even if he tried. The meaning of the words would elude him in the vague, unfathomable darkness of the abyss of language. Sitting in the passenger seat of the car, Dong wishes he had paid more attention to the language his mom loves and speaks. The language of sorrow and suffering. Perhaps, with a twist of his finger, and a tight embrace when she comes home on those winter days, he can turn it into a language of happiness. That is in the past. Dong shakes his head, focused on the open road, leading to nowhere and anywhere. "Where are we going, Mom?"

"We are staying at Dolores's house for the moment."

"At Lizzie's house?"

"Problem?"

"No, mom. I just…" Dong fumbles with his T-shirt. "I never knew you were so close with Ms. Dolores."

"Well, let's say we let a lot of water flow under that bridge. And it's not like we're staying there for free. I will help her with the housework on days she has night shifts. She says you can help her daughter study for tests. She has high hopes for her little one, although she admits that those hopes haven't been very fulfilled." Ms. Hoa is roaring with laughter. She pushes on the gas pedal, rushing forward. "What's the deal with you and that boy?"

"That boy?" Dong feigns innocence.

"You know who I'm talking about."

"There's nothing going on."

"You lied to me twice. Don't hit the third strike or there will be no more you and I, Dong." Ms. Hoa smiles, ruffling his hair. "Speak, I won't judge."

"I…" Dong stutters, then, taking a deep breath, he closes his eyes and lets his words flow out. "I love him. I've loved him ever since we were still neighbors. But we lost touch when he moved and we didn't talk again until recently. Lizzie and Ames told me about him and the party they were going to. And they showed me his photo. I thought, *Why not?* Looking back, there are a lot of answers for that question. But I ignored them all. I wanted him. I want him still. He is the light I see in the darkness I face every day at school. You may not know this, or you may notice and don't want to broach the matter, but I was bullied. I don't know why I used the past tense—it's still happening. I don't have a lot of friends. I hardly share my life with anyone, and eventually, the four walls of my room could barely hold the stories I've got to tell. You will probably laugh at this, but I wrote a bunch of letters to Simon. He never answered. I kept writing and writing to the void, hoping that in the echo of the bottomless chamber, I would hear his voice calling my name. And he did. That's why I lied to you the first time, and the time after that. Mom, I know it is wrong, but I can't stop myself from wanting him in my life. I know it—"

"It is not wrong, Dong," Ms. Hoa interrupts him, stroking the back of his hand to soothe his nervous tension. "How can it be wrong to love anyone? You are not harming anything in the process. But let me tell you my side of the story. The reason why I was angry. You know Simon's mother, right?"

"Yeah? Ms. Barbara? What about her?" Dong asks, realizing he has been crying this whole time. He wipes away his tears on his sleeves, waiting for his mom to speak.

"Yeah, Barb or whatever. When she discovered you and Simon sleeping together in her son's room that afternoon, she went crazy. She took you home to me, and you were crying. You probably don't remember this, but she and I were screaming at each other. I almost bit her head off. That woman was a force to be reckoned with. And I was not built to lose. The last straw was when she insulted you. Throwing all the blame on you, when you knew no better than to sob and tremble at my side. I lost it. I swore to myself, and to her, that I wouldn't let you, be it now or forever, get anywhere near that cauldron of hell. Dong, it is not wrong of you to love. But I am a mother, and it's hard for me to see you suffer from the path you choose. I know she is a mother, too, and she probably loves him in a way—perhaps the wrong way, like I did all these years—but she has no right to use that reason to hurt you. So, there it is. The reason I was angry was because I failed to protect you from the harm that could befall you, and then I turned myself into the worst kind of harm that could ever befall you. I guess what I'm trying to say is…" Ms. Hoa sighs, then says with a firm conviction, "I'm sorry for the pain I've caused you."

"But I also did terrible things to you, Mom," Dong protests. "I failed the test, I lied to you, I never listened to your side, I threw a tantrum without caring about your feelings. I was a terrible son, and I deserved the punishment."

"Dong, listen to me, darling," Ms. Hoa says, somewhat embarrassed at her usage of the unfamiliar endearment. "There's no such thing as failing to be a son. And there's no such thing as failing to be a parent. We were all given tests, and some of us excel at them more than the rest, but that doesn't make us less worthy of love, and it certainly doesn't justify the pain we suffer. We will spend our whole life saying sorry to everyone we encounter, and we will also spend as much time being thankful for their existence in our life. What I'm trying to say is we made mistakes, and we went through a long winding way to fix a very tiny hole, but we can learn something from it, can't we? So, don't let a failed test decide who you are, because to me, you are always more than a number on a white paper. We persist, Dong. And it's you and me this time."

Ms. Hoa stops at a red light and turns to flash her son a beaming smile. Dong feels his heart blooming in his chest, and each palpitation is bursting with a life of its own. Ms. Hoa's face doesn't have the same old knitted brows and stern gaze. Her eyes are more mellow. Her smile is gentle and filled with joy. But somehow, Dong still feels like this is the woman he knows. This is the woman he shares his blood with, the woman who holds him in her bosom and feeds him the last bites of meat when she must go hungry. Ms. Hoa didn't change into someone else; she simply returned to her true self, to who she used to be before the man. And Dong loves her, a love that can't be compared with any other type of passionate feeling.

"What about Simon?" Dong mutters, looking at the rearview mirror to see the boy in the blue T-shirt making a left turn.

"Well, he's got his parents to deal with, hasn't he?" Ms. Hoa says nonchalantly. "He's strong. He will survive."

"And I can be friends with Lizzie and Ames?" Dong hesitates, watching Ms. Hoa's reaction meekly through the corner of his eyes. The woman laughs again.

"We are staying at one of the girls' houses. It's a bit late for that question now, isn't it?"

"Mom?"

"Yes?"

"I love you." Dong squeezes her hand, meaning every word he says.

"Yeah, me too." Ms. Hoa coughs, still feeling awkward about expressing such strong emotions, but her teary eyes betray her.

She hopes she did the right thing. She hopes she has ended the generational curse of abuse and suffering. But an anxious voice in her head keeps nagging at her that this is only the beginning. The road is wide open, and she can take as many twists and turns as she likes, but she is not sure of the ending. She has the boy to worry about. The world is weighing on her shoulders, and it takes an ocean of strength within her to not break down right there in the car, telling Dong that she is not sure. That she wants the best for him, but she is only a lost person in this wild desert. She said she doesn't want him to suffer, but she knows there's no way to stop the suffering. Ms. Hoa squeezes Dong's hand, and watching the boy's contented smile, a gripping fear fills her heart. "Me too, Dong. Me too."

That night, another storm is waiting for Simon in his home sweet home. And this time, there's no savior running through the dark road to bring him away. Simon faces the challenge head-on, standing strong as he is, in his blue T-shirt and beige pants, his hands clenched tight, his jaws tense. He told Dong that he won't give up. He told Dong that Alexandra won't be leaving. And he intends to live true to his words.

Simon sighs as he leans on his dark blue Honda, watching the lights in the living room of the mansion he'd sooner call a lovely prison than a home. He whips out his phone and texts Dong: "Hey, you good?" In a matter of seconds, a text shoots back: "Yeah, you?"

Simon's fingers hesitate on the keyboard. He wants to text Dong that he is not so well, that he wants to go back to Mississauga and stay wherever Dong is, that he skipped school today—the first time in a long while—and has been hanging around all sorts of places instead of going straight home. That he'd rather do anything than open the damn wooden door leading to the lavish hell disguised as a happy paradise, but he can't win against time. The digital numbers on his phone say that it will soon be dinner time.

If his father is at work today, he will be home soon. He couldn't care less about his stepmom and his stepbrother. Sweet little Nathan might be at a friend's place, or maybe Vivian is taking him to the mall for ice cream. She'd never do something like that for him, Simon, the grown-up kid, who can live on his own, who will get by, who will survive, no matter what. He holds the phone close to his face. It has only been one night, but his world has changed so much. He never thought he'd need the warmth of someone to be able to go on, to persist, to walk.

Then the phone vibrates loudly in the hazy darkness. Simon fumbles with his hands, almost dropping the phone. It is Dong.

"Hey," the boy's voice booms from the other side, cheerful, a bit cheeky—it is all that Simon will ever need.

"Hey, so, yeah, hey," Simon stutters, not knowing what he is saying, not knowing what he should say next. A million words died on the road from Mississauga back to Oakville.

"What's wrong? You don't sound very good," Dong says, chewing something. Simon can almost see the boy standing in front of him, his head cocked to one side, his almond eyes staring with worry, his soft lips moving, a few crackers—or some bits of junk food—scattered on his pale pink flesh. He only needs to reach out his hand to feel Dong's flush cheeks bounce against his fingers and make his smile spread from ear to ear. What is stopping him?

210

"I—" Simon swallows. If he wants to start, he will need to start from the beginning. But having been lost for so long in this labyrinth, he no longer knows where the exit is and where the entrance resides. He is floating around, trying to find a way out, holding on to the only visible thread: his conversation with Dong, his voice, the laughter, the images. The love that he thought was dead but has been resurrected overnight like the ever-benevolent, ever-forgiving embrace of a gentle beast.

"Are you home from school yet?" Dong says, still chewing, but a tinge of doubt shows in his voice. He is catching on to something. *Quick, tell a lie,* Simon thinks. That is the one escape route he always uses. But his heart prevails where his mind is trying to win.

"I am home. Well, not inside, at least. I'm standing outside, looking in, like a dwarf not being invited to the king's Christmas party." Simon laughs, but the line is silent, so he keeps going. "I skipped school. I hung around all sorts of places today. I just—I don't want to go home. I hate it here. The sports team, the debate club, the private school, the parties, the popular girls, the jocks, the fake smiles, pretending to be who I am not—I hate the person I am turning into, and I can't stop the process. What do I do? I want to be with you. Oh God, I want to drive to where you are, but I can't do that, either. I hate being a child, and I don't want to be an adult. What am I, Dong? And how can you love someone like me?" Simon crouches down on the ground, plucking the wild dandelions, trying to make his voice light with laughter, but it just produces tears.

"You hate being perfect?" Dong says after a while. There is a click in the background. Perhaps he is inside a closed room now. Or perhaps he is outside, alone, staring at the same sky as Simon right now, but in a different city.

"Well, being perfect is quite lonely," Simon says. "Do you hate being perfect?"

"I hate being picked on," Dong says. "I hate being the odd one out, the chosen one.It sucks. Because it makes people think that you are immune to pain. You put a tag saying that the table is the best table in the world, so what? The table will always be a table, you know. But going back to you, I don't think being perfect changes who you are. Simon will always be Simon. If I throw a rock at you—hypothetically, because I can't imagine myself doing that—you will get hurt. And that means you're not perfect."

"So you hate being perfect?" Simon says, laughing, already forgetting half of his worries and burdens. He loves when Dong goes on an irrelevant tangent only to come back to the starting point at the least expected time, in the most peculiar way.

"I hate seeing you hurt," Dong says. Simon can hear him shifting the phone to the other ear. "And I hate people putting labels on things just for the hell of it."

"Dong, did I ever tell you about why my parents got divorced?" Simon holds his breath, waiting. Dong mutters a quiet "Mm-hm," urging him to go on. He blurts out, his eyes shut, his voice tremulous to the point of almost inaudible, "Because I am gay."

The line goes silent for a long time. Simon hears his heart beating in his ears. The crickets sing in the thick bushes, and he has finished off the dandelions at his feet. In a nervous fit, Simon proceeds to attack another tangle of newly bloomed dandelions, waiting for Dong to say something. His ear is sweating, and he can feel the phone slowly slip out of his clammy hand. Unable to bear the weight of the silence, Simon hastily yells, surprised by his own volume, "Well—I mean –"

"No, I understood what you meant," Dong says, calm and a bit teasing. "I was just waiting for the realization to settle in. Simon, your mom caught us lying together, cuddling on your bed, remember?"

"Yeah?" Simon says, scratching his head.

"And she dragged me home, berating my mom, yeah?"

"Right."

"And I wrote you love letters. And though you didn't write back, you keep them till now. Then yesterday you drove all the way from Oakville to my place, professing in the best possible way how much you love me. I mean, dude, it would take a miracle for a person to not think that you are gay. See where I'm going with this?" Dong cackles, "So, what else is new?"

"I –" Simon is stunted. Hearing the loud laughter echoes from the speaker, something inside him suddenly blooms. Like a spring finally comes over an eternal winter land, he savors the raindrops of Dong's beautiful voice on his bruised heart. Giving into the sweet temptation of the boy's happiness, Simon laughs, sitting on the damp earth, "Yeah, I'm pretty stupid."

"Well, that's not new."

"My dad remarried."

"Yeah."

"And she—Vivian—is a sweet person. She tries to be a sweet stepmom, but there's always something you are not built for, you know what I mean? Then Nathan came along. He is good. I mean, he has done nothing wrong to me. Sometimes, I even think he is cute. But it's hard to see that—that happy family of three—and picture me belonging somewhere in between.

213

There's no crack for me to fit in. I tried. I really tried. But each time, I failed miserably. I thought—this was only one time, though—that if I was not there, they would be happier. And you know how the spiral will only go downward. I started thinking then, that if I were not gay, my parents would still be together. Or—or if I had not been born—"

Simon stops. He realizes he is now fully bawling his eyes out. The monsters he's tried to keep inside his heart are crawling their way upward. He covers his mouth, trying to say, "Never mind," but what comes out betrays his futile effort. He sobs into the phone, "I only want to be loved." His cries shatter everything. Who will save the savior when all is left and done? "Simon," Dong says sweetly, "through all of it, the spiraling, the dark nights, the trying, have you ever thought about yourself?"

"What?" Simon sobs.

"Have you ever thought about yourself, Simon? I mean, adults do what they want to do to get the life they desire. What does it have to do with you being the cause of it all? We are not that important." Dong chuckles awkwardly into the speaker. Simon imagines he is scratching his nose as usual.

"But if I were not – if I tried a bit harder –"

"Things would've ended up the same. Simon, if your parents wanted to stay, they would've chosen that road no matter what. The thing is, you're holding so tightly onto love, yeah?"

"Holding onto love?"

"Right. Imagine love as water. Each of us has our own cup, with its unique shape and capacity. There are some people who are only capable of, say, five hundred milliliters of love. But there are also some people—very rare—who are capable of holding an ocean. But Simon, you are not born to hold an ocean inside you an ocean. And you know it always takes an ocean not to break."

"What do you mean?" Simon asks, stupefied, still stuck on the love-as-water metaphor.

"What I mean is you have to let it go sometimes. Your cup is full, so pour it out. If you can't love your stepmom as much as you want to, what's the harm in it? You said so yourself, there's always something you are not built for. And your stepbrother, what if sometimes he's not loveable? There are moments you think he's cute, and you can treasure him in those moments to compensate for the times you can't. So what if there's no crack for you to fit in? Create your own crack. Don't keep it all inside. You've loved enough, now let me be the lover, remember?"

Dong softly hums the tune of a familiar Leonard Cohen song. Simon feels a breeze of peace sweeping through his heart. Nobody has ever told him to just let it go. Nobody has patted his shoulders, saying that it was not his fault. Simon looks at the closed door of his home, dazed, his ears still keenly listening to the melodious humming of Dong. How can he not love the only person who's ever shown him what happiness is?

An engine sound rings near him, disrupting the temporary peace. Simon quickly stands up. His dad is home. He says hastily, "I've got to go. Talk to you later."

"Wait, Simon."

"Hm?" he says, trying to stay inconspicuous as his dad turns off the ignition and steps out of the car.

"Whatever happens, remember, it's you and me."

Dong hangs up, leaving Simon in awe. Because of what almost happened last night, Simon has forgotten how strong Dong is. The boy who will conquer the most hideous monster of despair on Earth—of course, he will have a way to conquer Simon, who's always been hiding behind a facade of normality. Simon stands up, his back straight, his eyes staring defiantly at his father, the tears barely having the time to dry.

"Dad," he says as a way of greeting.

"We need to talk," his dad replies, stern and weary.

"I know. I also want to talk."

Mr. Wiseman looks at his son, a bit taken aback. Then, with an unfamiliar awkwardness, he walks a few steps to the door, halts, and waves his hand to Simon. "After you." The boy nods, and with quick, decisive strides, he opens the wooden door leading to the brightly lit house that, just a few moments ago, had seemed so monstrous and petrifying to him. Simon firmly grasps the phone in his pants pocket, the warmth still lingering there, as if Dong is standing next to him in the hallway. The boy's voice gently soothes his pain: "Whatever happens, remember, it's you and me."

In front of him, Vivian is standing on the winding staircase leading to the second floor, a worried look on her face. Simon inhales. *It's fine,* he thinks. *I will let it go.*

Chapter 23: You Go Your Way

Mr. Wiseman closes the entrance door behind him. Simon can't help but think, *There goes my only escape route.* But he shakes the spiraling darkness out of his tired brain and walks briskly to the living room. "Vivian," Mr. Wiseman calls out, "can you come to the living room with us for a moment?"

"Nathan is waiting for dinner." Mrs. Wiseman bites her lips and her steps falter on the staircase, her gaze focusing intently on the second door to the right of the upper floor's hallway.

"Well, he's been waiting long enough. He can wait some more," Mr. Wiseman snaps then heaves a sigh, seemingly trying to exhale the whole burden on his shoulders out through his nose. Then, with a more somber voice, he says, "Just come. It won't be long."

"Or it will," Simon mutters, attracting a stern look from Mr. Wiseman, but he ignores it and keeps on walking, settling himself down on the sleek, stylish off-white sofa in the expensive, spacious living room. He looks at the floor, remembering the wild time when Dong was gasping sweetly in his embrace. It felt like ages ago.

Mr. Wiseman follows his eldest son's footsteps, but he halts, standing in the middle of the brightly lit room, rubbing his face, a lost man on his own path, trying to find a way out. Mrs. Wiseman leans on the wall, crossing her arms, not knowing what to do. Part of her wants to hold Mr. Wiseman's hands and persevere through this storm together, and another part of her, growing stronger every second, is burning to escape this suffocating room, to run fast, run far away from this Hell that she is about to step inside. She knows that love is unconditional. But no one ever told her that love would sometimes ask her to choose a side. Her eyes turn from Mr. Wiseman to the teenage boy sitting on the sofa, wondering what she should say next to detonate the bomb before the whole thing blows up. "So," Mrs. Wiseman says, then coughs, fidgeting. "Maybe we can talk about Simon's day at school?"

"There was no school. He skipped," Mr. Wiseman says curtly.

"There was no point in going when I was already two hours late," Simon retorts, not looking at either of his parents.

"Then why didn't you tell us? Why did you drive to Mississauga in the middle of the night? And refuse to see us? And furthermore, you let that boy talk to us as if he were—as if he were you or your representative. Simon, he is a stranger," Mr. Wiseman shouts, then in a fit of rage, he kicks at the coffee table. "Fuck," he mumbles under his breath.

Simon sits there, not really paying attention to his father's fury, not even sure that his mind and body are present within the same space as the two figures he calls his parents. The words keep floating through his ears and flying away. He is dreaming of an escape route. It is the same routine, repeated to perfection. He hates confrontation of any kind, and he'd pay anything not to stare at the demons holding his life in the face. *I hate seeing you hurt,* that little voice coos in his ears. *But Dong, I'm already hurt,* Simon thinks, trying to silent the noise of his breathing. *My heart is a devastated ruin that you won't want to look at for a second time.* He thought he had enough courage to let it go. But it seems Dong was right. He always is. It takes an ocean not to break.

"Are you listening to me?" Mr. Wiseman's cracking shout brings Simon back to the stormy reality. He looks up, and his eyes silence both Mr. Wiseman and his wife.

"I'm listening," Simon says, feeling a cry threatening to burst out of his throat. "I'm always listening. The question is, have you ever?"

"If you have any problems with your life, you should have told us, sweetie," Mrs. Wiseman says, attempting to appease the situation, her arms still crossing over her chest, her mind still focused on Nathan and the dinner the boy hasn't eaten yet. "We are always here for you."

"Oh, really? When is my next parent-teacher conference?" Simon asks, a tinge of total surrender in his voice.

"You should have shown us the paper first," Mr. Wiseman says, somewhat taken aback, but he quickly gets back the control of his authority.

"I gave it to you. I gave it to you three weeks ago. Then I gave it to Vivian. Then my homeroom teacher called. I guess at this point, I will have to write that invitation across the sky for you to notice. What more do you want from me? Stranger, you say? Fine, at least a stranger let me know that he needs me more than the people in this house will ever need me."

Simon jerks up, his hands clenched into a tight fist. He tries his best to contain his anger, but the anger has other plans. His mind wanders to various places—happier places. "Look at me," he cries, pleading. "Look at what I have become. Am

I not the portrait of perfection you always wanted? Now let me be me."

Mr. Wiseman stares at him, trying to find something to say back. He searches far and wide for some sort of consolation, but somewhere along the road, he realizes the consolation will only ease his conscience. And Simon is standing there, raw, naked to the bones, the hurt on his face like a thousand open wounds bleeding straight from his heart. Mr. Wiseman wonders where he failed as a father. He thought he would be better than the source of his son's pain. At least, that was what he promised himself when he parted ways with his ex-wife. That was what he told the boy when he decided to remarry. That is what he says to himself before he goes to sleep. He has done a good job, except his good job is based on his own criteria. He has never seen it from the eyes of Simon.

"Simon," Mr. Wiseman says, attempting a feeble comforting voice, "Listen here, it is not my intention to—"

"And I never blamed you," Simon replies before Mr. Wiseman can finish his sentence. "You deserve happiness. Everyone does. So here's the thing. You go your way, let me go mine."

"What are you saying?" Mr. Wiseman says, stunned by the boy's words, but more than that, he feels the pain slowly bloom from the heels of his feet.

"I'll find a way on my own. I'll create a place where I belong. I'll have somewhere to fit in. That's what I'm saying."

"Is it that boy's idea?" Mr. Wiseman grasps at straws in the dark, knowing he is wrong, but it is too late to turn back.

"What, is it a surprise to you that I can have an idea of my own?" Simon retorts.

"Listen, I think both of you need to—" Mrs. Wiseman pats

Mr. Wiseman's tense shoulders and looks at Simon with her pleading eyes.

But her effort is to no avail. In a quick stride, Mr. Wiseman crosses the room, and with a decisive blow, he slaps Simon twice on the face. Mrs. Wiseman gasps. Right then, a tiny yelp attracts both adults' attention. They look at the living room's entrance leading to the hallway. It is Nathan. The boy is coming to see why nobody is in the dining room yet.

Mrs. Wiseman runs to her boy, speaking in her soft, consoling voice. "It's nothing, dear, we are just talking. Why don't you go into the dining room first?" But Nathan is far from convinced. He looks with wonder from his father to his stepbrother, who is hanging his head low. His eyes cast an innocent worried gaze on his mother's face, then his father's, which is distorted by an anger he is far too young to understand. Nathan bites his lips, running to his stepbrother, standing guard in front of Simon, saying with as much firmness as he can gather, "Father, it is wrong to use violence. You say so yourself."

"No, Nathan, this is—" Mrs. Wiseman hurries to the boy's place, trying to explain. *If only Simon was not here*—she catches herself in the middle of the thought and curses herself. One day, she will learn to love the boy right. But when will that day come?

Simon pushes Nathan's arm away and steps aside. "It's alright, Nat. It's my fault. It is always my fault. You and— and the family have a nice dinner. I'm going for a drive."

He walks briskly to the door, almost running to his only exit. Behind him, Mr. Wiseman shouts, "You stop right there." But he is too far away to hear those threatening words. He is in a different place. He doesn't know if he let it all go or not, but he is certain he has spoken the truth. He doesn't want to intrude on his father's happiness, and he never wants to be a burden. Mr. Wiseman chose his path a long time ago, and Simon only tagged along for a brief period. Isn't it time he forges his own road?

Simon jumps into the dark blue Honda, fumbles with the ignition, then backs out of the driveway. Mr. Wiseman chases after him, shouting, "Wait, Simon. I said wait! We can talk things out. I promise—" But Simon doesn't need his promises. He knows they are there to be broken and trampled upon anyway. He drives in a blind haze, mumbling to himself, "It's alright, it's alright, it's alright—" The tears grow too much for him to bear, and he screeches to a stop in a parking slot, taking up two parking spaces. Above him is the dark sky, no sign of either clouds or stars. All around him is a vast emptiness. The withered, yellow grass undulating against the black canvas only heightens the solitude inside his heart. He feels so utterly alone that it makes sense to him how people can simply disappear without a trace, and no one ever notices. His phone rings constantly in his pocket, but he dares not pick it up. If it were his father, he wouldn't know what to say. A text comes through once, twice, multiple times. He opens the phone in frustration, swearing to himself that he will throw the phone out the car window if it rings one more time. But he halts in his tracks. On the screen, the latest message says: "Hey, no matter what happens, remember, it's you and me."

Simon laughs, then cries, then laughs with his tears ricocheting on the phone's screen. He's a mess. How can he save another person's life when he can barely save his own? The phone rings again. And without thinking twice, he picks it up. "Save me," he says, not even asking who the other person is, not checking the name on the screen, just going out on a limb and bleeding through his pain. "Save me."

"Where are you?" The soft voice rings like music in his ears. His heart is cradled in a nest of tender feathers.

"I don't know. I don't fucking know where I am, where I will go, or what my life will be. I don't fucking know anything."

"Your father's not there with you?"

"If he's here, I will either kill myself or do something terrible to him. You said I have too much love. It's the contrary. I don't have anything. Save me. It hurts so much I don't want to go on," Simon cries, heaving. A panic attack is the last thing he needs, but the last thing he needs is always the first thing that comes into his head.

"Simon, Simon, stay with me," Dong calls, trying to anchor Simon in reality. "I'm here. You have me. Don't ever say you don't have anything. You have me always."

"He hit me. For the first time in my life, my father hit me. It shouldn't hurt this much. I thought I was used to everything thrown my way. I thought—"

"No one is built that strong. And you don't have to be used to that. Pain is just a way to tell us that we are living."

"I told him that I'll be leaving. That I'll let him have his happiness as long as he lets me have mine. I'm perfectly fine with being on my own. I don't need his love to be happy. What more does he want from me?"

Simon sobs into the speaker. But Dong remains silent for a long while. Outside, the wind is growing more aggressive with each passing second. The weather is howling with rage at the teenage boy's suffering. "Say something," Simon begs at his wit's end. *Say you want me, say you won't leave me, say you need me, say...* Simon prays fervently in his head. A thought

223

crosses his mind. *What if he also leaves me?* He stares at his reflection in the rearview mirror. A child stares back at him, fearful and lost, desperate for a little bit of love. Is this who he is reduced to at last? Dong's voice breaks his illusion. "I will send you my address. Are you stable enough to drive?"

"I—"

"If you say you don't know one more time, I swear I will be the one who slaps you next, genius." Dong rolls his eyes so loud Simon can see it.

"I can drive," Simon says with a hitch in his voice, then, trying to calm himself, he repeats in a more confident voice, "I can drive. To your place."

"Good, then you drive here. I will pick you up from your broken place, put you in a hot bath, towel you, tuck you in a nice, soft bed, lie down by your side, embrace you through the night—"

"Dong, I—" Simon feels his heart resume its beating again.

"—then I will proceed to tell you a hundred reasons why you are wrong. Now get your ass here. The address is in the message. And Simon, if you think I am the only person in this world who loves you, you are deeply wrong. That's the first reason. I will tell you the rest later."

Dong hangs up the phone. A text swiftly comes through with a new address in Mississauga. Still bewildered at Dong's stern voice and firm attitude, Simon backs out of the parking lot and drives away. He puts his phone on the passenger seat and keys the address into the GPS. The screen flares up time and time again, but Simon's mind is too focused on Dong's tone to notice it. By the time he arrives at the address, the phone is out of battery.

Back in Oakville, Mr. Wiseman sits on the edge of his bed,

holding his phone, staring at the message screen, refreshing it every ten seconds.

"Simon, where are you?"

"Simon, let's talk things out."

"Simon, I shouldn't have hit you. I was blinded by rage."

"Simon, come home."

"Simon—"

He sends his last message ten minutes to midnight. It says: "Simon, I was wrong. It was my fault. It was always my fault." Mr. Wiseman waits with tension and anxiety until morning. There is never any reply, and he doesn't think there will be one. Not after the wounds he's inflicted on Simon, day by day, month by month. Word by word.

Chapter 24: A Million Reasons

Simon parks his car in front of the cozy townhouse. The lawn is decorated nicely with in-season flowers. The grass is green and lush. He has a feeling that this house and everyone who is living in it are full of life—always bustling about, always laughing at the dinner table, telling each other the troubles of the toiling day, encouraging each other to walk on. He folds his hands and leans his head on the steering wheel, suddenly losing the will to get out of the car and jump into Dong's embrace. Yet another place where he doesn't belong. Why does Dong want him to be here? He said Simon was wrong. A hundred reasons, in fact, are staring him in the face, scrutinizing him at his most vulnerable state, with no weapon to fend for himself. He is tired. Maybe he shouldn't have driven here so blindly in the night just because he is drunk on the sweet, honey-drenched voice of Dong. But then, where else would he go? Simon shifts the gear, and as he is about to turn on the ignition again, there is a knock on the car window. "Hey," Dong says, smiling at him tenderly, and it blows all his thoughts away.

"Hey," Simon replies, trying to find his voice, failing to stop the crack coming through. "So, hey, nice seeing you again. In so short a time. I mean, hey."

"Windows." Dong knocks on the glass, and Simon realizes he hasn't pulled down the car windows yet so whatever he just said was lost on the boy. With a flush face and a giant boulder of embarrassment on his shoulders, he coughs and draws down the glass panel.

"I was saying how nice it is to see you again. So nice. In such a short time. I mean, I never thought. So, hey."

"You okay?" Dong tilts his head to one side, an amused look in his sparkling, dark, unfathomable eyes. He is in his pajamas, with a large scarf wrapped around his shoulders. His hair is falling over his forehead. The soft lips that Simon was imagining a moment ago are right in front of him now, pursed with worry in a delectable shade of pink.

"I thought I was," Simon says, somewhat dizzy, lost in his own labyrinth of desire and unknown guilt, "but now I don't know."

"Guessed as much. I thought you wouldn't get out of your car, so I stood at the doorway, waiting for you. It was cold. Mind if I get in? Or do you feel well enough to come inside the house? Ms. Dolores, Lizzie, and my mom are inside," Dong says, rocking his body back and forth. His eyes are a tiny bit glassy, just enough to hold Simon's gaze captive. He tucks a strand of loose hair behind his ear, and Simon wishes it was his hand touching that soft skin, that warmth, that tender heat that burns through the flesh. "So, are you going to come inside? Or am I to get in your car?"

"Oh. Oh, I—I don't think I'm in a good shape to see a lot of people." Simon looks away, avoiding the eyes that are so dangerously tempting him to do things he should not.

"Great, then open the passenger door. I'm getting in."

"Wait, I—"

Without hearing another word of protest, Dong strides to the other side of the car, waiting. Simon begrudgingly unlocks the door, praying for the strength to get over this ordeal. *Sweet temptation, how treacherous thou art,* he curses a thousand times in his mind as Dong scoots in nearer to him in the passenger seat. The scent of sharp mint and sandalwood attacks him in a full blow, and he surrenders more quickly than he thought he would. *It is wrong,* Simon thinks to himself. *It must be wrong to want someone, to desire someone, to yearn for someone this much.* How else to explain the fire that is kindling in his stomach as he is trying his best to remember how to breathe normally?

"What are you doing?" Dong laughs, teasingly punching his shoulders, and it takes everything in Simon's power to not burst.

"You smell different."

"Oh, it's the shower gel mom bought. She went on a shopping spree with Ms. Dolores today after you left. We will be staying with Ms. Dolores for a while until Mom finds a nice apartment to settle in. I told her I didn't need something so fancy, but mom insisted. I think Ms. Dolores is behind all of this. Not that I mind. I'm just a bit uncomfortable with all the changes. But I guess I will get used to it soon. You don't like the scent?" Dong goes on a tirade of words. His voice is like warm milk sweetened with honey. The boy forgets to talk until Dong pulls his arm slightly, repeating the question in that saccharine innocent tone, "Hey, is the scent too much?"

"On the contrary," Simon says, swallowing hard. *God is testing me,* he thinks.

"Really? Lizzie says I smell like incense. But I don't think so." Dong sniffs his wrist, contemplating the scent for a moment, then says in his chirping voice, "It smells like burned wood.

That's a different sort of scent. Incense has a stronger smell. My mom lights it every day, so I know."

"Well, if I had a closer sniff," Simon begins, his voice hoarse, his throat dried with a yearning thirst. But he catches himself. "Never mind. I think you have a wonderful scent."

"Hm…" Dong purses his lips, seeming to question Simon's words, but the boy is avoiding his eyes like they are the most dangerous trap he's ever encountered, so Dong lets the matter of scent rest. Instead, he leans on Simon's shoulder, linking his arm with Simon's tensed one, murmuring softly, "You know, I was worried when I heard your voice over the phone. I thought you would do something stupid."

"Like what?" Simon asks, trying to distract himself from the ticklish feeling of Dong's hair brushing against his T-shirt. His heart is palpitating, and his mind no longer has the power to remember the reason he came here.

"I don't know. Like you might disappear. Like you might be leaving."

"Uh-huh."

"And you promised me you wouldn't be leaving."

"Yeah. I did."

"So I suppose things didn't go very well between you and your parents? Whatever it was, it must have hurt you enough to break you open."

"Yeah," Simon replies. Everything slowly comes back to him like a film rewinding in slow motion. He tenses up again, but Dong's fingers stroke his hand gently and hold him firmly in the reality of his dark blue Honda and a forest of sharp mint and sandalwood.

"You know, before yesterday," Dong says, "I didn't exactly have a good experience with my parents. I often wondered why I was even born? If they hated me that much, why did they decide to have me? And I won't speak for you, because you have a different life. Each of us is dealt a different set of cards. I can't say mine or yours is worse. But then, my mom told me today that she was wrong. Not because I was born—she said I was the best thing that ever happened to her. She was wrong because she didn't know how to handle that treasure. And it is important to say one is wrong when one realizes. She knows she hurts me. And to be fair, I hurt her in return. But if we are going to spend our lives apologizing to each other, why not make our lives better, you know? That's what I thought."

"And? What's the point of telling me all of this?" Simon asks, the anger coming back to his heart anew. "If you just asked me to come here just to teach me how to forgive and forget—"

"But I didn't." Dong squeezes the escaping hand, grasping Simon's arm firmly, holding him in place, not allowing him a chance to get away. "That's not my intention. You should know me better than that. Simon, that's your anger talking."

"Then what part of you is talking?" Simon shouts, then halts. Looking straight at him, through him, piercingly, are those unfathomable eyes, filled to the brim with love and passion, embracing him in a tight, fiery hold.

"I'm talking with love. I already told you. I hate seeing you hurt."

Dong reaches out his hands, cradling Simon's face, hugging his head close to his chest, patting his hair. The silence hangs in the air, and it is the most soothing silence Simon has ever experienced. He listens to the sound of Dong's fingers dancing on his skin, the sound of the night closing in, the sound of life passing by them as they sit there, watching everything unfold in its magical way. There's a crack in everything; that's how the light gets in. And Dong, with his gentle hands, his mellow demeanor, his soft voice and tender existence, has opened a crack large enough for the light to shine on Simon's eyes. He touches Dong's hand, pulls it to his lips, and indulges himself in kissing each finger, from the tips to the knuckles. For the first time since the morning, he feels safe.

"He doesn't want to hurt you, you know," Dong says, and Simon lets his voice carry him to the land of joy and warmth.

"Who?"

"Your father."

"He already did."

"Well, do you think you haven't done the same?"

"Hurt him?"

"Yeah."

"He's far too concerned with Nat to be hurt by little old me," Simon scoffs, still kissing the slender fingers that smell like Heaven to him.

"Listen, I think there are different ways to show love. Perhaps your father shows your little brother the love he thinks a boy his age wants. And in the same train of thought, he shows you the love he thinks a boy your age wants."

"Like private school and luxurious clothes instead of being there for me? He lets the money talk."

"And you're letting your anger talk. What's the point?" Dong pinches Simon's ear, then proceeds with his caresses. "What I mean is, how many people our age would boast about having their own car, attending the best school, participating in the best clubs, eating at the most expensive restaurants, and stuff like that?"

"Here it comes. Be grateful for what you have and don't

begrudge what you have not," Simon groans.

"No. It doesn't alleviate the pain you feel in your heart. It doesn't change the fact that your father is never there when you need him the most. But cut him some slack. You are trying your best, and he is doing his best, too. It's just, sometimes, the roads we are on lead us to different goals, and it is neither your fault nor your father's. There's nothing you can do about it. Forgiving or forgetting won't do shit. But maybe, if you can sit down and admit that you are wrong, things will be different. There are a thousand ways to move on, you know."

"So you are saying I'm wrong? You're on his side, then? That it's all my fault? I never asked to be on this Earth. He brought me here."

"And did he ever ask to be on this Earth? Simon, I know you are hurt but come on. I never said it was your fault. I said you and your father were both on the wrong track going nowhere at all. I'm on your side. But you are pushing me away. You think you are the only one who knows how hurtful it is to walk on a broken leg when the road is long and winding. But we've all been there—perhaps your father and my mother have been there much longer than we care to admit. Look, I'm just saying, you don't have to forgive or forget the things he has done, but you can at least hear him out."

"He hit me!" Simon sits up, shouting, no longer able to contain his rage. "He slapped me twice. In front of his wife. In front of Nat. I'm not a child. I don't need the humiliation. I don't need your meager sympathy and pity. I shouldn't have come. Shit."

"Simon, look at this." Dong calmly lifts his shirt and pulls his pants down a little, showing his lower abdomen. Simon opens his mouth, but before another word comes out, he is stunted and speechless. On the porcelain skin, there is a purple blemish. A sort of triangle shape, seared into the flesh, like a birth mark, except it is not a natural one. Simon doesn't recall that shape being there when they were young. He reaches out, touching the purplish mark, stroking it, his mind running wild with thoughts, his heart trying hard to not imagine the worst scenario.

"What is this?" He utters, a dark premonition welling up in his eyes, telling him it is better not to know.

"My father dropped a steam iron on me. After he learned about the incident at your house through my mom. I've never known if it was accidental or intentional. But my mom took me to the ER, and after so many years, it's finally healed. And that's that." Dong shrugs, pulling his pants up, but Simon stops his hands.

"How can you—how can he—how can a person—?" he stutters, trying to sort his thoughts, his words, his questions. What does he want to ask? He doesn't know. In his mind, the image of Dong lying there with the burn, in his dark room in the basement, crying silently for help, knowing that the help wouldn't come, stabs through his heart again and again, each time fiercer than the last, until his breathing stops. Simon gasps. The dark premonition turns into tears.

"I don't know. Sometimes, people do the most impossible things. He burned me. I healed. But the point of the story is, I'm not speaking to you from a place of cheap sympathy or pity. I—"

But Dong can't finish his sentence. Simon smothers him in a frenzy of kisses and broken sobs. "If I had known...if I had only known," he repeats in Dong's ears. His breath is hot and feverish on Dong's skin. The boy squirms uneasily in the

233

passenger seat. This is not how he thought it would turn out. He never thinks about the mark, not anymore. His mom's pain every time she saw it only makes him hide the mark more carefully. He knows it only brings suffering to other people's lives, so he refrains from mentioning it. He's promised himself to bury it in the bygone past forever. But something in Simon's stubborn demeanor, the unyielding force of his pride, turns Dong's mind over. He doesn't want to hurt Simon this much. He only wants Simon to know that it is possible they are bearing the same pain, that he understands, that Simon doesn't have to go through the torture of his solitude. And here they are, a beautiful mess, wretched from the start, wrecked by their own clumsy hands when they are too young to hold on to the love that burns far too bright, far too cruel.

Dong pats Simon's heaving shoulders, wondering all the while how this tall, giant frame can turn into a weeping puddle in his arms. He thought the burned scar would have a different effect. What had escaped his mind was the magnitude of the love this giant holds within his heart for him, suppressed tightly to the point of exploding with a simple touch. The tears are seeping through his pajamas, and Dong squirms uneasily in his seat. He feels the monster of guilt gnawing at his stomach and biting his skin. He shouldn't have brought the old wound up just to open a new wound in another person. Sometimes, the best of intentions, through the marvelously cruel hands of fate and misunderstanding, become the most lethal weapon, twisting its way into the depths of a person's vital point, making it bleed and fester.

Simon sniffles, gathering himself up, wiping his face, trying to smile although his lips are having a hard time lifting. "Sorry," he says, cracking. "I just—this is not about me. I ended up letting the hurt person comfort me. I'm a mess."

"It's okay. I was going to wash these pajamas later, anyway." Dong chuckles, pinching Simon's nose slightly. "Feeling better?"

"I guess." Simon nuzzles into Dong's hand, unwilling to let an inch of that warmth go. "I have no right to feel hurt. You are right, I have things so good."

"No. No, that's not what I want you to take away from this." Dong inches closer, his brows furrowed in consternation. "Simon, you have every right to feel hurt. You are entitled to your feelings. I just mean that people have their own burdens, Simon, and yours are not necessarily lesser or heavier than your dad's. Listen, why don't you stay here tonight, sleep on this whole thing, and let's see how the story changes in the morning, m'kay?" He cups Simon's face in his hands, smiling sweetly. The little twinkles return to his eyes and Simon can't pull himself away from the alluring tenderness.

"I'm just scared. So scared. What if one day, no one needs me anymore? Dong, I don't want to be abandoned." Simon falls on the other boy's shoulder, breathing in the scent of sharp mint, filling his lungs with the air of safety and joy.

"I guess that is the point, isn't it? People will come, and people will leave. Nothing is forever, and nothing is certain. That's the beauty of it."

"And will you , too?"

"Why would I?" Dong peppers kisses on Simon's temple, trailing the soft touches down to his lips, and gives him a light peck while smiling. "If I left, you would be a wreck."

"This is a mad man talking, but the moment I tasted your love, I was already a wreck," Simon scoffs, leaning in for a deeper kiss, carving the softness of the pastel pink lips into his overwrought brain, swearing to himself and to God above that he will never let these hands go.

"Are you sweet-talking me?" Dong giggles, pushing Simon's chest weakly.

"Well, am I successful?" Simon bites his lower lip, teasing the flushing boy.

"Well, I—"

A knock on the car window startles both of them. They jump, almost hitting their heads on the car roof. Outside, Ms. Hoa stands in all her overbearing stature, her curlers nestled in her hair, her worn cardigan billowing in the air, her mouth in a straight line, her eyes screwed up. Simon feels his stomach sinking to the car floor. In these twenty-four hours, he has accumulated enough debts against this woman to turn himself into her mortal enemy. And now her son is exchanging saliva with him as she comes out. He swallows his fear, trying to gather the courage he had when he set foot in her house yesterday—when he didn't have anything else on his mind but his lover. "Mother," Dong says meekly, drawing his attention back to reality.

"I was wondering why you were out so mightily late," Ms. Hoa grunts, somewhat angered, but more amused by the pallor on Simon's face.

"Oh, hi, Ms. Hoa."

"It is very late now," Ms. Hoa says in her nonchalant, brusque way. "Tomorrow is Friday, my boy has school, and I have work. What are you doing here?"

"He's running away. His father slapped him. Twice," Dong replies instead of a flustered Simon, opening the passenger door to get out.

"And your grandmother beat me black and blue. What?

Two slaps got him so scared he had to run away from home? Children these days." Ms. Hoa tuts, shaking her head disapprovingly but not stopping Dong from dragging Simon toward the house.

"I asked Ms. Dolores, and she said Simon can stay here for one night. He'll be staying in my room, so no worry, Mom."

"Of course, there will be worries. He was eating your lips—"

"Mom," Dong flusters, flushing up to his ears. Simon watches him, amusement and adoration shining brightly in his eyes, a low chuckle escaping his lips, but he quickly catches himself, not wanting to appear more insolent than he already does in front of Ms. Hoa.

"And am I wrong?" Ms. Hoa jerks her eyebrows, seemingly unaware of the catastrophically large tomato that her son is turning into. "I saw with my eyes how he nearly bit your mouth off of your face."

"Excuse me, I'm going to my room," Dong mumbles, frustrated with his mother and the smug smile on Simon's face.

"Yes, you are, but without him." Ms. Hoa holds Simon in place. "What will he do to you when my eyes are not around?"

"Mom, he won't do anything. He's grieving." Dong sighs, trying to appease his mom, but he can't hide the tinge of expectation in his voice. The boy he loves will sleep in the same room with him tonight, and yes, there will be things going on, and he won't give this chance up. Even it means going against the sweet, beloved, stout woman standing in front of him.

"Grieving from two slaps? Right, that sounds like just the right excuse to ask for your sympathy. And I've watched enough movies to know what kind of sympathy it will be." Ms. Hoa frowns, strengthening her grip on Simon's wrist as the boy has to muster everything he has inside to not guffaw out loud.

"Mom, I don't know what movies you watch, but it won't come to that," Dong quickly responds, his ears quivering slightly, red to the tip. Somewhere in his brain, a cheeky voice chirps, *But it won't be so bad if it comes to that.* He looks over at Simon, and the boy flashes him a beaming smile with teeth like a row of pearls reflecting the moonlight, and the cheeky voice affirms him, *Yeah, it is definitely going to come to that.*

"Not under my watch." Ms. Hoa scowls, already glimpsing what Dong is cooking in his head.

"Mom, he's only here for one night, I promise. Can we go inside, please?" Dong resorts to the most lethal weapon he holds in his hand—which he only learned that he has today when he was sobbing in his mom's bosom—and brings out the pleading, teary voice with the puppy eyes. "Please, Mom, it's late."

Simon sees Ms. Hoa's face change as rapidly as a chameleon changes the color on its skin. Her brows relax, her features soften, her eyes grow gentle, and her voice becomes soothing again. "Right, right, let's go inside, we don't want to cause a scene." The woman lets go of Simon's hand in a heartbeat and rushes toward Dong's side, enveloping him in her body, swaying him back and forth, cooing in his ear, "Go to sleep, my sweet little boy." Dong's soft laughter bubbles out of her bosom as he hugs her back and snuggles his head into her neck, and it makes Simon's stomach churn with a bittersweet envy. He knows he should be happy for Dong. He knows more than anyone that Dong deserves the love and tenderness that people are showering upon him. But deep down inside, a worm keeps wiggling through his veins and leaks its venomous pang of jealousy. He wants to be where Dong is. He yearns for the brightness in Dong's eyes. He'd pay anything for it to be his, to feel the warmth of a loving mother's embrace on his skin. Simon clutches his stomach; an immense loneliness slowly crawls on his skin. He never knew it would be this hard to be wholeheartedly delighted for another person's blessings. Even when that person is supposed to be the one he loves and treasures more than anyone else.

He sighs, laughing at his own pathetic state of being and his petty jealousy. Maybe Ms. Hoa is right. He is indulging too much in his grieving from the two slaps. And it will take a long time to explain to Ms. Hoa where his grievances begin. Looking at the pair of mother and son in front of him, Simon wonders why he bothered to drive here after all. He kicks a pebble under his feet, attempting to walk away and ask for permission to leave. But Dong turns to him, one arm still wrapped around his mom, the other reaching out for him, smiling with unconcealed innocence and a love so large, so tantalizing like the ocean breaking wave after wave inside his heart. The pale pink lips call out for his name, the voice beckoning him to come closer. "Simon, what are you waiting for? Get over here." In an instant, without even being aware of his actions, Simon takes the kind hand offered to him. Again, he is whole. Again, he finds that he is standing on his Earth and can feel its every move.

"Thank you," he whispers softly into the hug. Dong ruffles his hair, and as he closes his eyes, savoring the warmth of the fingers on his scalp, the jealousy dissolves quietly into the nothingness from which it stems.

Dong drags Simon to his room despite the glaring eyes and

the prickling reluctance of Ms. Hoa. Simon is sure that he can hear the phrase "Don't you dare do anything weird" being hissed out from her tightly-pursed mouth. He is reminded once more that she is giving in to her son, not to him. And if something happens to her son, Simon will bear the full extent of the dragon's wrath. Much like Ms. Hoa, he's watched enough movies to know the consequences of messing with a dragon's treasure trove. But the moment the door closes and the scent of sharp mint and sandalwood fills his nose like a long-lost lover, he can't stop himself from pulling Dong into a tight embrace and breathing in the boy as if he were Simon's entire reason for living. His mind tells him to let go but his arms possess a will of their own. He fears the emptiness in the air when Dong moves away, leaving him with nothing but an invisible space in the shape of a body that perfectly fits into his frame.

Dong pats his shoulders, trying to untangle himself from Simon's grip. He wonders what caused Simon's onslaught of intense affection, but there is one thing he is sure of: This is not coming from a good place. He slithers away from the boy's embrace, slightly wavers by the hurt in his eyes, but he is determined to do everything he can to draw the boy from the dark abyss that he is stuck in. "Simon," he says in a mellowing whisper, caressing the boy's ear, "maybe we should talk a bit."

"Why? We talked plenty." Simon follows Dong to the twin bed, sitting down beside him, scooting close enough that he is almost sticking to the other boy.

"Yeah, and we are getting nowhere with your situation. Have you contacted your parents?"

"I forgot." Simon whips out his phone. The battery is dead. "Well, not like they would care," he says, then tosses the phone on the bed. Dong picks it up and plugs it in the charger.

"That's the problem with you, see. You assume instead of trying to figure out the truth of the matter. I'm not much of a better person myself, but I've witnessed the same thing happen to me, and I know full well where it's going. It might sound a bit hypocritical of me, but Simon, I don't want the same ending happening to you."

"As in my parents getting divorced? Again?"

"No. As in you getting hurt more than what you are bargaining for."

"I told you. They don't c—"

"Simon, you are being willfully stubborn to prove a point in a battle you know you are losing. You just don't see it. You say they don't care because you are afraid of the feelings that will bury you alive when you realize how much they care. And I know you understand. You are far too intelligent to not know that."

Simon looks at Dong, speechless. In the boy's glistening dark eyes, as deep as a bottomless ocean, Simon can see the reflection of his true emotion. A bit of sadness, a whole lot of fear, but much more than that, the wish to be loved, to be understood. He wants to argue for his case, to tell Dong that he is wrong, that Simon never succumbs to such things as wishing for his parents' affection. That being vulnerable is not in his nature, not since the day his mother rejected his existence simply because he yearns for the same gender. He wants to tell Dong how hard he fought to get where he is, to be someone who can withstand the relentless stabbing of words and ridicule, to be strong, to be perfect, so that no one will ever dare look at him in the face and deny his right to be on this Earth. He wants to shout in anger and fury that Dong wouldn't understand the battles he'd been through. But the words won't come out. Dong's eyes pierce him straight to the core, chilling, freezing him in place. The purplish mark of the iron burning on Dong's lower abdomen appears in front of his eyes in all its glorious beauty and sadness. And Dong's words ring in his ears: *"You are being willfully stubborn to prove a point in a battle you know you are losing."* He stares blankly ahead. How could he not see it? All these years, he's been fighting a battle so futile and so meaningless until he lost the one ally he ever had: himself.

"Maybe you are right," Simon says, breathing softly. "Maybe it's not worth it in the end. Maybe being perfect is not the solution. Maybe—"

"Of course, Simon, being perfect is never the solution." Dong smiles, his eyes twinkling ever so slightly in the moonlit room, and it takes Simon's breath away. "Remember what our wise musician once said? There's a crack in everything; that's how the light gets in."

Simon feels his whole body shattering to the floor. He collapses on Dong's shoulders, his weight pushing the boy down to the bed. But that is the least of Dong's worries. Not when Simon is muffling his cries into Dong's shoulders, his tears burning new scars on Dong's skin, his pain smoldering and seeping through the boy's flesh. Dong silently embraces all the mess that Simon has become. Dong has never liked being perfect. Maybe he is one of the lucky ones because he escaped the claws of that monster. Simon, not so much. Dong feels the muscles of Simon's shoulders tensing up under his palms, then slowly relaxing into defeat. He knows it takes courage to fight a fierce battle, but he also knows it takes a special kind of bravery to admit defeat in front of your mortal enemy, who is just an exact replica of yourself. And Simon is doing just that. It's hard to be a silent observer in this whole ordeal, when his beloved is tearing himself to pieces, crushed by the great expectations that he wears as his strongest armor. But he ends up being the one to save him when he falls, Dong is willing to bear the burden. He hugs Simon, gently stroking his back, encouraging him to let his emotions go. "You know," he whispers close to Simon's ears, placing lingering kisses after each word, "you might have a million reasons you think you're wrong. But I will be that one reason to prove you right."

"Are you trying to make me feel better?" Simon laughs in short chops through his tears.

"Is it working?"

"Tremendously."

"How can I make it even more wonderful?"

"Why? It's good enough as it is." Simon nuzzles close to Dong's neck, indulging in the warmth he never gets anywhere else. "I don't deserve more."

"You can always ask for more. And whether you deserve it or not, why don't you let me be the judge of that?" Dong cradles the other boy's face in his hands, their noses touching. His smile grows so infectious that Simon can't help but glow. "Ladies and gentlemen, I judge that this man before me deserves every and any happiness the universe has to offer. Case closed."

"I know one way you can make it true." Simon gulps, leaning closer, their lips slightly touching, their breath mingling. Between them, the words are blooming on their own. "Dong, will you take me as your lover?"

Dong stares at him, bewildered, his breath catching in his throat. The world stands still in that one hanging second, then it catapults forward with the speed of light as Dong grabs Simon's face and kisses him with a passion so fiery, it almost burns them both. "You already are, you stupid child," he says, laughing between breaths. "Always is, always have been, always will be." Simon traces the plush lips with his own, savoring the taste of hot pepper and sweet bread on his tongue, wondering in his mind what his precious boyfriend had for dinner to be this delicious, throwing his thoughts out the windows the next minute as he tries to feel under Dong's pajamas, hungering for more of the flame. *If this is what it means to love,* Simon thinks as his fingers dance on Dong's ribcage, *I am willing to bear the pain, the suffering, the hell of it all. As long as he is here. The reason to prove that I am right.* "Dong, I—"

But before he can finish his ardent begging, a loud knock on the door breaks the room apart. Ms. Hoa's voice booms from the other side, "You boys asleep?"

The two boys freeze on the tiny bed, limbs tangled together, skin almost touching skin, lips still lingering on lips. They wait in a long suspenseful silence until Ms. Hoa's footsteps echo quietly down the hall. After making sure that his mom has closed the door to her room, Dong heaves a sigh of relief. He looks at Simon's contorted face and bursts out laughing, making the other boy surrender with his own jovial chuckle. "Well, that will be as much happiness as you can get tonight, lover boy," Dong says, pushing Simon to his side and curling into his chest. "Sleep then?"

"Mm-hm. I have all the time in the world."

The night goes on. But Simon no longer cares what the morning will bring. He feels like he has walked a long while through a very short, arduous road. As he wraps his arms around the body that lies so pliant in his embrace, Simon knows he is safe. He has finally found peace. For the first time, he makes a truce with his enemy. He has learned to forgive himself. As it turns out, it takes a room full of love, sharp mint, and sandalwood to knock that thought into his muddled, stubborn brain. He falls into a deep slumber, dreaming of Dong's voice as he sings to his guitar. The Leonard Cohen song is on repeat. The sweetness is restored.

Chapter 25: What's It Going to Take to Break You

Simon wakes up from the sweet voice dripping in his eardrums like the most potent honey. A soft melody rings in the room, bringing with it a sense of calm and peace like he has never known before.

"There's nothing I can do
If you only knew I don't mind making room
I just want more of you
What's it gonna take to—"

"Hey, you are up early," Simon grumbles, fumbling with the pillow in his half-asleep state, "Why do you hate sleep so much?"

"Oh, did I wake you? Sorry." Dong loosens his earbuds, facing Simon with a beaming smile. He is putting on his pants, an oversized shirt hugging him in the most adorable way, and Simon can't help the beating of his heart as his mind tells him, *This is what perfection looks like.*

"It is the most beautiful way to be woken up," Simon says, his eyes conveying a million words he can't utter. "G'morning."

"Sweet talker." Dong giggles, climbing into the twin bed they shared last night, cupping Simon's face in his palms. His eyes are twinkling in the still-dark room. "I have to go to school. Will you be here when I'm back or will you go home?"

"I want to be here, but I don't think I can be away from home one more day without my dad calling the cops. Where's my phone?"

Dong takes the fully charged phone from the nightstand and hands it to Simon. "Here's your phone, Your Highness."

Simon snuggles up to the comfortable warmth of Dong's body and his cozy oversized shirt, waiting for his phone to restart. The other boy keeps humming an upbeat melody softly into his ears, seemingly the continuation of what he was singing earlier. Simon perks up, wanting to ask the song's name, but a barrage of notifications stops him in his tracks.

Twelve missed calls. Thirty messages. The last text hits him straight through his eyes, hurting his brain: "Simon, I was wrong. It was my fault. It was always my fault."

He drops the phone on the duvet, staring blankly ahead. His brain is telling him he's won the battle, but his heart is wailing that he's lost the war. He can feel Dong's worried gaze following his apathetic movements, but his mouth refuses to open, the words refuse to come through, and no coherent thoughts form in his muddled brain. He hates how right Dong was, and he loves the boy for it. *Never mind*, Simon repeats like a mantra. *What does it matter? Whatever I try to do, I can't gather spilled milk into the golden chalice and turn it into wine.*

Smirking at the irony, he picks up the phone, scrolling through the missed calls and the unread messages, pondering the existential question that is now tailored to his situation: To call or not to call? He wonders if it will fix anything at all. The past is a foregone conclusion, and the future is not in his hands. Words are just droplets of salt carelessly thrown into the ocean of hurt. He knows better than to hold on to the belief that a simple apology will mend a generational war.

Dong punches his chest quietly like a cat's paws kneading on soft flesh. His eyes linger on Simon's face, wrought with worry and a keen sorrow that is always there, even when things are happy and blissful. "What's wrong?" Dong asks.

"I think my dad broke."

"What do you mean?" Dong sits up, alarmed, then he quiets down in a hushed tone. "How's your father?"

"I don't know. He said he was sorry. Damn right he should be."

"Simon, that's no way to talk about your parents."

"You talked about yours the same way just a few days ago."

"I didn't swear. I didn't cuss. And I certainly never thought that my parents should be sorry for anything."

"Well, what do you know about my parents, then?" Simon growls, then quickly withdraws his fangs and claws when the pain on Dong's face tears his skin apart. "I'm sorry, I was way out of line."

"You don't have to be. You are right. I know nothing about your suffering. I just—I think my origin and the way I was raised will haunt me to the end of my days. It's hard to think for yourself when you are taught since the day you were born that you owe your parents your life." Dong smiles gingerly. "Forget it. Let's not talk about things that will hurt us both. I'm sorry."

"Don't be. Just—gosh, I wish I knew how to say things in the right way." Simon tousles his hair. The strands are sticking up everywhere. He keeps hurting the person he loves most. Will it always be this way? "Dong, I don't want to put the blame on you. I guess this is too much for me. I don't expect him to care—my dad, that is. And if it seems like he cares now,

I still don't believe it. I think he is faking it, if you can fake an apology, that is. It's hard to trust the man who's always abandoned me. That's all."

Simon burrows his head into the crook of Dong's neck, using the warmth to ground himself in his shelter. As the wet sensation spreads through his skin, Dong realizes that Simon is breaking down slowly like the fall of a decaying angel, and he is trying not to show his agony. Dong pats Simon's head gently, unsure of what to do. He feels a gnawing sense of remorse as he reminisces about his less-than-perfect meeting with Simon's father. If he had acted a bit differently, with more tact and manners—the proper way he had been raised by his mother—now would be a perfect time to reach out to Mr. Wiseman and be the bridge that Simon needs. But a thousand if-onlys can do so much, and given the choice again, Dong doubts he would have acted differently. He thinks of Mr. Wiseman's oppressive anger, of Simon's attitude of surrender, and of the reluctance he shows every time the word "home" is uttered. *No*, Dong thinks, shaking his head, shooing away the disturbance. *Who would allow their beloved person to return to that?*

Dong feels the quiet tremor on his shoulders each time Simon tries to suppress a sob. It seems that God is punishing him for a crime he didn't commit. A crime someone pushed into his hands without allowing him a chance to defend himself. "Do you want to ask Ms. Dolores if you can stay?" he asks, giving up on hope, knowing that Ms. Dolores has done far too much for him, and there's only so much baggage a person can handle.

"Don't. I'm already pathetic enough," Simon says, breathing through a bitter laugh.

"I don't think you are pathetic. Simon, this is only temporary."

"Everything is temporary. What will be eternal, then?" Simon looks at Dong, almost too wistful and desperate to accept an earnest answer. Dong averts his gaze, biting his lower lip to prevent himself from bursting out with a frustrated scream. *Oh, the bubble of happiness, thou art a heartless bitch.*

"You don't have to force yourself to go back if you don't want to. It's your choice, Simon. Live your life the way you want. Don't be anyone's ghost," he mutters into Simon's hair.

"I am seventeen, going on eighteen. I don't have my own money. My private school's tuition is paid for by my father. The clothes I wear, the shoes I have on, the parties I attend—don't be anyone's ghost, you say, but Dong, I am living my life in borrowing mode. What else can I be?"

"You can be free. You are young. And no amount of money can take that away. Not yet."

Dong looks at him, a fierce fire in his eyes. It is the burning passion that is procured from generations of his people, always fighting war upon war upon war for peace. The desire to be free runs in his blood, seemingly since the first Vietnamese man claimed his stake on the unknown land. Resist and rebel, Dong's eyes say, echoing the marching shout and drums of soldiers from the long, arduous past.

He has never known how to back down. Such is the fate of his life. Such is the fate of his race. Blood and steel on soft earth, but once in a while, when a soft smile appears on his face, one might forget how fierce the lion's soul within him can roar. Facing a soul like that, Simon doesn't have any other option than to surrender completely to the side of endless victory—the victory of the heart. He sighs into the sweet embrace of his boy, small in stature but larger than life in his bravery and the dormant untamed fearlessness within him, feeling safe in the knowledge that he is sheltered from the storm.

"Should I call him back?" Simon asks, already knowing the answer.

"Well, yeah. He's your father."

"Sometimes, I wonder why you are so kind to the world while it never shows you kindness."

"Simon, oh, poor Simon." Dong laughs, merrily tousling Simon's bedhead. "It's the only way to move forward. Hatred can only get you so far. You know that more than I do, don't you?"

The dark-haired boy gazes tenderly at the larger frame in his arms. The sweetness of his touch and the love emanating from the tips of his fingers soothe whatever monsters are raging inside Simon. He sighs, surrendering to a force greater than himself. Growing up inside that house, he learned long ago there are things he can hold and there are things he can only stand on the sideline to watch fall. His mind wanders back to the last conversation, or rather, the bitter bickering between him and his father. The pain he caused and the hurt he suffered—he wonders if there will be retribution for them. If there is, Simon doesn't think he can pay the price Heaven asks. What will become of him then? *Freedom*, he thinks, *costs more than a simple word on a page in the dictionary. And yet people continue to fight for it.*

"I think I will go back home," Simon says after a deep moment of contemplation.

"When?"

"Today. In the afternoon. Or evening. Or never."

"There are things you should think rather than speak aloud," Dong scolds him, then he jumps off the bed and gets ready for school.

He puts the textbooks and the various notebooks neatly into his canvas bag, decorated with Lizzie and Ames's drawings and animated character pins. An adult personality hidden between the layers of childish impulses. Such is the boy Simon adores. Such is the treasure the world wants to bury. In the dimly lit room, the first light of the morning is slanting through the window blinds. The weather is growing colder outside. The dust is floating in the air with every movement Dong makes. The scent of books and papers, the sound of hands tapping the soft cover to swipe off last night's wrong answers, and the humming of a forgotten melody—they all lull Simon back to sleep once again. The last thing he remembers before closing his eyes is a tender kiss on his forehead, ripened with the scent of berries, and a voice whispering in his ears, "Sleep tight. Remember, whatever happens, I love you." It is so peaceful and warm, Simon wants to weep in his sleep.

The next time he wakes up, Dong is nowhere to be found.

Judging from the time on the clock on the nightstand, Simon deduces that Dong must still be in class. *Great*, he thinks, rolling his eyes, *I skipped another day.* He scrolls through his phone again, but there are no calls from either his father or his stepmom. He wonders how long it would take for them to forget that he exists. Perhaps one night is enough. Brushing off the voices inside his head, he gets off the bed and tiptoes out of the room. The house is empty. The hallway is eerily silent. It is daytime so he understands this silence to mean everyone is at work. He has the whole house for himself.

Swallowing hard, he clutches his heart in both excitement and trembling fear, imagining himself as the explorer of a new territory. A new world. An adventure no one knows, not even Dong. A journey that is his and his alone.

With that in mind, Simon heads downstairs and finds the kitchen, realizing he hasn't had breakfast yet.

Scrolling through his newsfeed while munching on a sloppy peanut butter and jelly sandwich, Simon expects to find some shocking posts from his friends about his absences these two consecutive days and the party he never attended. There is nothing. He chuckles to himself at his own naivete. What was he thinking? He is not that important. No one ever is. A girl in his class posted a photo with her friends and a handsome boy. He forgot the boy's name. She mentions him as her boyfriend, and he laughs the bread out. The same girl confessed her feelings for him just a few days ago. *Ah,* Simon thinks, *just how shallow life can be, and how deep I need to wallow.*

He cleans the dishes, texts Dong that he misses him already, and patters back upstairs. Rummaging through Dong's scant belongings and reveling in the illegality of the act, Simon finds a euphoric feeling. He hopes to find some secret diaries, a few more unsent letters, or something he can use to tease the boy later. More than that, he hopes to find a good enough reason to tell Dong why he is still here, at Ms. Dolores's house, when Dong gets back from school though he clearly said that he'd go home. The end justifies the means—isn't that always the path?

Absent-mindedly, he picks up the various books still in the moving boxes. Joyce. Hemingway. Faulkner. Dostoyevsky. Some other names he doesn't bother to remember. No wonder Dong has aged so fast; Simon has never met another teenager whose reading taste matches Dong's. Giving up on the boring masterpieces, better left untouched and revered in silence, Simon moves to the box in the corner of the room, marked "Miscellaneous" in red ink. He dives in headfirst because he expects the worst. But treasure is often found that way.

Inside the box, there are heaps upon heaps of notebooks and papers. The writings are clear and neat. Simon can see with amusement how Dong changes his pen colors often, but they are just different shades of blue. There are poems, short stories, essays, and sometimes, there are silly short pieces such as, "Who pushes Alissa into the suffocating door frame? Who knows? Life sucks. I want to eat ice cream." He laughs at the innocence of it all. Be it the deep musing in the uneven rhyme scheme, the amateur story structure but plenty of symbolism and metaphorical language, or the severe need to eat ice cream, Simon loves it all. This is Dong, contained in twenty notebooks, 200written pages, ten shades of blue pen, and the silliness that only Simon will ever know so intimately.

He turns the pages briefly, wondering who Alissa is and why Dong cares about that girl so much. A smoldering feeling rises up inside him. What is that suffocating door frame? But the rest of that notebook gives little hints except a few more passages on André Gide, whose name Simon has never heard of before. He surmises from the books that he is yet another great name in literature. He can do without that. What he wants to see and read is the life Dong has been living. As Simon agonizes over the budding realization of their differences in the years of their separation, a call comes through. He glances at the screen. It is his father. With reluctance, he presses the green button.

"Hey, Dad."

"Simon, hey. So. Um." On the other side, his father's voice is hesitant and wrought with worry. It seems he barely had any rest. He is hoarse and tired. A part of Simon is drowning in guilt.

"My phone ran out of battery," he quickly says, trying to ease the gnawing teeth biting at his conscience.

"Yeah. Yeah. No worries. I understand. I thought as much. Listen. Um. Where are you right now? I think I can come by to pick you up. We can have lunch or dinner together, just the two of us, and talk things out. You know, like old times. How about that?"

Just the two of us. Like old times. Simon chews on those words and tastes their bitterness on his tongue like they are poison. Trust is not a one-way passage, and he has given up on trying. His father has finally looked his way, but he no longer wants the attention. Selfish. Selfless. He is standing at a crossroad, deciding between the person he wants to become and the person people expect him to become. His father calls his name softly, "Simon?" Dong's whisper this morning echoes in his mind:*"Remember, whatever happens, I love you."*

Yes, he thinks, *trust is not a one-way passage.* And while his father burns the forest Simon bleeds to cross, Dong has quietly laid down another path for him to walk forward.

He grips the phone tightly in his hand, then with a firm voice and an unshakable determination, he says, "Let's have lunch, then. I'm at Dong's new place. There's no one here and I must leave anyway. I will come back home, and we can figure out where to have lunch. Talk things out. Make decisions. Do all the things we need to. But father, dear?"

"Yes?" the muddled voice answers him. No anger. No authority. Just a pure weakness and subdued power.

"You can't rebuild a burned bridge, can you?"

The line stays silent for longer than Simon can bear. Finally, he bids his father a quick goodbye and hangs up. He is hurt enough. Now, he will step on the pain to live again. What was the song Dong sang this morning? Right...

What's it gonna take to break your heart?

Simon burrows his face in the pillow, breathing in the scent of pine trees and peppermint. The tears flow free. He weeps without knowing. This. This is what it takes to break his heart.

Chapter 26: Conversation at Seventeen

When Dong gets back from school, Simon is nowhere to be found. The house remains silent for a brief second before Lizzie and Ames storm in with their bursting energy and their roaring laughter at their silly gossip about some mean girls.

Dong looks at the vast emptiness all around, feeling like something has been stolen from his life without his permission. He clutches his school bags. The heavy textbooks remind him of the burden he used to bear. His mom, Ms. Hoa, is still at the nail salon, discussing their living situation with her boss. Ms. Dolores is at the hospital, worrying about the life and death of other strangers. Absent-mindedly, Dong walks to his room, not heeding the girls' calls. In a dream-like state, he searches for signs of Simon's existence. The shirt, the sandalwood scent, the beaming smile when he turns the doorknob—anything to prove that last night was real. But Simon has vanished into thin air, leaving behind a well-cleaned room and a tidy bookshelf. The unpacked boxes remain where they are, which surprises Dong. He secretly hoped Simon would peruse them and find inside each layer of dust the longing he buried through the years they were apart.

With a lingering touch, he picks up the blanket and inhales the leftover woody scent on the fabric. Behind closed eyes, the boy he loves is still in the same room.

"D-dog, what are you doing?"

Ames calls him for the third time with a quizzical look on her face. Lizzie hangs on the door frame, sucking on a cola-flavored lollipop. When she speaks, her cheeks puff up and her words are slurred.

"Simon left again, eh?"

"I don't know," Dong says, the bewilderment barely audible in his hollow voice. "I told him to go home so I guess he did just that."

"When are we going to see Prince Charming again?" Lizzie pops her candy in her mouth and chews the leftover pieces. She seems carefree for someone who's hanging on for dear life with her exams.

"I will let you know when I know. Well, I have his phone number. It's not like he'll be gone forever." Dong smiles a crooked smile, and his hands fumble with the bedsheet.

The scent of sandalwood and peppermint weaved in the fabric is too overwhelming for him. He thought Simon would have waited for him and kissed him goodbye. All those sweet scenes from the movies he watched were deceiving. He bites his lips, torn between the great expectations of his dreams and the harsh reality of his cold bedroom. Alone he's always been and alone he's here again. He flips the duvet over, and to the three teenagers' surprise, a note falls out. Lizzie picks it up as it lands at her feet and she reads it out loud:

"'Got urgent business. I will call you later tonight. Or earlier. Depending on how shit goes down. Whatever happens, remember I love you. Simon.' Oh well, look who's madly in love with our little prince!" Lizzie coos.

"Lizzie, that's inappropriate!" Ames snatches the note from Lizzie's hand and returns it to Dong. The boy clutches it and holds it to his chest like it is a sacred treasure. Simon was here; he wasn't dreaming.

"D-dog, you overthink the littlest of things. Everybody saw him. My mom saw him there. If you were dreaming, then all of us must have been in a big hallucination. Parallel universe and whatnot. Please, give it a rest."

Lizzie rolls her eyes. She's too tired for this whole fiasco. Her mind wanders back to the test this morning, the essay she hasn't written on the Berlin Wall, and all the other walls, or wars, and the comparison between John Steinbeck and whoever that guy was who won a Nobel. She has too many things to do and too little time to do them all. And here's Dong, the one person she's counting on to help her fight the rest of the school year, brooding over his imaginary sorrow. She stomps her feet, knowing she's being unjust yet unable to bear the melodramatic mood further.

"Come on, are we going to tackle the mountain of home-work or not?"

"Oh Lizzie, give it a rest, will you?" Ames scolds her with a stern gaze. "Can't you see D-dog is going through a moment? And it's *your* homework. Do it yourself."

"It's your homework as well," Lizzie murmurs, quietly agreeing to disagree.

"At least I finished my essay on the Berlin Wall."

"The walls. Why does the world love building up walls so much?" Lizzie groans, taking out her notebooks and textbooks. "Can't we just shake hands and hug it out?"

"People don't work like that," Dong interjects from his dark corner of the bed, his eyes beaming up at the sight of his two best friends bickering over trivialities. This is where he belongs. This is his Heaven. "If people worked like that, we wouldn't have to write so many essays. And there wouldn't be so much history to learn."

"Spare me the lecture. Less talk, more action, please." Lizzie shows her blank pages to Dong. She has just put her name and the historical dates on it. Dong laughs at her quirky personality and her impulsive temperament. He's always loved her for that.

Ames stands by the door, looking down at Lizzie in fake contempt. Her essay is not better, but at least she put more effort into it. As she shows Dong her paper with a fully written page about the event, without going into the specific causes or giving her perspective, Lizzie laughs at Ames's attempt to be a scholar.

"So that's what you are going to do? Turn in a paper with content from the textbook, only rephrased?"

"And yours is better? The dates are wrong," Ames bites back.

"Oh, but it's genuine. I have my authenticity and integrity as a true learner." Lizzie acts hurt, but then she bursts out laughing again.

"You two are lost causes." Dong shakes his head and begins to lay out the structure for them to rewrite their essays.

As the three teenagers huddle together to fight against the Berlin Wall, or rather, one teenager dictates and the other two blindly follow, giggling all the while and chiding each other with their snarky comments about their writing, a storm is brewing in a cozy restaurant in downtown Oakville. Lizzie is right—people love building walls. Dong is also right—people can't simply shake hands and hug it out. Like Simon and Mr.

Wiseman with the high wall of indifference between them on the dining table of the Italian restaurant.

"You speak first, father," Simon says after a deafening silence amidst the ambience of piano music.

"After you," Mr. Wiseman mutters while flipping through the menu for the tenth time. He hardly registers the name of the dishes or what he wants for dinner. He only wants to prolong the time. To what end, he doesn't know.

"What's there for me to say? You are the one who wants a conversation." Simon sips on his water, cold and composed, far too old and mature for his young age of seventeen.

"I think it's high time we have a conversation, don't you think so? You are seventeen, eh? Gosh, how time flies." Mr. Wiseman chuckles nervously, wiping his forehead.

"Yeah. Especially when no one seems to care."

"Simon, look, it's not that I don't want to care. I love you; you must believe me. See, if I didn't love or care about you as much, I wouldn't pay for your school and—" Mr. Wiseman stops halfway. He chokes on his words as he faces the burning hatred from Simon's dark and unbreakable gaze.

"Yeah. That's pretty loving. Throw a heap of money on someone and surely they will love you back."

"That is not what I'm trying to say."

"But it is what you are saying nonetheless," Simon says with a voice as light as air, and it breaks Mr. Wiseman's heart. He flounders in the dark, trying to find the right words, but they keep eluding him. It's ironic how he can persuade the toughest bankers, but not his teenage son who can shut him up with a few simple words.

"Simon," Mr. Wiseman says in a futile attempt to salvage their relationship, "I want to explain my side of the story."

"Your side of the story? Let me distill it down for you. Your side of the story is you and Mom discovered that I'm gay. You both shifted the blame, as if I was the shame of the whole Wiseman family. Then you got a divorce, and neither of you took a moment to think or care about what I would think. Neither of you knew I took it all on me, thinking I was a faulty product. A black dot on an otherwise spotlessly white page. You remarried, got yourself another son. Sweet and cute little darling that he is—you forgot all about me. I was in the dark all those years, struggling to find a place to belong. Do you know how hard it is to be perfect? No, you were too busy living it. Your side of the story." He hisses each word between clenched teeth. "Don't make me laugh."

Mr. Wiseman closes the menu. There's no point in prolonging the meal or talking things out and hoping mere words of affection will save anything. He ponders on Simon's fury and his outburst. The calm and the composure with which he uttered the most painful sentences. Mr. Wiseman pinches his nose, stopping the oncoming tears. *"Throw a heap of money on someone and surely they will love you back."* The words are such a sharp piercing knife and Mr. Wiseman is helpless against the attack.

"I thought that was the only right thing to do. You wouldn't have wanted to suffer the arguments between your mom and me. And—" Mr. Wiseman says in defeat.

"But I still suffered, didn't I? Whatever. All things end."

"Simon, I didn't mean to hurt you. It's not that I don't accept you. Things take time. I had hoped that—"

"That I would change?" The smile on Simon's face borders on being vicious and filled with malice. It scares Mr. Wiseman. This is not the son he used to love and understand like the back of his hand.

"No. No, that's not—I simply hoped you would be happy."

"And I wasn't. Until now."

"That is a temporary solution." Mr. Wiseman can't help himself.

"To what problem? Father, I'm not a five-year-old boy. You can't paint a picture in gold and tell me that it's a pirate's treasure. I will find my way. Whether it's temporary or not, I will be the judge of that."

"Since when did I stop being the judge of that?" Mr. Wiseman raises his voice in despair, then lowers his head. He foresees the answer, but he can't accept the ending.

"Since the moment you said you wanted to have a conversation with me. The first one. Three years ago."

They proceed to eat in complete silence, each pursuing their own thoughts. Mr. Wiseman can't give up the dream of winning his son back. The nagging voice in his head tells him to push forward, but his heart laments that it is all too late. No one wants to gather the spilled water and call it wine. Simon, on the other hand, thinks about his future. He might have to give up on his private school and the parties. If he saves a little bit of money, he will have the bare minimum to enroll in a good college. He's dipped his feet into screenwriting and directing a few times, and he loves orchestrating a life on screen. Perhaps—no, this time, he will choose the life he wants to live, not the life someone wants for him. Munching on the tender steak, the father and son savor the last moment in each other's company. Mr. Wiseman grips his knife, unwilling to give up.

"You're always welcome at the house," he says.

"Thanks," Simon says, startled from his train of thought. "I will think about it."

"Think about it? What do you mean?" Mr. Wiseman asks, dropping his fork in surprise with a loud clang.

"Meaning I plan to leave the house."

"No, you won't."

"Yes, I will. I'm staying at a friend's, and after graduating high school, I will move to a dorm. Pretty neat, eh?" He smirks.

"Whose house? Where will your money come from? And what about tuition?"

"Alex's. From my part-time jobs' savings. OSAP," Simon replies with terse words.

"I won't allow it."

"And I'm not surprised. You hardly allow anything outside of your sketched-out plan and strategy. Father, sadly I'm not a piece on your chessboard. Thanks for the meal."

Simon wipes his mouth and stands up with determination. He places his share of the meal on the table, puts on his coat, and walks away. Facing the empty seat, Mr. Wiseman swallows all his unspoken words, feeling betrayed by his own blood. Something is broken, and he doesn't know how to mend it. In absolute despair, he breaks down at the table of the cozy restaurant and cries.

Life is about losing everything, and as a Wiseman, he knows that. But knowing never guarantees understanding, and accepting is a whole new region he is just now stepping into. He wonders where he went wrong. Since the day he abandoned Simon on his own, leaving the boy helpless to fend for himself at the new school, totally oblivious to the pain he was enduring, Mr. Wiseman has been spiraling. He thought it would make Simon stronger. More masculine. But did it make him more or less of a human? Mr. Wiseman never thought of that. Right and wrong. Black and white. How could he see through everything when the only color in his eyes right now is a blurry grayness of his Simon leaving, lost forever?

Outside, Simon texts Dong: "I cut everything off." He breathes in the sharp cold air of the night. He knows Dong won't accept his choice. The boy may reprimand him, even. But Dong has a mother who loves him back. Simon has nothing. No mother before. No father now. He runs to his car in the parking lot opposite the restaurant, feeling freedom blowing in his hair. *It's alright,* he thinks, biting back the fear, adrenaline surging through his veins. *I will make it through another night. Humans are born to survive, and I will live to testify to it.*

In the dark bedroom, Dong reads the text with a heavy heart. His finger hovers over the call button, but he decides against it. It is Simon's life, and he has every right to cut off anything he doesn't want. Dong thinks of Mr. Wiseman, the worry on his face, the care and the tenderness in his eyes when he asked about Simon's wellbeing on that day of Ms. Hoa's incident. He turns in his bed, chewing his nails with a strange anxiety. He knows it is wrong, cutting things off with someone who cares for you that much. But he also knows that he's never been through what Simon's been through. What he sees is but a fleeting glimmer of a movie, and movies are deceiving. After tossing in bed for a long while, he texts back: "Whatever happens, I trust you. Eternally. With love."

Sinking into a dreamless sleep, Dong's mind wanders constantly between the realms of the past and the future. What is lying ahead and who is waiting there for him? He prays in the dark that life will be gentle, and that he will live to testify to it.

Chapter 27: Alexandra Lost

Time flies like the unforgiving bitch it is and always has been, and before they know it, it's the end of May. Five months pass by the group of four youths like an arrow flying south at the speed of light.

Between the university applications, overnight study sessions with Ames and Lizzy, and final exams, Dong could hardly find space in his mind to miss or think about Simon. His terse text messages, "How are you holding on?" and the simple, curt replies, "I'm doing fine," can't convey the immense ocean of hurt and longing each of them was going through. Dong kept thinking there would be a tomorrow when he'd be free enough, kind enough, tender and loving enough to type a longer message, or call and talk to Simon for hours.

But that tomorrow never came.

Now, he sits in front of his desk with his laptop open, waiting for the result of another university application. Two rejections have come through, and he doesn't mind. He bet everything on the last one, which often takes longer to reply—the top university in the country. The one and only University of Toronto. Crossing his fingers, he counts the hours and minutes while watching his mailbox with bated breath. He doesn't hear Ames knocking on the door and her quiet entrance. "D-dog," she calls, a strange tone of detachment in her voice.

"Ames, what are you doing here? I'm sorry I didn't notice you coming in." Dong quickly stands up and pushes a bean bag to her place by the door, but Ames refuses the kind offer. "Is something wrong?" he asks, intrigued by her distant attitude.

"I just came to say goodbye." Ames looks at him, her mind running through the years they spent together. The laughter, the tears, and the conversations they shared in the school library. She bites her lip, trying to keep it all in, but the memories are bursting in her mind like an explosive.

"Goodbye? What are you saying? Oh, Ames, don't cry."

Dong rushes to Ames as the girl can't use the high indifference of coldness and detachment to defend her broken heart anymore. She holds on to Dong's shoulders.

"I'm leaving tomorrow with my mom. We are relocating to Alberta. Housing is cheaper there, and she said she could pay for my tuition if we moved away from the GTA. Oh, I don't want to, but it's Mom. She's been through so much since everything happened with my dad. And I dare not tell her that I don't want to. Why am I so useless? Dong, why are we so useless?" Ames sobs into the boy's chest, wetting his T-shirt.

"I don't know," Dong says, confused and at a loss for words. "I'd thought as long as I could get a university degree, it would be alright. Isn't that what we were taught to believe?"

"But Dong, where is the money for your degree coming from? If I have to watch my mom work another job, I'd rather have no degree at all." Ames bawls her eyes out. Her low bellows raise the anxious monster within Dong. He asks himself the same question, *Yes, where is the money coming from?*

"Listen, Ames," Dong says quickly, half reassuring her, half trying to reassure himself, "you can apply for OSAP, then work part-time for your tuition. After graduating, you can get a job and pay the government back. A university degree means more job opportunities with higher salaries, doesn't it? And you can secure a stable future for both you and your mom. That's where your strength comes from. Perseverance, Ames. You need to persevere. Don't give up. Don't say we can't do anything," Dong pleads, more to himself than to Ames.

"But who can guarantee that I will get a job after graduating, D-dog?" Ames questions him, doubt glazing her eyes. "You, sure. You have the best grades. Graduating high school as valedictorian. Applying to top universities. You will probably get a high-paying job. But me, I barely have anything to prove. My grades are barely good enough to pass. There are plenty of me in the sea, D-dog, while there will only be a few of you."

"Oh, Ames, don't talk about yourself as if you are nothing." Dong starts sobbing.

"But I *am* nothing. Not everyone will shine. Some of us have to accept being the darkness so a few of you can be light, don't you think? Did you ever consider that I was envious? Oh, D-dog, look at you, good at studying, both parents are alive. Your father is abusive, yes, but your mother loves you, and now, you have Simon who's doing everything to be with you. While I—what do I have beside my mom?" Ames screams as she pushes Dong away.

Dong stares back at her in bewilderment; he's never seen Ames so fierce and furious. A sudden anger rises within him; he doesn't wish for Ames's life to be this way. He is not the cause of her misery. Simon's weary smile comes back to his mind. *You haven't lived the life I lead.* He clenches his fists, trying to temper his breathing. Everyone is asking him to sympathize with them. Be it his mom, Simon, or Ames—they all want his understanding. But the question stands, and the question stays true: Will he continue to be this way forever, smiling and accepting whatever they throw his way, the guilt, the fault, the blame, and everything in between so his beloved can feel better about themselves? In a fit of rage, Dong talks back for the first time since meeting Ames and Lizzie.

"None of that is my fault, is it? Don't blame your misery on me."

"What?" Ames takes two steps back, taken aback by his attitude.

"I mean, sure, I'm sad about you leaving. The whole situation is a mess. I would never wish that for you or for anyone else. But I don't have any control over any of that, do I? And why do I have to feel guilty for being the best at studying? That's the only thing I'm good at. Look at me, do I have any other friends beside you and Lizzie? My mom loves me, sure. But it took me nearly killing myself for her to turn around and realize the way she loved me was pushing me to the edge. Why are you wishing for the life I lead? You don't know what I've been through!" Dong shouts the last sentence and deflates like a popped balloon. His breathing becomes ragged and uneven.

"Is that what you are thinking? Do you know what I've been through, then?" Ames asks, trembling with indignation. She feels unfair, but a part of her regrets what she's been throwing at Dong. She knows in her heart that Dong never meant to hurt her in any way. But it's so hard to look from the other side when anger is the only thing in front of her eyes.

"What I want to say is why can't we sit down and calmly talk things over? I'm as sad as you are about your leaving, Ames. You and Lizzie are my best friends." Dong hangs his head, nearly crying. He can't bear the heavy atmosphere. The air is suffocating.

"There's nothing to talk about. You—"

But before Ames can finish another hurtful remark, Lizzie barges into the room, panting with excitement.

"D-dog, did you check your email? Did you get in? Oh my God, I got accepted to McMaster. Hey, all thanks to you, old friend." She slaps Dong on his shoulders. "And Ames, did you check your email? D-dog got rejected twice already. Hey, why do you two look like you've just been to a funeral?"

"I haven't checked. Ames got here a half hour ago. I haven't had time," Dong says meekly, brushing Lizzie's arm off his back.

"Go on. Check it then. It's not like I'm stopping you," Ames replies curtly, folding her arms, closing off the world between her and the other two.

"Wait. What?" Lizzie, the cheery summer breeze that is passing through the winter storm in the room, can't help but wonder about the cause of the Cold War.

Dong walks to his laptop and opens his mailbox. A new email lies there for him to open, but he doesn't need to. The simple subject line "Congratulations! We offer you..." is enough to let him know that his wish has come true. The one and only Toronto has chosen him. But happiness can't come through. He stands there, listless in the slanting afternoon sun, feeling cheated of a prize he worked so hard to obtain. Lizzie stares at him with a quizzical look, wondering what has happened in his laptop that makes him so sad.

"D-dog, don't be sad, you can reapply next year, okay?" she says, expecting the worst.

"I got in," Dong mutters without strength.

"See? There's no way he wouldn't get the best of the best." Ames bursts out crying, running out of the room and slamming the door behind.

Lizzie looks after her, growing even more curious about what passed between Ames and Dong in that tiny frame of thirty minutes. She walks to where Dong stands, rigid as a statue, tapping his arm.

"What's wrong with her?" she asks.

"She's leaving for Alberta with her mom."

"She's what? Well, that explains the anger, but why is she aiming it at you?"

"Lizzie, do you ever feel envious of me? Like I receive all the good things, but I don't deserve it? Like you should have been the one blessed with a good brain or something?" Dong turns to look at her, smiling ruefully. His eyes shine with a soft sorrow, old beyond his years.

"What? No. Why would I? We were born with different abilities. You are good at studying. I'm good at communication and social skills. Fish will swim and monkeys will climb trees, why are you asking me this question? Don't tell me—it's Ames?" Lizzie asks, astonished by her own question. "No way, it can't be."

"Ames said she's always been envious of my life."

"That crazy girl. She's mad with grief."

"But she's right, isn't she? I just—I don't know. If I'm not as good at studying, maybe she will feel better. But I don't want to, Lizzie. I don't want to concede anything just for the sake of another person. This is my life; shouldn't I be proud of it? Why should I take the blame? Why should I feel guilty for getting accepted to University of Toronto?" Dong rests his head on Lizzie's shoulders. The girl pats his head, consoling

271

him like a wounded child who refuses to cry.

"You have no reason to feel guilt. Ames is not in the best place to think about anything else right now. D-dog, when people are hurt, they can only focus on their own pain. You know it best, don't you? Just let her go. People come and people leave. If it is meant to be, perhaps she'll return someday."

"Are you leaving too, Lizzie?"

"I will be living at McMaster, but I will come back home for the holidays, so we'll still see each other, right?" She smiles, cupping his face in her hands.

"How long do we have?"

"Well, let's leave tomorrow's questions for tomorrow. For now, congratulations for getting into the one and only Toronto. How's your mom's house search going?"

"It's going alright. I think we will be ready to move out by the end of this month. Thank you for helping us this whole time. You and your mom. We don't know what we would have done without your support."

"Come on. Aren't we best friends?" Lizzie laughs, hugging him close. She tries to hide the tears in her eyes, but Dong can see them. And he can also hear the quiet sobs in her chest as she cheers him on.

That night, Dong stares at his phone screen for ten minutes straight before pressing the call button. He waits with mounting anxiety. Two rings. Three rings. Many rings go through. Then Simon picks up, and he is greeted by a gruff voice instead of the usual soft and loving tone.

"Hey."

"Hey, um, I hope I'm not bothering you?"

"In fact, you are," Simon says. Dong chuckles, thinking it is their usual banter. But after an eerie silence on the other line, he realizes it is not a joke.

"Oh, is that so? Should I call back at another time?"

"No. It's okay. I was thinking of driving to your place anyway."

"At this hour?"

"What? Your mom still controls you as much as ever?" Simon teases and Dong can imagine his smug face with that haughty smirk.

"No, I was just afraid that it would tire you out. Your voice sounds like you need a rest."

"It's fine. Just settling into my new place. Will be there in a few—well, in twenty minutes."

"What—"

Simon hangs up before Dong can raise his questions. Dong's mind starts racing with a million thoughts. A new place? What about his parents? His school? Twenty minutes, does this mean he is close by? He bites his nails, shuffling his feet in the duvet, trying to piece the puzzle together. He is smart and he feels sure that he can get to the bottom of this. But the more he thinks about Simon's situation, the more he is befuddled. They have only texted each other since Simon had his argument with his dad. Dong realizes how little time he's actually spent on Simon. People come and people leave, Lizzie said. But will Simon leave, too? What is Dong doing, sacrificing everything for Toronto? Unable to bear his racing thoughts, Dong jumps out of bed and heads for the door.

As he walks out of the entrance, a car stops in front of the driveway of Ms. Dolores's house. He squints his eyes in the darkness. A shadow comes out of the driver's seat, locks the car, walks to the opposite side, leans on the passenger window, and lights up a cigarette. A pair of wise eyes pierces through Dong's soul. The shadow is Simon. Dong runs down the path leading to the dark Honda Civic, unaware of the run-down exterior and the different color, too busy focusing on the cigarette, the jean jacket, and the rugged appearance of the person who has grown apart from him in a span of five months. Simon grins, but Dong feels like weeping.

"Hey," the taller boy says. His voice is rough and hoarse. The tone has lost the soft edge of innocence, but somehow, the warmth still lingers.

"What happened? Oh, Simon, you are smoking. And the car. And the clothes. What's going on?" Dong fusses over Simon like a mother hen. He touches his jacket, his faded shirt, and every inch he can grasp without offending the other boy. A voice echoes in his mind: *People come, and people leave.* He fears the worst and hopes for the best.

"Well, stuff." Simon takes a puff of his cigarette, mindful not to let the smoke get in Dong's face. "Care to join me for a drive?"

"I don't mind, but—"

"Then hop in. It's not much but it'll give us privacy to talk."

He opens the passenger door, and with hesitant steps, Dong climbs inside. The car jerks into motion and with a swerve, Simon drives them out of the comfort and peaceful neighborhood. Dong looks back at the passing lights, clutching his seatbelt. The shrouding silence in the car claws at his heart. He can feel the visceral grip on his throat. Soon, they are on a highway. He wants to ask where they are heading, but a look at Simon's profile in the dark makes him swallow all his words.

"Eyes on the road." Simon turns on the signal light and exits the highway. They are driving back to Oakville.

"My eyes are still on the road."

"Yeah. Remember the scenery closely. This might be the last time in a long while you see it." Simon smirks, more to himself than to Dong.

"What do you mean?"

"Here we are."

They stop at a park. Dong detects the sign, Gairloch Garden. The night is clear and crisp. The summer breeze is whispering in the dark leaves of the old maple trees. Dong sits still, asking no one in particular, "Now what?"

"Get off and take a stroll, or we can sit here forever."

"What do you want me to do?" The despair in Dong's voice is audible in the still night air.

"No, what do *you* want to do, Dong?"

"I don't know. I seriously don't know. What happened to you? Why don't we start with that?" he screams, then burrows his face in his knees, hiding his quiet cries. Something is trickling through the cracks in his armor, and he's losing it quickly.

"I cut things off with my father. I told you that much."

"Then?"

"Then, I finished my high school diploma. Living out the rest of his money. He already paid for the year. Just got my degree. I will be attending an art college in September. No more privilege and luxury and all that glittering shit." Simon laughs. "I quit. Here's the real me."

"You mean, the run-down car, the jacket, the rugged appearance, and the smoking habit?" Dong lifts his head, his eyes glazed over with tears. How much did Simon have to endure all these months without telling him? The pain and

275

the suffering shine in his eyes like a trademark no one wants to claim; a burden he bears as a sacrifice for his freedom. "You gave it all up for what?"

"I want to be a person. That's all," Simon says, drawing another hit. "I traded my expensive car for a cheaper one, saved enough money for a shared room with a roommate. I signed up for OSAP, took on part-time jobs. No mother. No father. Alone I was born and alone I am here again. Don't cry, it isn't as bad as all that. I'm living my life how I want to. And you should do the same."

Under the dim streetlight, Simon kisses the teardrops on Dong's reddened cheeks—the first sign of tenderness since the trip started. The feeling of chapped lips on his soft skin puts one word in Dong's mind: solitude. So this is what Simon has been through—abandoned and forsaken by everyone and anyone who claimed to love him no matter what. Even Dong, who is no better. All those tumultuous months he never thought about calling Simon just to hear him weep. He focused on the exams, the grades he'd get, the applications to the universities, the choices he needed to make to get onto another path. The way out of this little town.

He grips Simon's jacket, breathing in the new scent. The smoke, the sandalwood, the piercing mint, and something uniquely Simon. Something like a whole night sleeping out in the car under the starry sky, dreaming about another place— any place would be better. He wishes he could be the shelter Simon needs, but it is all too late for a new beginning. The night is closing in on them. They are struggling in a new battle under the same sky with different enemies. How can he convey to Simon everything he has buried in his heart for years? The love that keeps on burning is as cruel and bright as it was the first time he saw Simon standing there, playing basketball with his group of friends.

"Are you leaving me?" Dong finally manages to say his voice weak and exhausted.

"Do you want me to?"

"I don't. Do you?"

"I don't deserve someone like you, Dong." Simon ruffles the other boy's hair, kissing his forehead and letting the touch linger there longer than he should. "By the time you finish university, you might want someone else. Better educated, higher degree, taller, more handsome—"

"But he would not be you," Dong cries, desperate and distressed. "He will never be you. How can you say that? Simon, you are the one I love. You are my Alexandra. My one and only Alexandra."

"Maybe Alexandra was lost long ago."

"Then I will find her." Dong cups Simon's face in his palm, his eyes sparkling. In a fleeting moment, Simon thinks he sees the hope and the reason to keep on going. As he reaches out his hand to touch the light, Dong leans in and places a deep kiss on his lips, speaking between breaks. "This time, let the more loving one be me."

As greedy as the first human born on Earth, Simon swallows each kiss eagerly. He sits up, pulling Dong's head closer, devouring the sweet fruit of his lips as if this were their last night together. The ragged breath fogs up the car windows. He doesn't want to let go. In the most urgent moment, he realizes what he doesn't want to lose the most, what he's been fighting for all this time, why he's sacrificing everything to become who he is, the cause and the meaning of his life: to be by Dong's side, to live with him. Yes, all things end, but wouldn't it be so much sweeter if they could end in each other's embrace?

"I never want to let you go," Simon says, wiping the tears from Dong's eyes, their foreheads touching. He leans in for another brief kiss, but Dong stops him.

"Then promise me."

"Promise what?"

"In six years, I will be starting my medical residency. I applied for a major in psychology at the University of Toronto and got accepted. I will specialize in Children Development." Simon smiles sweetly at the words. He expected nothing less from his angel. "Don't laugh. I will be helping kids like you, Ames, Lizzie, and me. In six years, what will you be doing?"

"Screenwriting. Or directing."

"Okay, aim to be a director then. Have a short film out. I will be watching. Then come to me. Propose on your knee. I don't need a fancy ring. You just need to be there, and I will say yes. You hear me? Promise me, Simon, that you will do it."

Simon looks into those strong, determined eyes, wondering why the only one who has never given up on him is the one who doesn't have any blood relation with him. The only link between them is a mere word of love and this vague promise. Who knows what the next six years will bring? Right now, he's at the bottom of a pit. Dong is standing on a high ladder, ready to climb higher. Even in his situation, Dong is willing to reach out his hand, patiently waiting for Simon to catch up. Maybe Simon will walk, crawl, or worse, fall down time and again on that road. Still, Dong is there. Like a light shining through the cracks in his armor, Dong keeps looking at him, urging him on, never giving up. How can he refuse such a look? How can he surrender a love like that? No, he is wrong. He can't quit.

Not yet. Staring into the eyes that are the salvation of his life, Simon says firmly, "I promise."

"Seal it."

"With a kiss."

Dong smiles into the rough touch of Simon's dried lips. The lips of a working boy, fighting so hard for a chance to survive and be himself, for a new start, a new life where he doesn't need to fear and yearn for perfection. Hanging on Simon's neck, Dong lets the rest of the world slip off his shoulders. The moon bathes them in her gentle silvery light. In the distance, someone is playing Leonard Cohen on the speaker:

"Even though she sleeps upon your satin
Even though she wakes you with a kiss
Do not say the moment was imagined
Do not stoop to strategies like this"

Perhaps in six years, they will all forget about this summer. The heat of youth and the promise to be together. Each will be burdened with different responsibilities. Adulthood may be polite, but it is rarely kind to anyone who bothers to listen to its advice. But as all fairy tales of old, six years will go by like the heartless bitch that time is, and Dong will achieve his dream of being a child psychiatrist, working to save children who suffer like he once did. Ames lives another life in Alberta with a new circle of friends. She is happier, and she has long forgotten about the hurtful words she uttered that day before she left, but Dong has forgiven her for everything. Lizzie is the same as before: the bursting energy, the cheeky attitude, and it doesn't help her much in earning many handsome admirers, but she makes do with her mother, Ms. Dolores. She is thinking of having a child through IVF. She loves the idea of being a mom, but she doesn't want to shackle herself to one person. "To be free," she always says.

And one day, in the unforgettable heat of summer, when Dong opens his condo's door for a pizza delivery, there kneels the hero of his life, Simon, with a ring in his hand and a bouquet of peonies. A lopsided grin on his bearded face. The clock rewinds to the times of old, and they are seventeen-year-old boys again, fiddling with their shirts, shuffling their feet at the first love confession. True to his word, Dong says yes. True to his word, Dong is the more loving one.

Thus concludes the chronicle of a love foretold.

About the Author

Thanh Dinh is a Vietnamese-Canadian poet and writer whose work explores grief, diaspora, queerness, political memory, and the sacred violence of survival. Her debut poetry collection, *The Smallest God Who Ever Lived*, was named a Top New Release on Amazon and praised for its lyrical boldness and emotional intensity. She later ventured into fiction with *Chronicle of a Love Foretold*, the short story collection *Love, Anyway*, and the noir literary suspense *Kill My Darling*.

You can connect with me on:
- https://writerlybookspub.com
- https://www.facebook.com/writerly.books

Also by Thanh Dinh

Upcoming Novel

Kill My Darling
Angela never meant to kill him. But love makes monsters of us all. When the body of Bambi Raymond—rapper, addict, and cult-like figure—sinks beneath the dark water, Angela is left to carry both his ghost and his enemies. As lies twist into truths and revenge burns hotter than grief, she learns that the most dangerous man in her life may not be Bambi at all.